Mill Town

a novel

~

Kenneth P. Smith

PHENIX BOOKS

MIDDLETON HOUSE PUBLISHING, Ltd, Co.
Greenville, SC

Kenneth P. Smith

MILL TOWN. Copyright © 2022 by Kenneth P. Smith

This book is a work of fiction. The characters, incidents, and dialogue are drawn from
the author's imagination and are not to be construed as real. Any resemblance to actual
events or persons, living or dead, is entirely coincidental.

No part of this book may be used or reproduced in any manner whatsoever without
written permission except in the case of brief quotations embodied in critical articles
and reviews. For information, address Middleton House Publishing, Ltd., Co., 1990
Augusta Street, Suite 204, Greenville SC, 29605

Phenix Books®, an imprint and registered trademark of Middleton House Publishing,
Ltd. Co. Printed in the United States.

Library of Congress Cataloging-in-Publication Data has been applied for.

ISBN 978-0-9981071-0-3

Dedicated to Blanche Smith, my mother, who gave me my love of books.

Other Books by Kenneth P. Smith

- *None But the Living (2017)*

- *Bad Creek (2020)*

Author's Note

On February 15, 1947 in Greenville, South Carolina Willie Earle, a 24-year-old black man and a World War II veteran, was arrested in the stabbing death of a local cab driver. The arrest was based solely on circumstantial evidence, and Earle denied having any part in the crime. In the middle of the night on February 16, a convoy of mostly taxi drivers drove from Greenville to the jail in Pickens County where Earle was being held and forcibly procured his release. He was taken to an abandoned slaughter house in rural Greenville County, where he was subsequently beaten, repeatedly stabbed, and then shot to death in the wee hours of the morning. This was the last racially motivated lynching to occur in South Carolina.

On May 21, 1947, a jury of the Thirteenth Circuit Court in Greenville—all white males—returned a verdict of 'not guilty' on all counts for the twenty-eight men who had been arrested and charged in the lynching of Willie Earle. The case was subsequently closed.

PROLOGUE

Two blocks west of Main Street in a squat, blonde-brick building was the Brown Derby. Half a block beyond, ran the railroad tracks that marked the commonly acknowledged rather than official boundary between Corinth and Free Town. So the Brown Derby was not technically in Free Town, but in the minds of the white people of Corinth it might as well have been. The Brown Derby was a pool hall and it was owned and run by Moss Bledsoe. Moss was a big man who wore a constant scowl and seemed to always be in a bad mood. To say, he was irascible.

The eight pool tables in the large, smoky room were well-maintained, with clean green felt surfaces and were checked regularly to see that they were level. To the left of the front door, which was painted glass, a counter ran along most of the front wall where two huge jars sat, one of pickled boiled eggs and the other of pickled pigs' feet. Behind the counter was an ice-cooler of bottled beer. Moss was positioned on a high stool beside the beer cooler where he collected payment for the eats and the beer; from here he could survey the entire room. A pool table was twenty-five cents a game. He brooked no trouble in his place, keeping a taped-wrapped picker stick always within reach, and was known to have no hesitation in using it. Brawlers took it outside on the street, where they had to deal with the local cops—all white—and usually ended up spending the night in jail. The clientele was all black men of various ages and this is the way Moss Bledsoe wanted it. He was black himself, and had not much use for white people.

The Greyhound station was a few blocks south of the Brown Derby, but closer to Main Street. On the ground floor of a two-story building, it was a large, but cramped dimly-lit room with rows of wooden chairs on the right side. On the left were more chairs and two large double glass doors—the left door was inexplicably always locked—that led to where the buses pulled up and parked to disgorge themselves of weary passengers and board those bound for outward destinations. At the glassed-in ticket counter at the rear sat a man in a dingy and wrinkled white shirt with a black clip-on tie. He was reading a detective magazine. Four or five people were scattered about in the chairs, waiting on buses to somewhere.

Outside the terminal, which was located on a corner, a bus pulled into one of the three angled parking slots. The ticket agent glanced up from his reading as the bus's headlight glared through the glass doors. He reached for the microphone on the counter near the window.

"Express bus from Atlanta, Georgia arriving at Gate One. Leaving for Charlotte, North Carolina in ten minutes, boarding in five," he said in a memorized monotone, and returned to his reading. Three of the people sitting in the chairs roused themselves, gathered the few belongings they had, and headed for the doors.

As the bus door opened with a pneumatic hiss, two men stepped down onto the pavement. Both were wearing jeans. One had a leather jacket over his tee-shirt and the other wore a flannel shirt with the sleeves turned up above his elbows. His jeans were also rolled to a cuff just above his ankles. They were both white and young, with dark hair slicked back from their foreheads. The shorter man, wearing high-heeled western boots, carried a small canvas ditty bag and the other a slender wooden case with brass latches. They entered the lobby of the station and sauntered up to the ticket window. The agent did not look up from his magazine.

"Hey!" said the short man. "You open for business or what?"

The agent placed the magazine on the small table beside him and stepped to the window. He looked at the two men, sighed, and finally spoke.

"Yeah, bub, what can I do for you?"

"Is there a pool room around here? I mean, close by," drawled the man with the wooden case.

"A pool room? Now let me see," said the ticket agent, scratching the stubble on his chin. "Well, fact is, there is one right up the street. Only one that's within walking distance. But I wouldn't recommend it, not to the likes of you two." The agent chuckled.

"What the hell does that mean?" asked the shorter man angrily.

"On nothing personal, I'm sure. It's just not a place for, uh, white boys like yourselves. That's all I mean."

"You mean it's a nigger joint?"

"Yes, I guess I do. A nigger joint."

"Which way is it?"

"Like I said, I don't recommend it."

"Why not? Nigger money's same as white money, ain't it?"

"Well, I suppose it is at that."

"Which way then?

The agent looked down, pursed his lips and then looked back up at the two men.

"It's a place called the Brown Derby. Blacks only, so far as I know. Just go back out those two doors where you came in, take a right and go up three block and then a block over on to your left. Can't miss it, but I wouldn't go in there if I was you."

"But then you ain't us, are you?" one of the men returned sarcastically.

"No, I reckon I ain't."

Moss Bledsoe sat on the high stool behind the counter pouring over a parley card and did not notice the two men as they entered the pool hall. They stood there in the doorway for a moment, surveying the place. There were black men shooting pool at the first seven tables and they didn't notice the two men either. At the back table a lone man bent over the table, apparently practicing his game. The two men then strode over to the counter where Moss was with his card.

"Hey, mister, we'd like to shoot some pool. That is, if you ain't too busy to give us a table."

Moss looked up, seemingly not surprised, but not pleased at all at the appearance of the two white men. He stood up and placed the partially filled-out parley card on the counter.

"Ain't nothing available. Maybe you two ought to come back tomorrow night," said Moss, his voice deep and unfriendly, "or maybe not at all." The two men looked at each other.

"Look, we don't want no trouble. Just a friendly game or two. We'll be moving on," said the white man in the leather jacket. "We ain't from around here."

"No shit," said Moss sarcastically. "You look like trouble to me. Both of you."

"Just want to shoot some pool. That's all."

"You just a couple of hustlers looks like to me," said Moss, noticing the cue case at the taller man's side.

"We play for money, but we ain't hustlers. Everything's fair and square."

Moss didn't say anything for a moment. He then sighed, with a disgusted smirk on his lips. "Look, if you can get anybody in here to shoot with you go ahead and try. But you're just not going to hang around here, understand? If you can't get a game then get the hell out of here," Moss said, then picked up the parley card and returned to his stool.

The two men turned and walked over to the wall where several cue racks hung. The man with the case opened it, took out a two-piece cue stick and deftly screwed the ends together. The other man took a cue stick from the rack and held the larger end to his eye, looking the length of the stick.

"Straight?"

"Yeah. Who woulda thought?"

They then moved closer to the first table, standing just away from it, watching the game that was in progress. The four black men playing totally ignored them.

"Anybody want to shoot a game of eight-ball for a quarter?" one of the white men finally asked loudly.

One of the black men was leaning over the table, eyeing the cue ball and sizing up his shot. He then pulled his stick away, placing one end on the floor and leaned on it.

"No," he said flatly, bent back over the table and took his shot.

"Hell, man, it's just for a quarter," insisted the white man.

The black shooter stood erect, placed the end of the stick back onto the floor and looked directly at the two white men. "I said no and I meant no. We ain't shooting pool with no crackers." The other men around the table smirked, looking at the two white men with hostile faces.

"Okay," said the white man and they moved down to the next table where they received the same hostility and answers. And at the next table and the next. Finally, they reached the last table where the lone black man was practicing shots.

"We looking for a game. Seems none of your friends wants to play us. Want to shoot a game or two for a quarter?"

The black man completed his shot and looked at them with a wide grin.

"Sure, I'll play you for a quarter. Nine-ball though. One at the time."

"Okay, you got it."

The black man extended his hand and with a broad smile introduced himself, "Name's Loomis. Loomis Cartee." The two white men looked at each other with a smirky grin, ignoring Cartee's outstretched hand, which he quickly withdrew. "Want to roll for the break?" asked Cartee.

"Sure," said the smaller white man, placing the que ball between the head rail and the first diamond of the pool table. He then gently stroked the ball, kissing it softly off the opposite foot rail, returning to about two inches from the head rail.

"Ooo, that'll be tough to beat," chatted Cartee, who stroked the eight ball the same way as the white man had done with the que ball. Cartee's ball rolled slowly back to him, past the resting que ball, and stopped barely touching the head rail. The two white men glanced at each other again, this time there was no smirk. "Guess I'll break," said Cartee as the white man racked the balls for the game.

Cartee made two balls on the break and then proceeded to pocket the remaining seven balls in succession, calling the pocket of each shot. The larger of the two white men leaned against the wall chuckling as Cartee ran the table. The other man stood helplessly by, watching, leaning on his custom-made two-piece cue stick. The game had taken all of four minutes. Cartee picked up the quarter lying on the table's side rail.

The big man stepped up to the table and racked the balls for the next game. He looked over at Cartee at the far end of the table. "How about a dollar a game instead of this penny-ante quarter crap?"

"That would be all right with me. Make it light on yourself," grinned Cartee, placing a wrinkled dollar bill on the rail.

After an hour of play, Cartee was up fifteen dollars.

PART 1

CHAPTER 1

~

At the edge of the small backyard near the alley that ran back along the row of mill houses were six chicken coops, each housing a hen. A tall, thin man in clean overalls went from coop to coop gathering an egg from each. His movements were slow and methodical as he placed the eggs carefully in the large bowl he held. The bowl was half full of crushed newspaper. After he gathered the egg from the last coop and placed it gently in the bowl, he bent over slightly to re-engaged the latch on the wire door of the cage and trudged slowly back to the house.

He climbed the steps leading up to a small back porch, and to the door which opened directly into the kitchen. The woman at the stove, her back to him, was pouring coffee into cups.

"Got six this morning," he said.

"That's good. Set them over here," she said as she turned and placed one of the cups of coffee on the table beside a folded newspaper.

"I'm sure glad we got those hens," he said. "What with no meat to speak of, these eggs have come in real handy. Gives us something that sticks to our ribs."

"The war won't last forever with only Japan left," she said, and started breaking several of the eggs into a large clean bowl.

"No, I guess not, but it sure seems like it sometimes, don't it?"

"I got grits on and some biscuits. Go wash up," she said, ignoring the man's comment.

"All right." He picked up the coffee from the table and took a sip. He then placed the mug back on the table and went through the bedroom where the bathroom was and washed his hands just as slowly and methodically as he had gathered the eggs.

When he came back into the kitchen, he took his seat at the table. She placed a plate of scrambled eggs, grits, and two biscuits in front of him. He coated the eggs and grits with salt and pepper, and began to eat.

"This looks mighty good. We got any butter?"

"Margarine. I forgot to put it on the table." The woman stepped over to the refrigerator, took out a saucer with half a stick of margarine on it and placed it on the table. She then scraped the remainder of the eggs from the frying pan onto her plate, ladled out some grits, and sat at the table across from him.

"You ain't going eat any biscuits this morning?"

"No."

"They awfully good, especially with butter."

"Margarine," she corrected him. "We haven't had butter in two years."

"Yeah, I know. I just like to pretend like it's butter. Actually, it really ain't too bad."

"It's not butter," she said, and he shrugged.

They ate the breakfast without any further conversation. When they finished, she got up and took both plates to the sink and began to wash them. He walked over to the stove and refilled his cup from the coffee pot, and sat back down at the table, taking a cigarette from a pack of Lucky Strikes that he pulled from the bib pocket of his overalls. He lit it and leaned over his coffee cup, staring into it. With his thin, large hands wrapped around the coffee mug he finally looked over at her. She was busy at the sink, her back to him.

"Well, I guess they'll be coming home soon," he said, staring back into the mug.

"Who?"

"The boys. You know the boys."

"What boys," she asked.

"The soldiers. The boys in the service."

"Oh."

"Yep, they'll all be coming home. That's for sure."

"Not all of them," she said so softly that he might not have heard her, but he had. She really wasn't interested in conversation, not this conversation anyway, as she washed the dishes.

"Well, I'd say the ones been fighting in Europe for sure. But we ain't licked the Japs yet," he said wistfully.

She looked up from the sink, out the window, across the yard. "No, we haven't."

"But we will. And it won't be long neither, I reckon. Not too long, anyway 'til we do."

"I don't know. It seems like it's been a long time," she finally said. "It does to me."

"Yeah, a long time."

Both were thinking of Tom, but neither mentioned his name. They had not heard from him in more than two months and were worried. They read the paper first thing every morning looking for news of the Marines. Tom was their oldest boy and he was somewhere in the Pacific. There was not much information, not about specific units anyway. Still they read the paper first thing each day and listened for news on the radio in the evenings. But mostly what they heard was propaganda; no real news. Not of the war in the Pacific anyway. They knew the Japanese were pretty much beaten. Everybody knew that. But they wouldn't surrender. They just wouldn't. People in the mill village kept saying they'd have to land the Marines on the Japanese mainland. Then it'd be over. How many Marines would it take? Not sure, but a lot. The people didn't say this to them. Not directly anyway, because they knew that they were worried about their oldest son.

He took a deep draw of the cigarette and exhaled a white cloud of smoke which drifted to the ceiling and seem to hang there. The coffee was cold now but he lifted the cup to his mouth and drained what was left.

"I just don't know what we going to do with all of them. When they get back, I mean."

"They'll go to work and get married, raise families like everyone else," she said flatly as she wiped the plates dry and stacked them on a cupboard shelve beside the sink.

"That's what's bothering me, where they all going to work. Ones that come back here are going to want to work at the mill, I reckon. They'll all young and strong. Yeah, they'll want mill jobs."

"Well, that makes sense, doesn't it?" she said.

Kenneth P. Smith

"Yeah, I reckon it does, but a lot of the women will have to be laid off to make room for them. We took on a bunch of them when the war started."

"Men got to work."

"I know they do. You're right about that for sure. So I guess they'll have to make room for them. All those young men. They all going to need jobs."

When he said this, she turned and looked at him. "Why, Claude, you're not worried about yourself, are you?"

"Some, I reckon." he said hesitantly.

"You've been a good hand for over forty years. They're not about to let you go. Now you just forget about it."

"Well, Jewel, I'm sixty years old. I'm doing about all the looms I can handle and they know it. Maybe a younger man could do more. I'm just a little worried about it, that's all. Just thinking about it."

"Don't be silly. You're the best fixer they've got. They're not thinking about getting rid of you, so you just stop it. Now! You hear me? Stop it!"

"I don't know."

"Well, I certainly do. I won't hear any more of it."

"They's talk the Sterling's may sell out to one of the big companies up North. Then what?"

"The Sterling's aren't ever going to sell out. They've owned the mill since '05. They look after their people. Always have."

"Look at the Galway Mill. They done it over in Corinth, didn't they?"

She looked down at him for a brief moment and then turned away. "It's nearly eight. You better get a move on. I got house cleaning to do." She left the kitchen.

Kenneth P. Smith

"All right," he said and slowly pushed himself from the table. His hat was hanging on a nail next to the back door. He placed it on his head, pulling it down securely close to his ears, and left the house.

The bright spring sun was on his shoulders as he strode to the mill off in the distance, the low constant hum of the machinery in his ears even this far away. But he wasn't thinking about spring, the sun, or the low gentle roar from the mill. He walked briskly, with his hands stuffed into the pockets of his overalls. This was the only life he knew. He had worked at the mill so long it now seemed almost a part of him. And the village. The mill village. It and its people were all he knew too. It had been good to him, to his way of thinking. Paid him a wage when he was nothing more than a kid. It was hard work for sure, then and now. But they took care of him then, and he and his family now. Kept him on during the Depression and that was no small thing, with so many people out of work. No siree! Sure, they often had paid him in company script instead of real money. It was good only at the company store, but it still let him put food on the table and coal for the fireplace. They never went hungry. No siree!

But he felt things were changing. Things beyond his control. He was growing older and was not as quick as he once was. As a loom-fixer he knew he was doing all he could do to keep up. He just prayed that the workload would not increase. But there was something else. He had spoken about it to his wife at breakfast, and it was not just the expected influx of men, all young and strong, that would soon be sent home from the war and looking for jobs. The fact was, as he saw it, that the mills, mostly all family-owned, were beginning to vanish. They would not really go away, but the big corporations were starting to scarf them up. One by one across the South. It had already happened to the Galway Mill over in Corinth. And if it happened to the Galway Mill, as large as it was, it could surely happen to the Sterling Mill. The big companies wouldn't care about him, or how long he'd been there. They were only about production. Production and profit. They wouldn't give a hoot about the people. They'd put him out to pasture for sure. He hadn't been able to save much money and even though there would eventually be a monthly check from the government, he knew it would be small and probably not enough to live on. He meant to work, at least a few more years. But he was afraid.

The eight o'clock whistle blasted, breaking the still of the morning, as he walked through the gate and disappeared into the bowels of the large red-brick monster.

As she went about the household chores, she thought briefly about her husband's anxiety toward changes that she too knew were coming. But she dismissed it as unwarranted worry. Nothing they could do anything about anyway. Her thoughts turned more toward her son. She hoped, prayed, that he was safe. She knew from his letters, reading between the few lines that he wrote, that he had been in harm's way. In fact, he had been wounded, but she was unaware of this.

But the war was almost over. That's what everyone was saying. In the newspaper and on the radio. Except she was not so sure. What would landing American soldiers on the shores of Japan be like? She knew the Marines would be the first to go in. They always were. It scared her to think about it. She told herself that he would be home soon, safe and sound. Her family would be together again, just like before. But it was hard. Why hadn't she heard anything from him in so long? It almost made her angry to think about it. It wasn't fair. The not knowing. Tears were running down her thin cheeks as she wrung out the mop and hung it high on a nail on the back porch.

CHAPTER 2

~

He stood in the doorway leading from the kitchen to the sitting room, leaning against it. He wore a clean white shirt and pressed brown trousers which hung loosely on his too-thin frame. His father sat across the room, bent over the radio, trying to tune it. His mother was on the small sofa thumbing through a thick Sears catalogue. She looked up at him and smiled slightly, but his father was preoccupied with the tuner and didn't seem to notice him standing there.

"What are you doing, pop?"

The older man did not stop his fidgeting with the knob, "Trying to tune in the ballgame. Sometimes at night I can pick up Milwaukee. Not clear or nothing, but enough to hear what's going on. Sometimes."

"Still a Braves fan, huh?"

"Reckon I am."

"Pop, mind if I take the car for a little while? I don't plan to be out late."

"The key's in the same place. On the hook by the refrigerator."

"All right. See you, Ma."

"Be careful, son," she said to his back as he turned and took the key from the hook. She heard the backdoor close softly behind him. The catalogue still lay in her lap as she watched her husband fiddling with the radio.

"Can't get nothing but static. Must be the weather," he grumbled, sitting back in the chair. "I'll try it again in a little while."

"He's different, Claude," she said.

"Who's different?"

"Tom. He's changed. You must have noticed it too."

"Well, Jewel, he's likely been through a lot. Three years fighting Japs. Probably seen some bad stuff. Aw, he'll be all right."

"I don't know. He's not himself. Not the boy who left here three years ago. Like he's away someplace else, not here. I worry about him. Lord knows, I do."

"Now don't worry yourself none. He'll be all right."

"He's been home almost a month now. He just sits out there on the porch swing during the day, staring. At what I don't know. Just looking away. Hardly says a word to me all day. At night he goes off some place. I believe he's drinking too"

"Yeah, well, it's about time he went to work. I believe I can get him on at the mill. Can't just sit around here forever. I'll talk to him."

"I don't know, Claude. He's changed. There's something inside of him, deep I think that's different. Sometimes I feel like I don't even know him anymore."

"He'll be all right I tell you. It'll just take some time. He'll get to working and forget about everything. Meet a girl. You'll see."

The Casablanca, with its red flashing neon sign, was much the same as any other roadhouse that dotted the landscape of America during the forties and fifties. A long, low concrete block building, painted, and set back off the highway, leaving plenty of room for parking in the dirt or gravel space in front and to the sides of the building.

Inside, across the wood-plank floor from the front entrance, was a long bar with stools. To the left was a random array of tables, with booths lined against the front wall. Beyond this was a large dance floor with a small raised platform at one end for the band, when there was one. Tonight there was no band at the dimly-lit Casablanca, but the juke box blared a sad, hollow-sounding country and western song.

Tom walked in without looking around or seeming to notice anything or anyone, and took a seat on a bar stool. Several other men sat a few stools down from him, drinking and laughing. He did not acknowledge them.

"Evening, Tom," said the bartender as he placed a glass of beer on the bar in front of him.

"Hello, Mac." Tom smiled briefly and lifted the glass to his mouth.

"Whatcha know good?" said Mac who pulled a beer glass from the murky water of the sink and began rubbing it with a soiled, damp drying cloth. Tom shrugged slightly and shook his head. He drained the last of the beer from the glass and stared into the empty glass in front of him on the bar.

"Well, nice talking to you," said Mac jokingly. "Ready for another?"

"Yeah," answered Tom, almost inaudibly.

He drank two more beers quickly and felt nothing from them as he sat there gazing into the empty glass. He glanced up once and caught his reflection in the mirror behind the bar. At first, for an instant, he did not recognize the man staring back at him. Then he realized he was looking at himself. He quickly looked away, back into the beer glass. It was only then that he seemed to become aware of the loud music as someone dropped a coin in the jukebox which started blaring a dance song. It was only then that he seemed to be aware that there were other people in the place.

He picked up the beer that Mac placed on before him and strode to the end of the bar and looked out over the small crowd of people, some of them now on the dance floor. Holding each other close, some embraced and moving slowly in the shadowy light, ignoring the rhythm, until they looked like just one creature. They looked like they were having a good time. He wondered if they really were. Mill workers likely, most of them. Getting a head start on the short weekend ahead. The juke box music was incessant, but they'd be a band tomorrow night. It would be just as bad. Probably worse.

He then glanced over at the row of booths along the far wall. Mostly in shadows of the dull lights that hung from the ceiling above the dance floor. In one of the booths, in the back corner, sat a woman. She was alone and something about her seemed familiar. Did he know her? Someone from somewhere that was a long time ago now? She caught his eye, then squinted as if she wasn't quite sure of who she was looking at. Then she broke into a wide smile and motioned for him. He gulped down the last of the beer and sat the glass on the corner of the bar. He approached the booth.

"Hello, Tom. I wasn't sure that it was you at first. It's been a while. You're thinner than I remember."

"It's me, or what's left of me," he said and laughed self-consciously. He stood close to the booth, looking down at her. "I wasn't sure it was you either. It *has* been a while, I guess."

"Yeah, it sure has," she said. A short awkward silence followed. Then, "Won't you sit down?"

"Sure, for a minute," he said. He sat down opposite her and fidgeted with his hands crossed on the table, staring at them.

"When did you get back? I heard you were home."

"About a month ago, I think."

"Oh, that long. I didn't realize."

"I haven't been out much. Just here. How have you been?"

"Me either, I mean I don't get out much, but I'm fine."

"Looks like you're out tonight," he said.

"Yeah, a *real* party. Stella, you may remember her. She was a couple of grades ahead of us." He shook his head vaguely. "Anyway, I worked with her at the mill for a little while after we first graduated, and she's been trying to get me to go out with her. I don't know, I really think she just feels sorry for me. So finally, I said okay and she dragged me in here tonight. Said we'd have a good time. Well, we're here about all of ten minutes and she starts dancing with this guy. He sits with us a while and then they go back on the dance floor. Then they come back to the booth and she hands me her car keys. Tells me she has a ride home. They walk out the door, all hugged up and laughing. So here I am, alone, but I'm getting ready to leave."

She reached down beside her for a small leather purse and held it against her breast. Maggie Harper was a pretty woman, though she now looked older than she was. She wore her dark brown hair long, but pulled back from her face. Her large brown eyes still had a certain sparkle, and he remembered in school she was smart. Prettiest and smartest girl in the senior class. He thought it then and he thought it now as he looked directly into her face.

"Can I buy you something to drink?" he asked finally.

"No, but thanks. I should never have come here. I don't know what I expected. I guess I just wanted to get Stella off my back. Do you come here much?"

"Some. About the only place I go." he said.

"A big dancer, huh?" She flashed a broad smile.

"No, just a few beers. That's about it."

"Me neither. I mean other than work, I don't go out any place much." She looked down at the purse that she held tightly.

The waitress stopped at the booth and he ordered another beer. They didn't talk, but looked out at the couples out on the dance floor. The waitress brought a bottle of beer and placed it in front of him. He picked it up and took a sip, and held the bottle, looking at it and flicking off small parts of the wet paper label with his thumbnail.

"I guess you knew about Eddie?" she finally said, without looking at him.

"Yeah, I knew. Ma wrote me about it. Seems like a long time ago now. I'm sorry."

"Over two years. We hardly got to know each other. You know how it was, with the war and all. He was just a boy. I don't think I ever really knew him." Her eyes filled with tears. He looked away, embarrassed for her, or maybe for himself.

"We were friends. Not best friends or anything like that, but I liked him," Tom said.

"Yeah, he talked about you. How smart you were," she said and smiled again, but it was a sad smile.

"I don't know where he got that idea. I sure don't feel smart. Not then or now."

"Well, he thought you were."

"Y'all got married our senior year, didn't you?"

"April twenty-third. We all knew what was coming. Remember?

"Yeah, I remember," he said.

"I'll never forget that graduation night. The buses just waiting outside the auditorium for all the boys who'd been drafted. It was awful. Just awful."

"It *was* pretty bad. I'm sorry what happened. For Eddie, but for you too."

"You didn't leave that night, did you? On the buses, I mean."

"No, I had joined the Marine Corps a few weeks earlier. I had almost a month before I had to report," he said, and then chuckled slightly. "Talk about stupid!"

"So I guess you just never know, do you?" "But you're here," she said, "and Eddie's not."

"No, I guess you never know," he said softly, staring at the beer bottle on the table.

"I'm sorry, Tom. I shouldn't have said that."

"Oh, no. You're right. It's just so random. There's no other way to explain it. I've asked myself a thousand times. Why me? I'm real sorry about Eddie."

"I don't even know how he was killed. They never told me. He had only been gone nine or ten weeks. They just said he was killed 'in the line of duty'. He may not have even been overseas yet. I hadn't got a letter from him in three weeks. I hated that war." Tears streamed down her cheeks.

"Me, too."

He took another sip of beer and she just looked out on the dance floor. There didn't seem to be much else to say. She then slipped out of the booth, stood up, and wiped her eyes with the back of her hand.

"It's been nice talking to you, Tom. It's good to see an old friend. Maybe I'll see you around some time, but it won't be in here. Maybe in town someplace."

"Yeah, maybe. I'm not sure how long I'm going to hang around here in Whittier. Got some things to figure out."

"Going to college?"

He chuckled. "No, nothing like that. Truth is I don't rightly know. Probably end up working in a cotton mill, here or someplace.

"You'll do it. Figure things out, I mean." She hesitated for a brief moment. "So long."

"Bye, Maggie."

As she walked to the door several of the men sitting at the bar turned and watched her go. They then turned back to the bar, mumbling to each other and chuckling lewdly. Tom sat in the booth, alone, staring at his hands folded on the table. Yes, he was here and Eddie wasn't, he thought. Why? He knew, with all that he'd been through, that he shouldn't be here either. He could see their faces as they passed before him. All alive and laughing, but now all dead. Bodies mutilated, sometimes beyond recognition. His friends and buddies. They all wanted to live as bad as he did, get back home, make a life. He did not understand it. He would never understand it. If he could just stop seeing the faces. He drained the bottle of the last of the beer as the waitress approached the booth.

"You want another one?"

For a long moment he just sat there staring up at her, more like he was looking through her to somewhere far away.

"I said, do you—"

"Yeah, bring me a beer," he said as if suddenly waking from a shallow sleep. The waitress rolled her eyes and walked away.

Kenneth P. Smith

CHAPTER 3

~

Tom pulled the car up off the street, got out and strode across the dirt yard to the porch steps. It was a moonless night and the house was dark as a tomb. His mother always left the porch light on, but tonight there was no light. Odd, he thought as he stepped onto the porch. Then he was startled, but only slightly, by a voice from the darkness, from the end of the porch where the swing was. It was Shelby Jean, his brother Bud's new wife.

"Hello, Tom."

"You scared me for a second there, Shelby Jean. What are you doing out here this late?"

"I've been out here since Bud left for work. Just swinging and thinking. I couldn't sleep, I guess." She spoke just above a whisper, her voice was thick and throaty, and strangely mellow in some way. He could not see her from where he stood. "You been out to the Casablanca, I'll bet. You have, haven't you?

"Yeah," he said as he lit a cigarette. He leaned on the banister, but did not move toward her. She rocked gently in the swing.

"I wish I could go to the Casablanca sometimes. I want to dance. Just to go someplace."

"Why don't you get Bud to take you?"

"He's not interested. I guess it's that foot of his. Says he can't dance. He seems to do anything else that he wants to do, but when I ask him, he just says, 'No, I don't think that's a good idea, Shelby Jean'," she said, mimicking her husband. "His idea of fun is going down to Joe's on Saturday evening for hamburgers and milkshakes. I swear, if I never eat another hamburger it'll be too soon."

He smoked the cigarette and gazed across the yard into the blackness. She continued to swing ever so slightly. She could make out his silhouette across the porch, and she watched. Finally, she said, "I'm so bored I can't hardly stand it. I'm young. I want to do things. Go places. See the world."

"Not that much to it," he said.

"But you've seen it, Tom. You really have."

"I've not seen much of anything. Nothing interesting."

"Oh, but you've seen the Pacific Ocean. That's something."

"Yeah, maybe that's something. I don't remember much about it though."

"You've seen California. I just want to go to California. They say it's always warm there. Is it?" she asked in the darkness.

"Where I was, it was, but I wasn't there very long."

"You traveled across the whole country, Tom. You have!"

"What I saw, I saw through the window of a Greyhound bus going about sixty-miles an hour, and a lot of it at night. I didn't see much."

"Tom, tell me about the Pacific Ocean. You've seen it."

He took a final drag on the cigarette and flicked it out onto the yard where the tiny embers glowed for a few seconds and then were gone.

"Shelby Jean, I spent most of my time there on a ship, and most of that below deck. Except when we made an assault. When I think about the Pacific Ocean, I think of death. That's all."

"I'm bored, Tom," she said, ignoring his comment. "And sick and tired of this place. This town. This little pea-patch of a town. I mean I appreciate your daddy building me and Bud that little bedroom upstairs in the attic. I mean it, I really do. And your mama's good to me. Treats me let I'm one of her own, but I won't ever get out of here. Bud's only dream is to make second-hand at the mill and get on the day shift someday I don't know if I can stand it. I really don't."

"You married him," he said.

"I know I did, and I love him. I mean I guess I do. But I didn't know it was going to be like this."

"What did you think it was going to be like, Shelby Jean?" He lit another cigarette.

"Oh, I don't know. I didn't think about much it at the time, I guess. I just wanted to get away from my mama and daddy. Papa drunk all the time, slapping us around. And mama just taking it, even defending him. She was as bad as him. Still is. I had a chance to get out and I took it. Can you judge me for that?"

"I can't judge you for anything, Shelby Jean." Then they were silent again.

"Can I ask you something, Tom?" she finally said.

"I suppose you can."

"You seem lonely. Are you?"

"I don't know. What's lonely?"

"You know, like you need somebody or want somebody. Like you just tired of being by yourself all the time."

"Then no, I'm not lonely," he said.

"Well, I am. I'm lonely and bored," she said, her lips in a pout.

"You're just young. It'll come. You and Bud can make a home. Have things. Maybe you'll have a baby soon."

"God, you sound like Bud. I *am* young. I'll settle down one day, but I ain't ready to just yet. I'm sure ain't ready for no baby. I don't want to work the second shift in some nasty old cotton mill, or live the rest of my life in this god-forsaken town. Surely, you can understand that."

"I do understand it," he said softly, barely audible.

"Then take me with you to the Casablanca tomorrow night. Bud won't care. He thinks you walk on water anyway. I just want to dance. That's all, just dance and have a good time."

He could hear the squeaking of the swing's chain rubbing against the eye-hooks where it hung from the roof of the porch. She was swinging harder and faster now.

"Shelby Jean, I can't take you to the Casablanca. You wouldn't like it anyway. Besides, you're too young."

"Yeah, but not too young to get married and start having babies. That's right, ain't it, Tom?"

"No, that's not right. I can't take you to the Casablanca. Bud will take you there sometimes."

"He won't. I told you he won't," she said and they were quiet for a few moments. Then she stopped her swinging. "I think you lied to me just now," she said.

"About what?"

"About being lonely. I think you are lonely. Real lonely."

"I didn't lie to you, Shelby Jean." He flicked what was left of the second cigarette into the yard and stood up. "I'm going in now."

"Tom, come over here and sit beside me," she said. She had stopped swinging.

"No, I'm going in the house and go to bed."

"I wish you would."

He turned and pulled open the screen door and went into the dark house. He was gone and she began again to swing gently in the porch swing and humming to herself.

CHAPTER 4

~

Ford—Bradford Chatsworth Sterling III to be precise—
came from a long line of Sterling's, a family that
represented what passed for society in the upcountry. His
great-great grandfather, Nathan Sterling, had migrated to
the area from England via Pennsylvania sometime in the
early eighteen-hundreds, after marrying Mary Chatsworth
of Philadelphia. After moving South, with money
borrowed from Mary's father, Nathan built and ran a grist
mill and opened a store, becoming quite prosperous in
the process. He later bought land. Added a cotton gin,
and became rich.

With family money and funds from Northern
investors, the original Bradford Chatsworth Sterling built a
cotton mill on the Wausaki River near the village of
Whittier in nineteen hundred- one. His son, the second,
ran the mill until a bad heart forced him to retire in
nineteen thirty-nine when he turned it over to his son. All
the Sterling's, so far, had become civic-minded and
gentlemen. Ford Sterling was not much of either.

You would be hard-pressed to find anyone in Perkins
County who didn't know, or know of, Theo Hatcher.
Hatcher's small law office was in downtown Whittier. He
was friendly, displayed a home-spun skepticism of the

human condition, and even in the winter always wore a slightly rumpled, blue-striped seersucker suit—he owned three. It would be difficult to say precisely what brand of law Hatcher practiced. Like most small-town lawyers, he had done a little of everything over the last thirty some-odd years. It could be said that he was a generalist, and he liked to think of himself as such. At various times he had also served as a magistrate court judge, ran twice for mayor (won once, which he later confirmed was a-plenty), and had served on the school board several times. But mainly he practiced small-town law and liked it. Many of the people in and around Whittier had employed his services at one time or another—closing on the sale of a house, getting bail set for a wayward brother-in-law, divorces, and helping settle property claims were just a few of the areas where his legal expertise was needed and used. He was also the personal attorney for Ford Sterling.

Hatcher worked for Sterling's father and when he had to retire early and turn things over to his son, Hatcher just seemed to come with all the other property and equipment that became Ford's charge at the time. He smiled to himself when he thought back to that time. But it was more than that. Hatcher had known the Sterling's all his life and their families occasionally mixed socially, although he knew that he would never be in the inner circle of these wealthy mill families. Just their lawyer, and that was all right with him.

The diminutive Hatcher slumped in the large leather chair in one corner of Ford Sterling's office. His friend and client sat at his large mahogany desk, but had turned in his swivel chair toward him. Even though he was seated and eight feet away, Hatcher noted to himself that Sterling seemed to be looming over him. It always seemed that way. He had that effect on people. Sterling held a lighted, black cigar in his left hand.

"I don't really know why you want me here, Ford. You're not planning to sign anything today, are you?"

"Hell no, I'm not signing anything. I expect they'll likely bring a letter of intent. But you're my lawyer, aren't you? I might need to consult with you. Have you take a look at it. I just want you in the room. I guarantee you he'll have a lawyer with him. Hell, he's probably one himself."

"But I know next to nothing about corporate law. You know that," said Hatcher, his hands resting on either arm of the chair.

"Yeah, I know, but I just want to make sure that all the t's are crossed and i's are dotted."

"That *is* corporate law, Ford."

Just then Miss Goodson, Sterling's secretary, tapped on the door which was partially open.

"They're here, Mr. Sterling. Their car just pulled up in the parking lot?"

"How many of them, Mabel?" Sterling asked as he swung around to face her.

"Two, I believe.

"Okay. Have them wait in your office for a minute or two."

"All right," she responded and then disappeared.

"Who's supposed to be in this meeting, anyway?" asked Hatcher.

"Well, the main one is Madison something or other. He's the chief financial officer of Arlington. That's all I know, but I'll bet the other asshole is a lawyer." Ford took a bottle and a shot glass out of his desk drawer and poured a shot. "You want some of this, Hatch?"

"No. I'll pass," said Hatcher glancing at his watch. It was half past ten.

Sterling cinched up the knot in his tie and smooth it across his amble belly, but he did not get up from his desk. He leaned back in his chair, pushing himself slightly away from his desk, puffing on the cigar. The intercom on his desk crackled and then Mabel's voice.

"Mr. Ford, Mr. Madison and Mr. Abernathy are here."

"Okay, Mabel. Tell them I'll be with them in a minute." He switched off the intercom and turned back to Hatcher. "I'll just let them cool their heels for a few minutes. Don't want to appear too eager, you know."

"Whatever," said Hatcher offhandedly, half shrugging.

Sterling placed the smoking cigar in the large blue ashtray on the credenza behind him and turned back to his desk. He then began mindlessly shuffling papers and pushed them into a neat stack at the far corner of the desk. He looked at his wrist watch, and then seemed to be examining his fingers nails. After about five minutes of this he reached over and switched on the intercom. In his most charming and social voice he spoke, his southern accent a little thicker than usual He knew that they could hear him.

"Miss Goodson, please show our guests in."

Very quickly, Mabel ushered the two visitors in to Sterling's office.

"Good to see you again, Madison," Sterling said graciously as he stood up behind his desk and extended his hand. He then quickly turned to the other man. "I don't believe we've met. I'm Ford Sterling."

"This is Frank Abernathy, our general counsel," said Madison. Sterling shot a glance at Hatcher that said, 'See, I told you so.'

"Pleased to meet you, Abernathy." He turned to Hatcher who had not risen from his chair. "This here is Theo Hatcher." Hatcher nodded to the men, but did not get up. He wondered who the two men thought he was and what he was doing in the meeting, information that Sterling had purposely failed to offer. Sterling waved a hand across his desk. "Please sit down."

"Thank you," said Madison as the two men took seats in the two leather straight chairs in front of Sterling's desk.

Sterling stepped from behind his desk over to a large, polished oak cabinet. "Can I offer you gentlemen something to drink?" He had opened the cabinet door, revealing several bottles of whiskey and glasses.

"No, thank you," said Madison quickly, and Abernathy just shook his head.

"How about you, Hatch?"

"No, thanks, I'm good. A little early in the day for me." Hatcher knew that his comment would irritate Sterling, who glared at him for a quick second.

"Suit yourself. I guess I'll just drink alone." He refreshed his glass with a generous pour of bourbon and returned to his desk. "Well, gentleman, let's get down to it. What have you come up with?"

Madison slid his chair up slightly, leaning a little closer to Sterling's desk. From his briefcase he took a piece of paper and slid it across the desk to Sterling.

"This is a letter of intent, Mr. Sterling. Bottom line is that the Arlington Corporation would like to purchase your mill. This letter outlines our offer in general terms.

Of course, a more detailed due diligence will need to be performed before closing, but your balance sheet is impressive and I don't see any problems. If you'll just sign there where indicated, we can start the wheels rolling right away. We'd like to close in ninety days, if possible."

"Whoa now, you boys like to move fast! I like that!" said Sterling. He reached over and picked up the letter and began reading it, sipping the whiskey as he read. When he had finished, he turned and handed it to Hatcher. "Read that, Hatch, and tell me what you think."

Hatcher toke the letter, settled back in his chair and perused it. In a moment, he passed it back to Sterling. "Looks like all the t's are crossed and the i's dotted to me." Sterling didn't miss the sarcasm in Hatcher's comment.

Sterling, holding the letter in front of him again, leaned forward in his chair, staring at it. He then took a deep breath, sighed heavily, and took a long drink from his glass. He looked up at Madison, who sat stiffly in his chair, legs crossed at the knees.

"Three million bucks, huh? That's it, three million?"

"Yes, three million dollars. One million in cash and the balance in Arlington stock. Our stock, by the way, is trading well above the current Dow of one sixty-three."

"Three million dollars," Sterling repeated. He drained the last of the whiskey in a short gulp and placed the empty glass on the desk. He then loosened his tie and leaned forward with his elbows on the desk, toward Madison. "Madison, you ain't even in the ballpark. Our real estate alone is worth a million!"

With humorous interest, Hatcher was watching things unfold. He had seen it in Sterling before, when he didn't get what he wanted or felt he was being cheated or taken advantage of. He knew how explosive he could be. It would build. He waited on the explosion.

"Well, that's another thing, Mr. Sterling," said Madison coolly. "Arlington Corporation is not in the real estate business and does not intend to enter it. The offer excludes the mill houses and related property.

"What the hell am I supposed to do with nearly three hundred mill houses?" Sterling was livid. His face had suddenly become red and it wasn't from the liquor.

"That's not really our concern at this point. We feel that the offer is a fair one. For both parties."

With this, Sterling seemed to relax some, sitting back in his chair. He looked down at the empty glass on his desk, and said calmly, "I happen to know that y'all paid twenty-five million for the Galway mill. The Allgood's got real healthy on that deal. Real goddamn healthy."

"That is quite a different situation, Mr. Sterling, I assure you. Your mills are different. Galway's production is five times yours. You haven't updated equipment in a while. You have looms that are going on twenty-five years old. The Galway plant has all new looms. New Sulzer looms."

"We *have* Sulzer looms," Sterling shot back.

"Yes, but old ones and they will all have to be replaced soon. By the way, Mr. Sterling, where is your brother? As the treasurer of Sterling Textiles, he should be in this meeting."

Here it comes, Hatcher said to himself, but Sterling was somewhere else now. Hatcher couldn't believe he had been able to calm himself. He must really want to sell the mill, he thought.

Kenneth P. Smith

"Well, let me make something real clear, Mr. Madison. First of all, my brother is in Maine fly fishing. He does that a lot. And secondly, I run this company and I decide who attends my meetings. I've got a brother and a sister, and they trust me to run things. Understand?"

"I assure you, Mr. Sterling, I did not mean to imply...,"

"You didn't imply anything, Madison. You said it. I trust I have made myself clear enough," said Sterling calmly.

Sterling started to pour himself another drink, thought better of it, and set the glass back on the desk. He looked hard at Madison, and Madison did not look away. After a tense few moments, Madison cleared his throat.

"What about the offer, Mr. Sterling?"

Sterling stood up behind his desk. "Gentleman, this meeting is over. Here is your letter of intent." He handed the piece of paper back to Madison. "If you gentleman will excuse me, I have work to do."

"So you are rejecting our offer?" asked Madison as he stuffed the document back into his brief case.

"Lock, stock, and barrel."

Madison stood up and turned briefly and looked at Abernathy, and then back to Sterling.

"I'm sorry you feel that way, Mr. Sterling. Please contact me if you should change your mind." Neither man extended his hand to the other. Madison motioned for Abernathy and they both walked out of Sterling's office. Sterling slumped down in his chair when they were gone.

"That went well, don't you think?" said Hatch sarcastically, leaning back in the oversized chair.

"Screw you, Hatch. Those son of a bitches!"

"Sons of bitches, I believe it is, Ford."

"Whatever it is, I don't like it. I won't give my mill away. It's worth more than three million. I know it and they know it. Damn 'em all."

"Why don't you make some kind of counter offer. Hell, it's just like horse trading, the way I see it."

Sterling glared at Hatcher for a moment. He then rolled the empty liquor glass around in his large hands, gazing out the window beyond where Hatcher sat. He signed deeply and spoke calmly.

"No, I'll not counter their offer. Not yet anyway. I know these types. New York corporate suits. I figure the board at Arlington has decided they want my mill. No, I'll just wait. They'll be back. I guarantee it. They'll be back. They want my mill!"

"By the way, Ford, what's the figure you have in mind? Just curious."

"Nothing less than five million, and I keep the houses."

"I thought you didn't want the mill houses. You said—"

"I know what I said. They don't want 'em. Times are changing. He was right. These big companies don't want to be in real estate—mill houses. I can sell 'em and make a bundle. They'll be back, Hatch. Mark my words."

"You may be right. I guess we'll see." Hatcher got up from his chair. "Well, enough of this small talk, but I must say I have enjoyed my foray into corporate law, albeit a brief one. I've got to go. We'll talk later." He wasn't sure if Sterling even heard this as he walked past him and left the office. Sterling just stared out the window, deep in his own thoughts.

CHAPTER 5

~

Claude had already collected the eggs and sat down at the kitchen table with Jewel to eat the breakfast she had cooked. It was Saturday and he did not have to go in to the mill today. Jewel noted his subdued mood.

"You're not eating your eggs, Claude. You feeling all right?"

"Yeah, I feel okay. Just not real hungry this morning."

They both looked up at the ceiling from where a low but constant sound was coming– something bumping against the wall.

"Damn he ain't been home from the mill ten minutes and they already at it," said Claude.

"Oh, Claude, they're just young. That's all."

"Shameless is what they are! Always going at it."

"We were young once, or have you forgotten?" she said with raised eyes brows.

"Naw, I ain't forgot. We just didn't advertise it all over town. You'd think at least they'd slide the bed away from the wall some."

"It's a small room," she said.

The noise grew louder and more rapid. Jewel looked down at her plate, smiling, and Claude shook his head and took a sip of coffee. Suddenly the noise stopped. Claude glance again at the ceiling.

"Well, at least Bud's quick about it," said Claude. Jewel continued to eat in silence. "When I built that room for them in the attic, I reckon I shouldn't have put it right over the kitchen. They need to get their own place if you ask me."

"They will as soon as they get on their feet. I heard Shelby Jean talking just the other day about it. She'd like to move to their own place. I expect they will soon enough."

"I'm surprised she ain't got a young'un in her yet with the way they're always, uh, caring on."

"Like I said, they're just young."

They finished their breakfast and Jewel stood and cleared the table. She placed the dishes beside the sink and then poured Claude more coffee. She poured a little into her own cup and sat back down at the table. He pulled the pack of Lucky Strike from his pocket and placed it on the table after taking one out and lighting it.

"I believe Mr. Sterling might have sold the mill yesterday. Least that's what I heard might have happened," Claude finally said.

"Now just where did you hear such a thing, Claude Pruitt? In the mill water-house?

"Well, what if I did?"

"Water-house gossip. That all it is. Water house gossip."

"Not the way some of the boys are telling it, it ain't."

"What are they saying now?"

"Enoch Griffin had to go to the doctor's yesterday morning. When he was walking back to work, he cut across the mill office yard. He saw a car—a big, fancy car—pull up and park in front of the office."

"So?"

"He says two fellers got out and went into the office. They both had on suits like it was Sunday and carried leather cases under their arms. He said one of them was here—at the mill I mean—a couple of months ago."

"How did he know that?"

"I ain't sure. Maybe he had another doctor's appointment."

"I wouldn't believe anything Enoch Griffin said he saw. Talks all the time and wouldn't work in a pie factory. I swear I don't know how he keeps his job at the mill."

"He's a pretty good weaver, but that ain't what I'm talking about. I declare, Mr. Sterling's done sold the mill."

"I doubt it, Claude. But what if he has. So what?"

"Don't you see, Jewel, things are changing with the cotton mills. Like I said before, they all being bought up by these big New York companies. Ain't going to be no more owner-mills like the Sterling's pretty soon. And they're already getting rid of mill houses. Some of them are, anyway."

"Well, that's not a necessarily a bad thing, is it?"

"I don't know. Maybe not. But with this war being over I believe all hell's going to break loose. I don't know what's going to happen."

"Ah, Claude, you worry too much. They're still going to have to make cloth. I don't see how it makes much difference who you work for. Besides, what's Ford Sterling ever done for you?"

"I've kept my job all these years. Put food on the table. That's what!"

"I suppose you've forgotten about those years of stretch-outs and getting paid in company script instead of *real* money."

"Them were just hard times. Hard times for everybody. We had to get through the Depression. We all did, Jewel. You never went hungry, did you?"

"No, but I never got to travel all over the world like Mrs. Sterling does either."

"It was just to Europe or Itlee someplace like that, I think. Not exactly around the world."

"It's all the same to me. I've hardly been out of Perkins County."

The door to the back bedroom off the kitchen opened; Tom came in and sat at the table opposite his father. His trousers were wrinkled as if he'd slept in them. He wore a clean t-shirt, wrinkled trousers, and shoes but no socks. His hair was mussed a little and his eyes blood shot. His mother took a cup from the cupboard, filled it with coffee, and set in on the table in front of him.

"Thanks, Ma." Jewel nodded as she turned to the sink and started washing the breakfast dishes. He sipped the coffee.

"You out late last night?" his father asked.

"Yeah, pretty late."

"Go to the Casablanca?"

"Yeah."

"Get drunk?"

"No."

Without turning from the sink his mother said, "Son, I wish you'd stay away from that place. It's such a dive. I hear about trouble there all the time."

"Ah, it's all right, Ma. I'm not going to get into trouble. Just a couple of beers, that's all."

"Seems like you spent a long time drinking a couple of beers. You must really be a slow drinker," chuckled Claude. Tom did not respond to his father's comment. He sipped his coffee.

"We got some eggs left. Let me finish these dishes and I'll cook them for you. Got some grits in the pot on the stove," Jewel said, still at work at the sink.

Tom pushed his chair away from the table and walked to the stove, and then took down a plate.

"Don't cook me anything, Ma. I'll just eat some of these grits. It's all I want."

"All right. The butter's on the table. At least what passes for butter these days."

He ladled out the grits onto the plate and coated them generously with pepper. He sat back down at the table and began eating.

"Don't you want some margarine?" his father asked him as he lit another Lucky.

"No."

Claude picked a piece of tobacco off the tip of his tongue and deeply inhaled the smoke from the cigarette. He exhaled the blue smoke and it drifted slowly to the ceiling. He drained the last of his coffee from his cup. He looked at Tom.

"Got plans for today, Tom?" his father asked, squinting at him over his coffee cup.

"No, not really. Thought I might walk downtown and look around. Haven't been there since I got home. See if anything's changed since forty-two."

"Not much, I can tell you that. You can take the car if you want to, but don't be gone too long. I'm going to change the oil this afternoon right after dinner."

"No, thanks, I'll walk. It's pretty out."

"Going to be hot. On up in the day, I mean."

"That all right. I'm used to it."

"Well, I reckon you would be, at that. Probably hotter way out there in the Pacific, huh?" said his father, trying to nudge Tom to talk about the war.

Tom did not respond to Claude, but continued to eat the grits in silent. When he had finished, he took the plate over to the sink.

"You didn't eat much. Sure I can't fry you some eggs?" asked Jewel.

"No, I'm fine, ma." He turned and walked back into the bedroom, closing the door behind him. In a few moments he came back into the kitchen. He had put on a shirt and socks and changed trousers. He kissed his mother lightly on the cheek and left by the backdoor.

"I'm worried about him, Claude. He's just not himself. He's changed, like I said before."

"Yeah, something's not right. I believe he just needs to go to work. It'll do him good."

"I don't know," said his mother.

"Well, I got some putterin' to do out back. Might clean out those chicken pens. They sure need it." With that, Claude picked up the pack of Lucky Strikes and put them in his shirt pocket. He then pushed himself up from the table and went outside.

Jewel, alone at the table, sighed deeply and took a sip of her grown-cold coffee. She loved her family, at least her two boys. She cared for Claude, she cared deeply, but she knew that she had never loved him. Not the way a woman should love a man, the man she marries. But the boys were hers and she loved them. Bud, her younger, born with the slightly deformed foot which somehow, she still irrationally blamed herself. He needed her. Or did. Now he had Shelby Jean, for which Jewel was thankful. He would be okay. Deep in her heart she knew that she loved Tom more and she felt guilty about it. He was more like her in so many ways. He had always had a sensitivity that only she saw. He wanted more, or she thought he did, than a life on a mill hill. He could be somebody. Somebody with dreams. She had had dreams too. Long ago. She had just been too weak, she said to herself, to pursue them. They no longer existed, but were like a dry autumn leaf crushed beneath the weight of a heavy boot. Just unrecognizable fragments. Ah, so long ago. So long ago now, she could hardly recall them at all.

CHAPTER 6

~

"Whoa now, Daisy," said Pluris Tinsley as he pulled back hard on the rope reins. The mule took another step and then stopped. The animal stood motionless in the dying sunlight as the man detached the ropes and removed the leather collar from around its neck. Shouldering the collar, he led the mule into a stall of the small barn and then hung the collar on a spike on a post, head high. He closed the barn behind him and walked across the narrow yard to the back porch. He pulled open the screen door and went into the house, taking a chair in the kitchen. His wife was rolling out dough beside the sink, but he was not looking at her. He stretched his legs out in front of him. Staring at his dust-caked brogans, he absent-mindedly shaved off a slice of a tobacco from the plug he had taken from the pocket of his overalls.

"You want some coffee?" the woman finally said.

"No, not right now. How long before supper?"

"Thirty minutes, maybe," she said as she twisted an inverted drinking glass into the flattened dough. She was making biscuits. "Got to get these here biscuits in the oven. I thought I might cut up and boil some cabbage to go with the beans."

"I like cornbread," he said.

"Well, we're having biscuits this evening. It won't kill you to eat my biscuits once in a while."

"I like your biscuits."

"If you're through outside you ought to go wash up. Take them nasty shoes off your feet."

"I'm about through, I reckon. I'll go water the animals, then I'll be through. Where's Jewel?"

"She in the front room doing her school work."

"All right," he said.

When he came back in to the house after taking care of the animals, the plates and bowls of food were on the table. His daughter, Jewel, was sitting at the table. She took a sip from the glass of milk that was in front of her.

"Hey, papa," she smiled, almost shyly.

"Hey, girl. Finish up your school work?" he asked, taking his usual place at the table.

"Yes, sir."

Mrs. Tinsley poured coffee for him and then herself, and returned the pot to the stove. She sat down at the table opposite her husband. He ladled out the beans onto his plate and passed the bowl to his daughter. He took one of the large biscuits from the plate, opened it with his hands and placed a slab of butter on both pieces with a knife.

"I heard they're hiring down at one of the plants in Corinth. A bleachery, I think," he said, and took a bite of the biscuit.

"Hiring what?" his wife asked. There was a slight edge to her voice.

"Workers, that's what. People to work in the bleachery. Regular wage work."

"So?" she asked, somewhat disinterested.

"Well, the truth is I been thinking about it. Working for wages, I mean."

"You talked about it last year and the year before that. Nothing ever came of it though."

The young girl was listening to this conversation intently but kept her eyes on her plate of food. Sometimes her father talked of moving down to the city and taking work there. It frightened her to think about moving from the mountains. And from her school. After this year, she would only have two more and then graduation. She did not know many people who had graduated high school. Certainly neither of her parents had. She listened.

"I'm tired of trying to make it on this farm. If you want to call it that. Trying to plough this red, rocky dirt. Smelling mule farts all day. Worrying about the rent. It's late again, ain't it?"

"Yes, it's late."

"Wouldn't you like to have things, Edith? Like a good stove maybe. A decent dress. Wouldn't you, Edith?

"I would, I reckon.

"Well then, I'm going to talk to Jess Martin and see if he won't let me borrow his T-Model so I can drive down to Corinth. I'll put in my application at the bleachery. I reckon y'all might as well get ready to be moving."

Jewel looked up from her plate. "I don't want to move, Papa. I want to stay here and finish school. I want to graduate."

"I reckon you can go to school somewhere in Corinth. That is, if you don't go to work right off. What do want all this schooling for anyway? You got almost nine years as it is. That's more than me and your ma have all together. Ain't you learned enough?

Kenneth P. Smith

"No, Papa, I haven't. I want to graduate."

"And then what. Go to work in a cotton mill. Get married and have a bunch of young'uns. Don't need much schooling for that."

"I want to be a teacher or maybe a journalist, Papa. I already talked to Mama about it." She glanced over at her mother, as did Pluris. "That's right, isn't it, Mama?"

"We've talked about it some, I reckon."

Turning back toward the girl, Pluris said, "That stuff takes a college education I believe."

"That's right, at least some college."

"We don't have no money for you to go off to some college. You best forget about it, girl."

"Miss Henderson said she believed I can get a scholarship. I make all A's."

"What's a, uh, a scholarship?" he asked

"They pay for my schooling. In college."

"Well, I ain't never heard of such. You ain't going to college, so forget it."

"She can dream, can't she, Pluris. Ain't nothing wrong with the girl having dreams," said his wife.

"Nothing wrong with dreams, I reckon. Long as you know they just dreams," he said as he pushed himself away from the table and stood up. "I'm going over to see Jess and see if he won't let me borrow his automobile. If he will, I'll be leaving for Corinth at first light." He took his hat off the back of the chair and walked out back, letting the screen door slam behind him.

The girl and her mother looked at each other. There was pleading in her eyes as she looked at her mother. Then her mother turned away and got up from the table. She started taking the dishes to the sink.

Kenneth P. Smith

"It's more than a dream," the girl said softly, almost to herself.

That evening after supper Pluris walked the two miles to the Martin farm, which was mostly bottom land and much more prosperous than his own. A half-hour later he was driving back to his farm in Jess Martin's Model-T. When he got to the house he steered the car round to the back and parked it near the barn. He got out of the car and started walking toward the house, but then stopped for a moment, looking back at the Ford parked there in the fading light. He wondered if he would ever have the money to buy an automobile. He then turned and walked to the house.

Pluris Tinsley got up in the dark the next morning, which was nothing out of the ordinary, fed and watered the animals and was on the road in the Ford when the sun burst over the low rim of Nine Mile Mountain. It was nearly sixty miles down to Corinth, the first fifteen of which was a winding, rutted dirt road. He'd pick up the paved county road at Hickory Mountain, just below the state line, but it would be a slow and bumpy ride until then. The sun was well up when he finally pulled onto the county road and turned toward Corinth.

It was a warm, pleasant morning as he sped south, the air filled with the aroma of the pine trees mixed with the heavy sweet smell of honeysuckles. The mountains had given away to the rolling hills of the Piedmont and he honked his horn at the few cars he met on the two-lane road and at a mule wagon too. He was excited and was already feeling the freedom of a man who had decided to take charge of his own fate. It wasn't too late. He thought about leaving the farm and the mountains and said *good riddance,* to himself. And he thought about a new, a better life that seemed to be just around the corner. Just down the road he was on now. The farm work was hard on him and his wife. Working for regular wages, they could put all that behind them. It would be—it had to be—a better way to live. Maybe Jewel could go to school in Corinth, but she'd probably want to go to work in the mill once she saw what having regular money in your pocket could do. She could have things too. Just like her mother would. She'd be a lot better off working and forgetting about all this education nonsense, he concluded. He drove on and didn't think about it again.

He slowed the automobile as he approached Russellville with its one needless traffic light. He passed by a café and was suddenly aware of being very hungry. He hadn't eaten anything since supper the night before and he had a dollar in the bib of his overalls, folded, and stuffed into his pack of Brown Mule. He slowed and glanced over at the café and the people stirring about inside, and then up at the sun through the windshield. *No, I better not stop,* he thought. *Sun's getting pretty high. I best get on down to Corinth.* He then licked his dry lips and pressed down on the accelerator pedal. Russellville shrank rapidly in his rearview mirror.

He steered the pickup into the gravel parking lot and pulled up alongside a low, red brick building. A sign—*Plant Office*—hung on a welded angle-iron frame and swayed gently in the late morning breeze near the front steps. He stepped onto the narrow porch, took off his hat and buttoned the top button of his shirt. It was his best shirt, the one he wore to the infrequent church meetings he attended back home. He smoothed his hair with both hands, pushed open the door and stepped inside.

The room was large and sparsely furnished except for the wooden chairs lined against the wall to his right and the large desk at the back wall where a man sat reading some papers that he occasionally shuffled. When he closed the door behind him the man looked up.

"Howdy," said Pluris, holding his hat low in front of him, but not moving away from the door.

"Howdy. What can I do for you?" asked the man behind the desk.

"It's a mighty fine morning, ain't it?"

"Yes, I reckon it is. Can't enjoy it much sitting in here doing paperwork though." He placed the papers he was reading on the desk in front of him. "Can I help you with something?" the man repeated.

"Yes, sir, a fine morning it is," said Pluris. He was nervous. The man cocked his head to one side and just looked at him. Then Pluris said, "I reckon you can help me or tell me who can. Fact is, I'm looking for work. Work with wages."

"That's the only kind you'll find around here. But I'm afraid you're out of luck. We just hired on a bunch of men, so we ain't hiring right now. Probably hire some more come fall. You can come back then."

"I need to go to work now. You see, I've been a farming, or at least trying to. But it's beat me. I'm ready to come on down here and go to work. I heard that National Bleachery was hiring. That's why I come here. To work for wages."

"Well, you heard right. We were hiring, but we done hired all the men we need right now. Like I said, we'll likely take on some more people come this fall. Be glad to talk to you then."

"I need work now. I'll make a good hand. I ain't afraid of work, hard work. Done it all my life."

"I'm sorry but –"

"Reckon I can talk directly to the man who does the hiring? Explain things to him."

"The point is, you are talking to him. I'm the personnel man here. I do all the hiring. And some of the firing too, I reckon."

"Oh, I see," said Pluris.

The man sat forward and leaned with his forearms on the desk. "Do you know where Whittier is?"

"I reckon I do. It's down the main highway, ain't it?"

"That's right, US Forty-Seven. Only it ain't 'down'. It's 'over', west of here. Anyway, I'm pretty sure the cotton mill over there is hiring men. It's a fairly new mill and business is good. Just like it is here. Cotton mill's the Sterling Mill. You might have heard of the Sterling's."

"No, I don't reckon I ever did."

"Well, anyway, I suggest you drive over there and see what's going on. They'll likely put you on."

"Route Forty-Seven you say. How far is it from here? Whittier, I mean."

"Ten miles, maybe eleven. Good road all the way. You ought to go on over there."

"Yes, sir, I reckon I will." Pluris turned to leave. As he grasped the door knob he stopped and looked back at the man, "Much obliged."

"Good luck," he replied and picked up the papers on his desk.

The winding dirt road was strewn with rocks and rutted, mostly by wagon wheels. No one had spoken since they had left the farm at daybreak. Jewel sat on the rear seat which was packed to overflowing with curtains, clothes, and the last few items her mother had packed from the kitchen. Pluris had sold most everything else including the furniture. With the money from the sale they could buy new or at least good used furniture for the mill house in Whittier.

Finally, at Hickory Mountain, they turned south on the narrow, paved county road.

"There's Lanford's store up ahead. Y'all want to stop there?" asked Pluris

"No," said his wife. Jewel did not respond.

"Okay, then. I reckon we're on our way then." He honked the horn as they sped by the store. Silent tears filled Jewel's eyes.

So it was that in nineteen-thirteen the Tinsley's arrived in Whittier on a warm early-summer day in June. When they arrived, they found that the small, four-room mill house contained two beds and some pieces of furniture, mostly odds and ends left by the previous occupants. They finished furnishing it with used items purchased from the company store.

True to what the man at the bleachery had told him, the Sterling mill was hiring and Pluris took a job in carding on the third, or graveyard, shift. He also had arranged jobs for his wife and daughter in the spinning room, where most of the women and young girls worked. They wouldn't make as much per hour as he did, but it was first-shift work. And that was something. There was never again any talk of Jewel returning to high school.

Kenneth P. Smith

CHAPTER 7

~

He strode down Broad Street, hands deep in his pockets, oblivious to the heat of the afternoon that seemed to hang over the town like a heavy immovable curtain. When he had landed back in San Francisco he swore to himself that he'd never complain about the heat, not after the Pacific. And now, the heat, he never even thought about it much.

There were few things about Whittier that differentiated it from any other small Southern mill town. The main thoroughfare, called Broad Street, ran for five blocks with stores and shops on its left, or western side, and a railroad track ran along the other. On the other side of the tracks were a few less prosperous businesses and it was also where the mill village began. There were side streets, about two blocks deep with other shops and stores, some abandoned and boarded up. Beyond these was the neighborhood where the Sterling's, and others of their social status lived. A quarter mile further on was the high school and beside it the elementary school, known in those days as the grammar school. To the north, across the railroad tracks and beyond the cemetery was Flood Town, where all the black people lived.

He hadn't been downtown since he'd returned home from the war. Looks just the same, he thought. Nothing ever changes in Whittier. He strode by Freeman's Family Store, the only real department store in town. In small black letters on the lower part of one of the front doors were printed neatly, *Negroes Use Side Door.* Tom stared at this for a moment and then moved on up the street. He passed the pool hall where the letters were a little more adamant about the status of race relations than at Freeman's: *Whites Only-No Negroes Allowed.* The drug store next to it had no sign, but Tom knew that the lunch counter inside was for white people only. He had run into some black Marines at Peleliu. They were there mainly assigned to supply details or some other support unit, but when things got really rough they fought the Japs along with the white Marines. They did all right too, thought Tom. He hadn't seen that skin color made much difference in men then.

When he came to the small book store, The Book Nook, he stopped and looked at the few books on display in the window. There were none about the war and he was glad. In the center of the display was a jacketed copy of *Gone with the Wind.* He had seen the movie in San Francisco before his unit shipped out to the Pacific. He hadn't like it very much. It had seemed romantic and contrived. More a movie for women, he thought. He wondered if the book was any better. He pushed open the single glass door and stepped inside.

In the center of the store was a desk and a small counter with a cash register. The girl at the register looked up when the bell attached to the door made a thin, tinkling sound.

Kenneth P. Smith

"Why, hello, Tom. It's nice to see you again."

"Hey, Maggie," he said, a little startled. He hesitated. "You work here?"

"Well, yes I do."

"That was a stupid question. Of course you work here." He grinned shyly and shook his head. "I thought I'd just look around. That okay?"

"Sure. Are you looking for anything in particular I can help you with?" she asked.

"Ah, no. No, I'm just killing time. Say, isn't this old Mr. Fulcher's ice cream shop? Or was?"

"Yes, but he passed away almost three years ago. It was empty for a while, but Mrs. Hendricks bought it. This is her bookstore."

"You don't say. Is she still the librarian at the high school?"

"No, retired last year. Then opened the bookstore. She says it was her a life-long dream. To own a bookstore, I mean."

"I'm kind of surprised to see you here. I was thinking you worked at the mill."

"I did for a while after Eddie—. Ah, but when she opened the bookstore Mrs. Hendricks offered me a job, so I took it. Jumped at it, actually."

"You like it here?"

"Yes, very much. Pay's not much, but I like it. I like it a lot."

"It suits you," he said.

"Yes, I think it does," she said and glanced down at the papers scattered on the counter. "Well, I guess I'd better get these invoices recorded and put away. Are you sure there's nothing I can help you with?"

"I saw where you have *Gone with the Wind* in the window. Have you read it?"

"Oh, yes. Twice," she laughed.

"Liked it, huh?" he laughed.

"It is wonderful. I loved it!"

"I saw the movie, but couldn't really get into it. Might have had something to do with where I was at the time. I don't know."

"And where was that?"

"California. Just before, uh, before we shipped out. It doesn't really matter."

"Well, you saw it and didn't like it much," she said lightly.

"Maybe the book's better though."

"I saw it at the Rivoli in Corinth. I loved the movie, too, but you're right, the book is better."

"I don't read much. Not anymore. But I like books. Got it from my mama, I guess. She used to read to me a lot. I mean when I was little. She really loved books."

"Still does," said Maggie.

"What do you mean? You know my mama?"

"Yes, as a matter of fact I do. She comes in here. Not often, but every once in a while."

"Are you sure? Are you sure it's my mama?"

"Well, her name is Jewel Pruitt and she used to talk about her son Tom who was off in the war. She still comes in and we chat some, not too much. She looks at the bookshelves and picks one out, and she'll ask me if she can sit and look through it. I tell her, 'Of course you can, Mrs. Pruitt', so she does."

"Damn, I never knew. Does she ever buy anything, a book?"

Kenneth P. Smith

"No, she never has, but that's okay. I like for her to come in the store."

Tom stood there for a moment as if he were looking way off somewhere. He then shook his head like he was waking from a dream. He looked back down at Maggie.

"I'll just look around," he said, almost absentmindedly.

"All right," she said and gathered up the invoices in a neat stack.

He walked away from the counter and disappeared behind a shelf of books from which he began to randomly take books and thumb through the pages, not really looking at them at all. Nothing seemed to interest him. Finally, he placed a book back on the shelf and strode to the door of the shop where he stopped and turned back toward the counter.

"See you, Maggie."

"Didn't find anything?" she asked, looking up from her work.

"No, not really."

"What about *Gone with the Wind*?"

"Ah, I don't think so. Not now, anyway."

"Well, check back later. We're always getting new books in."

"I will. So long." He opened the door and was gone.

Walking back along the store fronts that he had known so well, he knew that he was somehow disconnected or at least that's the way he felt. Other than maybe for the bookstore, nothing had changed much, but it all seemed strange to him now. He was on the outside looking in. How could he come back here and just go on as if nothing had happened to him? He wondered what they all thought—his mother and father and all the others. Had he just gone away for a few years and now was supposed to just float in like nothing had occurred in the intervening time? Take up where he had left off. But he had not left off anything. When he had left Whittier he was a kid. Just a dumb kid. Sure, they knew he had been off to war. A far away war. It was over, he had survived, now here he was as if he were maybe just returning from a long trip. Nothing had really changed. He thought that Maggie understood. Maybe. He surprised himself a little that he should think of *her* after only their brief encounter at the Casablanca and then at the bookstore. Yes, *floating*. That was the word. It was how he felt. He was floating.

When he reached Broad Street he turned and walked back past Joe's. The early supper diners were already gathering. Ahead, an older man and woman got out of the car that had pulled up and parked at the curb. As he approached, they crossed the sidewalk in front of him. He had to stop to let them pass. They never saw him. He hesitated for a brief moment when they were gone, disappearing into Joe's. He thought how lonely he was. Not lonely really, but alone. Maybe Shelby Jean had been right. He then shook his head as if waking from a bad, shallow dream and headed home, to the mill village.

"Where you been so long, son?" asked his mother on the porch, not looking up from her knitting.

"Nowhere. Just walking around downtown." He stepped up onto the porch and leaned against the banister, facing his mother's rocker.

"And what did you see, just walking around?"

"Not much. Nothing's seems to change much in Whittier."

"That's certainly true enough. Lots of folks like it like that way, I suppose."

"I guess so."

He turned away and sat on the top step, his back to the woman. He pulled a cigarette from his shirt pocket and lit it. For a while they both were silent, her knitting and rocking slowly in her chair, him smoking and thinking. Finally, he took a long drag of the smoke and snuffed it out with his foot on the lower step.

"What's bothering you, Tom?" she asked, still at her knitting.

"Nothing."

"Something," she said.

"I don't know," he said softly. The trees in the yard rustled as a slight breeze came up, gently caressing his face. He breathed it in and for the first time that day realized how hot the air was. The sun—he could still see it—but it was slanted far westward now, just above the tops of the houses. "Pop inside?"

"No, he's goes down to Jarrard's store to see his buddies. Bunch of old fogies, gossip worse than women."

"Gives him something to do, I guess."

"Gives him a chance to drink beer, is what it does. And tell lies," said Jewel, chuckling. "He'll be home directly with some news he's heard about the mill or something. Most of it hogwash."

"Yeah," said Tom. "I see they've got a bookstore now downtown."

"Yes, there is one now. Did you go in it?"

"Yes, ma'am, I did. Ran into Maggie Harper. She works there."

"I believe it's Porter. Maggie Porter."

Kenneth P. Smith

"Yeah, I guess it is. I forgot she's married."

"*Was* married," corrected his mother.

"Yeah, was," he said.

"Did you talk to her?"

"A little. She said that you come into the store sometimes."

"So what if I do? I reckon I can go into a store when I've a mind to."

"Sure you can, Ma, but I just never..."

"You never thought about me looking at books in my old age. Is that it?"

"No, I guess I didn't. It just struck me as a little strange at the time. But then I thought about how, when I was little, you used to read to me. I mean, right here on this porch. At least that's what I remember. Do you remember, Ma, do you?

"Of course I do. Fairy tales and nursery rhythms mostly as I recall. I would read, but you already knew them all by heart. But you always wanted to hear them again—from out of the book. Anyway, I haven't thought about it in a long time. About you and books, I mean.

"Like I said, it just seemed strange at the time. I don't know."

"Is it strange to have dreams, Tom?"

"I wouldn't know the answer to that question, Ma. I truly wouldn't."

"I think we all have dreams in our lives. Mostly when we're young and don't know any better."

"You got dreams, Ma?"

"I guess I had dreams once. At least *a* dream."

"I don't recall you ever mentioning it."

"No, I suppose I never did. You see, Tom, when a dream dies you just let it go. It's not anything anymore. So you just forget it. That's all. You just let it go."

"Doesn't sound like you forgot it."

"Oh, but I have. It's like it's somebody else's dream now. Not mine at all." She lay her knitting in her lap and gazed out past where Tom was sitting, past the rooftops, over the tree tops where the clouds were changing hue, their edges tinged with an iridescent and indescribable pink.

"What was your dream, Ma?" Tom finally asked.

She didn't answer him immediately, but continued to look out at the horizon, or what she could see of it from the porch. She sighed and picked up her knitting and began again.

"Nothing. It was a long time ago and no purpose is served by dragging it up now. It's dead. Like a body, it's dead. So I'll just let it lie in peace."

"All right," he said and lit another cigarette. Dusk was creeping in like a stealthy cat, as shadows of the house and trees began to slowly vanish.

"Getting about too dark to see out here," she finally said.

"You could turn the porch light on."

"Yeah, I reckon I could, but I'm won't."

"You want me to?" he asked.

"No, I'm done knitting for the day. I'll just sit a spell and wait on Claude. He'll be along directly."

Tom rose from the steps and walked past her across the porch to the front door. He lightly touched his mother's shoulder as he passed.

"She's right pretty, don't you think?" she said.

Kenneth P. Smith

He stopped in the doorway and looked back at his mother. "Who?"

"Why, Maggie Porter. Who else would I be talking about? I said she's right pretty."

"Right, I guess so," he said.

"You got a dream, son?" Jewel asked after a long moment of silence.

"No, ma'am, I don't have a dream." He then went into the house, quietly pulling closed the screen door behind him.

CHAPTER 8

~

"Hatcher Law Firm," said Dorothy pleasantly, but business-like.

"Let me speak to Theo, Dorothy. This is Ford Sterling," said Sterling as if he needed to identify himself to her after all these years.

"Just a moment, Mister Sterling. I'll see if he's available," came her stock answer as the gatekeeper. She heard Sterling's deep impatient sigh on the other end of the line. She clicked on the intercom. "Mister Sterling's on the line for you." Hatcher picked up the receiver.

"Hello, Ford. What can I do for you?"

"Hatch, can you get over here right away?"

"Well, actually I'm in the middle of something right now. What's up?"

"I just got a certified letter from Arlington. A letter of intent to purchase my mill. Told you I would. I've got some questions. Legal questions. Just come over here, will you, Hatch?"

Hatcher knew Sterling to be in impatient man, difficult to put off. Delayed gratification was not a concept he readily grasped. I might as well go ahead and get it over with, he thought. With the phone wedged between his ear and shoulder, he began gathering the sheets of paper spread before him on his desk into a neat stack.

"Okay, Ford, I'll be right over."

Hatcher slipped on his seersucker jacket from the coat rack and stepped into the outer office. "I'm going over to the mill to see Ford, Dorothy. Shouldn't be long I expect." He then left the office, got into his car and drove the few blocks to the mill. Sterling's secretary ushered him in without delay.

"Hey, Theo. I really appreciate your dropping everything for me. Here it is," said Sterling, passing the letter across his desk to Hatcher, who took it and sat down in his usual chair off to the side the desk. He pulled a pair of reading glasses from the vest pocket of the jacket and perused the letter.

He then refolded it and placed it back on Sterling's desk and shrugged.

"Well?" asked the mill owner.

"Like you said, it's a formal letter of intent to purchase the business."

"Yeah, yeah, I can see that much. A real one this time. But is it legally binding? I mean the terms."

"No, it's not a contract or agreement. It's just like the one they sent you before. Only the terms are different." said Hatcher.

"Just like before, huh? I knew those Yankees would come crawling back. But not binding, you say," bellowed Sterling.

"What it does, Ford, is specify the terms that Arlington will agree to in purchasing the mill. Nothing legal, mind you, but it's a sort of an agreement to agree—if there were such a thing legally, which there isn't. That is, if you *do* indeed agree to what they say they'll offer."

"Goddamn right I'll agree to it. Be a fool not to. You see the price they're offering me."

"Prepared to offer. Nothing legal here, not in this letter. Just intent, like it says."

"Five million. Cash. That's just for the mill and the real estate it's sitting on. And I keep the mill houses and the company store."

"Did you notice the non-compete wording. You'd be out of the textile business permanently."

"Yeah," Sterling laughed, "like Brer Rabbit. Do anything to me, but don't throw me in the briar patch. I'll gladly walk out of this damn mill and never look back."

"What about your brother and sister? They're in agreement as well?"

"Hardy and Bessie? This kind of money? You kidding me, Hatch? They'd kill me if I didn't sell!"

"All right. Just asking," shrugged Hatcher.

"Look, Hatch, we've got over three hundred mill houses. All occupied by mill hands who aren't going anywhere." Sterling rose from his desk and started pacing back and forth. "The way I see it I can sell the houses for, oh, I don't know, say two thousand a piece. If they can't come up with the cash, which I would reckon hardly any of them can, I'll finance the damn thing. If they're not interested in buying, I'll rent the place to them. Say, twenty-five a month. Talk about cash flow!"

"Sounds good, Ford," said Hatcher as he got up from the chair, ready to leave.

Sterling ignored him and continued to talk out his plans. "And then there's the company store. It nets near thirty-thousand a year, give or take. That'll just be gravy. By god, this all looks good to me!" He then noticed

Hatcher was ready to leave the office. "Where you going?"

"If this is what you want to do, Ford, then I'm happy for you, but right now I got work to do myself. I need to get back to the office."

"I'm going to need you through all this and after the sale too. With the real estate and everything."

"Well, I'll be around. No plans to go anywhere anytime soon," chuckled Hatcher.

Sterling sat back down at his desk as Hatcher turned to leave. "One more thing, Theo. They say they'll close the deal ninety days from my acceptance. Is that the way you read it?"

"That's what it says. They just want some time to complete their due diligence. That's about it."

"So, I just need to sign the letter and send it back to them?"

"Yep," said Hatcher.

"Then what?"

"What do you mean?"

"You're the lawyer. What happens next?"

"Arlington will draw up an agreement, a contract. You and your brother and sister will sign it. I expect after you sign it this place will be crawling with accountants and suits until you close. You up to that?"

"For what they're paying, I don't give a damn about any of that. They've seen the books. I've got nothing to hide. The Sterling Mill is a money maker and they know it."

"All right, I'll be seeing you, Ford," said Hatcher as he closed the office door behind him.

After Hatcher was gone, Sterling unfolded the letter again and re-read it slowly. He then leaned back in his chair, with the letter dangling from his hand, turned and gazed out the window, across the mill's grassy yard and the town beyond. After spending a few moments in thought, he picked up the fountain pen on his desk and signed his name in a broad, scrolling script on the black line at the bottom of the letter. On the intercom, he called for his secretary who appeared at the door almost instantly. He handed her the letter.

"Mabel, I want you to send this letter back to Arlington right away. Now. You post it personally. Certified. Understand?

"Yes, Mister Sterling, I'll take care of it immediately." As she walked back to her desk, Mabel quickly unfolded the letter. Her eyes fell near the bottom, to the bold signature of Bradford Chatsworth Sterling III. For all intents and purposes, the mill was sold.

CHAPTER 9

~

Tom was sitting on the porch steps when his father pulled the Ford into the yard. He stood up and strode toward the automobile. Claude Pruitt looked up at him briefly from where he sat behind the wheel and then looked away.

"Where's your ma?"

"Lying down, I think."

"Talk to her any today?"

"Not much. There's not much *to* say, I guess."

"I reckon not, but she's taking it mighty hard. I guess we all are, but him being the youngest and all, it just seems to be the hardest on her." With this, Claude opened the car door and got out. "I know we got to be going, but I'll just step inside for a minute to see her."

"All right," said Tom. "I'll wait in the car."

They did not speak to each other as the car sped through the traffic of US Route Forty-Seven in the twenty-five-minute drive to Corinth. The traffic thickened as they passed the Corinth City limits sign that unabashedly proclaimed Corinth to be "The Textile Center of the World". Finally, Claude exited onto Washington Street, past houses with their front doors swung open in the heat, people sitting on the stoops sipping ice tea. People coming and going in the shops and stores that were huddled among the houses gave off a sense of life and energy. A group of children played hopscotch on lines of chalk drawn on the sidewalk. Men with brown paper bags twisted tightly around small bottles milled about the entrance to a barber shop.

They seemed to catch every traffic light, but were oblivious to the bustle about them. Washington Street was a long, dead-end strip of wide, busy pavement during the day. But at night, once past the neighborhood, could be heard jazz and blues—black people's music they called it—emanating from the small clubs and bars that lined the street. As the night wore on men could be seen sitting on the sidewalk, their backs against the bricks of a building sleeping or sipping from their little paper sacks. And women, mostly blacks but some whites too, waited patiently beneath the street lights at the corners.

At the end of the street the train depot sat behind a high chain-link fence that made it seem like an island, separating it from the hurried bustling of the city street. It was an ugly, squat Victorian building. Its red brick dulled by years in the sun and the paint of its green wood trim curled and faded. The Southern Crescent stopped here once a day on its sojourn from New York City to New Orleans and once again when returning. The giant locomotive, green and gold, gleaming in the afternoon sun, seemed strangely out of place beside the low, sad depot. One had the sense that it was somehow anxious to be on its way, and not sit here very long so as not to be associated with such a shabby, unkept place.

Kenneth P. Smith

The car turned into the gate, slowed and pulled up to the curb in front of the depot.

"Well, here we are," said Claude, both hands still gripping the steering wheel.

"I'll be back Wednesday evening," said Tom as he reached back for the small canvas bag in the rear seat.

"I ought to be me going myself. I really ought to. I'm his daddy." Claude looked away, biting his lower lip. "Was his daddy."

"Let's not go into it again, Pops."

"All right. You need any money?"

"No," said Tom. "I should be back around nine o'clock.

"On Wednesday?"

Tom nodded, got out of the car and disappeared into the station.

He sat there by the window gazing at a countryside of farms and small towns flashing by in the waning light of a summer's twilight. With the impending darkness, the clicking monotonous rhythm of steel wheels against steel rails, he vaguely wondered to himself whether he would be able to sleep on this long journey. He thought not. Why would this night be any different from all the others?

He pulled the folded telegram from the breast pocket of his jacket. His mother had handed it to him that afternoon. He had not read it. He opened it and looked at it.

Stanley C. Pruitt killed last night STOP Perpetrator unknown STOP Body at city morgue needs family id and claim STOP

New Orleans Police Department 715 Broad Street, NO, Louisiana.

Kenneth P. Smith

Stanley C. Pruitt—Bud, his brother—was dead. The telegram had been delivered to his

parent's house the day before. Handed to his mother at the door, like a clerk offering her a discount coupon from the grocery store. Bud dead. Just like that. He folded the telegram and placed it back in his pocket. He then closed his eyes and tried to think of nothing.

The train rolled on relentlessly between stops as dusk and then darkness settled over the rural countryside, and houses and towns became indistinct, blurred shadows. Tom couldn't sleep and was restless. Finally, as the train was slowing at yet another station, he went to the lavatory and washed his face. Combing his hair in the mirror and looking into his own dark eyes, he felt lost somehow, floating again—nothing seemed real to him. He stared at himself in the mirror for a long moment. Then he felt the movement of the train cease. They must be at the Atlanta terminal. He needed a drink.

He entered the club car and found it crowded with drinkers, smokers, and card-players. He worked his way through the throng and found a small table in the back corner, next to a window. He first ordered a beer from the stooped, black steward, but then changed his mind for a whiskey, straight up. He then pulled a cigarette from the pack and lit it and gazed out onto the brightly lighted platform of the station where porters hurriedly loaded luggage amongst the good-byes being said. As he finished his smoke, the steward returned with his drink and placed the glass on a small cloth napkin on the table.

"They running you a tab at the bar, sir. Will there being anything else for now?"

Kenneth P. Smith

For a brief moment Tom looked up at him as if he hadn't heard him, as if his mind was somewhere far away. He then shook his head absentmindedly. "No, no, nothing. I'm fine," he finally said and the steward vanished almost instantly. Tom took a long drink and turned and looked away, back out the window.

"Hey buddy, this seat saved?" Without waiting for an answer, the man slid into the seat across the table from Tom. "Damn car's crowded, ain't it?" He took out a large, black cigar from his coat pocket, bit off the end and chomped down on it. "Got a light, buddy?"

Tom turned to face the man and placed his lighter on the table in front of him. The man lit the cigar, rolling it between his thumb and forefinger as he sucked on it against the flame.

"Now that's a damn good cigar. Ought to be. Cost me fifty-cents at the bar." He then extended a large, meaty hand across the table. "Name's Wilbur Jackson," he said affably. He had loosened his tie and his collar was open. With his blood-shot eyes and red nose, it was apparent that he was well on his way to being inebriated.

Tom shook his hand. "Tom. Tom Pruitt."

"Well, I'm please to meet you, Tommy-boy. I'm from Richmond. Seems like I been on the train for days. Boarded this morning actually. Boy, don't seem like it though. Where you bound?"

"New Orleans," said Tom, dryly.

"Well, ain't that something. Me too. Going to the annual convention. I'm a chiropractor, you know. Up in Richmond."

"All right."

Kenneth P. Smith

"You going to the Big Easy on business or pleasure, Tommy-boy?"

"Business."

"Well, yeah, me too. *Some* business, that is. Don't want to miss the pleasure part though, if you know what I mean. They's some fine-looking women down there. Not just street hookers neither, loitering on a corner in the Quarter. No, siree. You can dial 'em up from your own hotel room. They'll come right on up. Now that's sweet, don't you think?"

Tom smiled thinly and shrugged. "I guess so, if that's what you're looking for."

"Damn right, it's at least one thing I'm looking for. Say, Tommy-boy, you ever been to New Orleans?

"No."

"Well, let me tell you right now you ain't going to believe it. Why, you can buy a drink on the street at eight o'clock in the morning. Not that I would ever do that, mind you. There's a little bar I go to down off Royal Street. Never closes, but from six to six-thirty in the morning to sweep out and empty ash trays. Damnedest place you ever seen. They got this old guy. I mean, he's like a street person or something. Comes in every morning exactly at eight. Puts five nickels on the bar and the bartender gives him a shot of whiskey. He throws it down in one gulp and leaves. Does it every morning. Seven days a week. Now ain't that something?"

"I suppose it is," said Tom. He then lifted his whiskey to his mouth, but set it back down without taking a drink. "It was nice talking to you, Mr. Jackson." Tom stood up and placed two quarters on the table. "I've got to go now."

Kenneth P. Smith

"Why, you ain't finished your drink, Tommy-boy. Sit back down and let's chew the fat. Hell, I'll buy you another drink."

"No, thanks. Maybe I'll see you around." With that, Tom turned and made his way through the crowded club car, and left. Once in the passageway he felt a slight jolt as the train started moving again, then at last it was again hurling south through the darkness.

As Tom stepped from the train onto the platform, he wasn't prepared for the wet heat which seemed to hang in the air like a thick hot shroud. Suddenly, he was conscious of his breathing—if only to make sure that he still could. Memories, feelings really, flooded over him. He had felt this kind of heat before. This heavy, thick heat which seemed to permeate and consume everything. Made everything a shimmering mirage. It was death. It was Tarawa. Everything but the smell. But he could smell it. He knew he always would.

People brushed passed him. He looked at his watch. Nine-fifteen. He couldn't remember the last time he had eaten. Sometime the day before. He was hungry now, but he would take care of his business first.

With his bag, he strode past a small-barred window under a sign that read, *Information*. He looked at it briefly, but moved on toward the huge doors that led out of the terminal. He stepped out of the terminal onto the glaring, hot sidewalk. He could just make out the street sign on the corner some distance away. Canal Street. As he walked toward the corner, a policeman was crossing from the other side. Tom quickened his pace to catch up with him.

"Excuse me," said Tom, breathing heavily.

Kenneth P. Smith

"Yeah, what can I do for you?"

"Where's the police station?"

"Which one? We got several. It's a big town, you know," said the cop, pushing his visored cap back on his forehead.

Tom took the telegram from his pocket, opened. "Uh, it's on Broad Avenue. 715 South Broad."

"Oh, well then. That's the main house. You'll probably want to catch a street car. It's a ways."

"I'll walk."

"Suit yourself. Just turn around and stay on Canal for, I'd say, fifteen or sixteen blocks. Until you get to Broad. Then take a left for about six blocks and you'll see it on your right. Can't miss it. But it's a hike, I'm telling. In this heat."

"Thanks. Thanks for the help."

"You ought to take a street car," said the policeman as Tom turned and walked up Canal Street. After a few blocks he took off his coat and flung it over his shoulder, and hurriedly pressed on. The sidewalk and streets were filled with people, cars, and trucks. All moving. He didn't seem to see or noticed them. He just wanted to get this over with.

The large police station was surprisingly cool as he pulled open the large glass wood-framed door and stepped inside. Huge fans circulated overhear, creating artificial breezes in the big room. People, mostly uniformed cops, were everywhere. The place was definitely open for business. To his left was a long counter with desks and policemen working behind them. He walked over to the counter and stood there for a moment. No one seemed to notice him, or cared that he was standing there. Finally, a big, red-face policeman got up from his desk and languorously plodded up to the counter.

"Yeah, what can I do for you, mister?"

"I need to see somebody about getting my brother's body home," said Tom.

"Your brother's body, huh? Now just how would I know anything about that?"

Tom, still holding his coat, fumbled in the pocket and produced the telegram. He handed it to the policeman.

"Hmm," said the cop, scratching head. "I believe you need to go up to homicide. They'll help you up there."

"Where's homicide," asked Tom.

"Second floor. Just take those steps there behind you. Tell the duty officer—better yet show him this telegram. He'll direct you." He handed the telegram back to Tom, who folded it and turned toward the stairs with it in his hand.

The stairs led up to what was also a large room filled with desks. Men, both in uniform and wrinkled suits, milled about or were sitting, talking on the telephone or pecking away at typewriters. The uniformed officer at the desk looked up from his paperwork and took the telegram which Tom handed him. Neither man spoke.

"Down the hall, Room 204. Lieutenant Lachance."

Tom put on his coat and walked past the duty desk and down a long hallway. Lieutenant Lachance's office was the third door down, on his left. Tom sighed deeply and tapped on the closed door.

"Yeah, what is it?" came the deeply-accented voice behind the door.

Tom opened the door and stepped just inside a small, cramped office. Lieutenant Lachance was at a desk piled high in papers and forms. In this disarray, there did not appear to be another square inch to place anything else. A floor fan oscillated laboriously in one corner, causing some of the papers on the desk to flutter each time its slight breeze passed. The lieutenant himself was hunched over the desk filling out a form with a fountain pen. His light tan straw fedora was pushed far back, reveling a head with little or no hair. His tie was loosened, and his white shirt, the sleeves rolled to the elbows, displayed a darkened circle of sweat under each arm. After a brief moment, he looked up at the man standing in the doorway.

"Well, come on in. I knew it must be a civilian since nobody around this place ever knocks. What can I do for you?"

"My name is Tom Pruitt."

"Congratulations, Mr. Pruitt," he said as he leaned back in his swivel chair, "but that doesn't tell me much, now does it?" Lachance placed the form on the desk in front of him.

Tom advanced into the office, to the edge of Lachance's desk. "I'm here to see about my brother." He placed the telegram flat on the form that the policeman had been working on. Lachance leaned forward and read it, and then looked back up at Tom.

"Sit down, Mr. Pruitt," he finally said, motioning to the only other chair in the room. "So Stanley Pruitt is—was—your brother?"

"Yes, sir. We called him Bud." Tom hesitated. "Can you tell me anything about what happened to him? My folks will want to know."

"Well, Mr. Pruitt, I can tell you what I know and it ain't much. He was found cut up with a knife. Not stabbed, just cut. When you're cut up the way your brother was you bleed to death pretty damn quick. He had been dead several hours when a beat cop found him. There are no witnesses, or at least none's come forward yet. And likely won't. They don't talk to policemen much over there. I wish I could tell you more, but that's about it. At least for now anyway."

"Are you still working on it? His murder, I mean?"

"Yes, of course we are. But I got to be honest with you, Mr. Pruitt, we get about seventy homicides a year here. That's better than one a week. We solve most of them, I guess, but too many go unsolved. Especially, the kind your brother was involved in?"

"What do you mean, involved?"

"Your brother was from out of town. Didn't know anyone in New Orleans as far as we know. And," Lachance hesitated, "he was killed over in the fifteenth ward. Across the river in Algiers. There's just nothing to go on. He was probably just in the wrong place at the wrong time, but we'll keep on it as long as we can."

"He knew someone in New Orleans," Tom said.

Lachance leaned back in his chair, rubbing his chin between his thumb and forefinger. "And who would that be?"

"His wife. He has a wife. Shelby Jean. She ran off. Left him a note that she was going to
New Orleans and wouldn't be back. That's why he was here. To find his wife and take her home."

"Well, now that's good to know. It's something," said Lachance, suddenly interested. He pushed aside some papers as if he was looking for something. He finally found it, a small leather note book. "Say her name is Shelby Jean?" He began to scribble in the notebook.

"Yes, sir."

"Can you describe her?"

"She has light brownish-blonde hair," said Tom.

"A dishwater blonde?" Lachance interrupted.

"I guess so. Blue eyes. I would say she was five-three or five-four."

"Okay, but what does she look like? I mean the whole package. Is she attractive? Homely? What?"

"She's very pretty."

"I suppose she talks with that hick accent? I mean, you know what I mean. Like Georgia or Carolina. No offense, Mr. Pruitt."

"She's from South Carolina. Like my brother."

"Well, now we got a little something to go on. Would you happen to know if she was in Algiers? Maybe working there?"

"I've never heard of this place, Algiers."

"I didn't think so, but we'll check it out for sure." Lachance scrambled around on his desk again and finally came up with a crumpled pack of Camel's. He extended it to Tom, who refused the cigarette. The policeman pulled one from the pack, lit it, and threw the dead match onto the floor beneath his chair.

"About my brother?" asked Tom.

"Yeah, I guess we need to take care of that. Now where is that paperwork?" He began to shift through the papers on his desk again. "I know it don't look like it, but everything I need is on this desk, somewhere. Just got to find it," the policeman chuckled. Finally, he found the paper he was looking for and he hurriedly filled in some of the blank spaces on it. "Mr. Pruitt, we'll need to go down to the morgue so I can get a positive I.D. You up to it now?"

"I'm as up to it as I'll ever be."

"Okay, let's go and get it over with," said the detective.

Tom followed Lachance down the hall, across the large office and down the stairs to the cavernous day room. Here they turned back to another set of stairs that led downward.

"It's in the basement."

"All right."

The morgue was very cold and had a strong sharp, medicinal odor. At the far end Tom could see a man in a long rubber apron, cigarette dangling from his mouth, hunched over a body stretched out on a long stainless-steel table. It didn't seem to bother him to be in the morgue. It was only bodies, dead bodies, and he had seen too many for too long for it to bother him now. Besides, it was his job. Just a job.

He followed Lachance to a bank of large stainless- steel drawers. They all had paper cards taped on them, with a name written in large letters. He pulled open the one whose card read 'Pruitt'. He pulled back the sheet covering the body and looked at Tom.

"It's my brother. It's Bud." Lachance quickly pulled the sheet back over the face and pushed the drawer shut.

They walked in silence back up to Lachance's office. He went behind his desk and Tom sat down in the straight-back chair. The policeman turned and retrieved a clipboard from a hook on the wall behind his desk. He placed the form on it and handed it to Tom.

"Just sign there where I marked with an 'X'." Tom took the clipboard, scribbled his signature, and handed back to Lachance. "Just one more thing, Mr. Pruitt. I'll need to collect fifty-dollars from you, if you've got it. He'll be on the first train out in the morning. We'll send a telegram back to your folks right away, but you might want to call them anyway. I mean about arrangements and such."

"All right."

"You can use the phone down in the day room, if you like. It's long-distance, but it won't cost you nothing."

"Yes, I'll do that. Thanks."

Tom pulled some bills from his trouser pocket and counted out five tens onto the desk.

"Well, I guess that's it. I'm real sorry about your brother, Mr. Pruitt. A young man like that shouldn't have to end up this way. No sir, he shouldn't and that's a fact." He wrote out a receipt and handed it to Tom.

They shook hands and Tom turned to leave. At the door, he stopped and looked at the detective. "Let me ask you something, lieutenant. Where is this Algiers?"

"Whoa, now, son! You leave New Orleans as soon as you can and forget about Algiers. It can be a rough place and you don't want no part of it, I can tell you that for sure. Look what happened to your brother over there. No sir, you don't want any part of Algiers."

"You never did say exactly where you found Bud. Where was he? Where did he die lying in his own blood?"

"I suppose you got a right to know that. We found him in an alley just outside a dive called the Yellow Parrot. Not an alley really. It's just a narrow wharf between the dive and the river. That's all. The Yellow Parrot is a rough place, Mr. Pruitt and I mean rough. I'm warning you, don't go over there. Forget all this and go back to South Carolina. Tomorrow."

"Do you think he was in the Yellow Parrot that night?"

"We don't know. Not yet anyway. That crowd over there sees nothing, hears nothing, says nothing. Like the three monkeys, if you know what I mean. Scared or something, I guess. I don't know. They don't like cops or strangers. A real low-life runs the place, owns it actually. To tell you the truth, Pruitt, he was a suspect. Still *is* I would say, but we got nothing on him. The story on the street is that he's good with a knife. Real good, but like I said, we got nothing to go on. And to be perfectly up front with you, we likely won't get anything. I'm sorry, but that's just the way it is sometimes."

"What's his name? The man at the Yellow Parrot."

"Bouchard. Ronnie Bouchard. But I'm warning you, Pruitt, don't get involved over here. This is a police matter. Go back to Carolina. We'll let you know if anything turns up. I swear to you we will."

"You said nothing will," Tom said dryly.

"I'm not an optimistic man, Pruitt. Twenty years dealing with this kind of shit tends to make a man just a little cynical, you know. I've been honest with you."

"Yes, I believe you have. Thank you, Lieutenant Lachance," replied Tom. He turned and walked down the hall and down the stairs. He made the call home on one of the phones in the day room. He spoke briefly with his father and then went through the large doors of the stations out into the hot, simmering street.

Kenneth P. Smith

CHAPTER 10

~

Tom strode down Canal Street, head down and hands thrust deep into his pockets, seemingly oblivious to the wet heat and people around him. He walked back past the train station without noticing. At the edge of the Quarter, on a corner, he entered a small restaurant. It was a shabby place with a few patrons at tables which appeared to be scattered about randomly. Across the room from the entrance, a bar ran nearly the length of the room. The bartender looked bored and was mindlessly polishing glasses. The row of bar stools was empty. Tom took a seat at one end. The bartender looked up, sighed deeply, and placed the glass he was cleaning on the shelf behind him.

"What's your pleasure, mister?"

"A beer."

The bartender pulled a glass mug from a narrow shelf overhead and placed it under the tap. With a foamy head, he set it down heavily on the bar in front of Tom. Some foam splashed out.

"Want to run a tab?"

"Can I order something to eat?"

"Sure. Menu's kind of limited this time of day. Got some red beans and rice leftover from lunch. Want to try it?"

"All right."

The bartender exited through a door behind the bar. He soon returned and set a plate heaped with red beans and rice on the bar before Tom.

"Want any hot sauce with them beans?"

"No, they're okay," said Tom, and he began to eat. The bartender drifted back to his post polishing glasses. Tom finished his meal and the beer, and lit a cigarette. He looked over at the bartender. "Can I ask you something?"

"Sure."

"Is there any kind of hotel nearby where I might could get a room? Just for the night."

The bartender flung the damp cloth over his shoulder and set the glass he had been wiping on the bar and strode back down to where Tom was sitting. He took a long look at Tom.

"You know you're in the French Quarter. But then again from the looks of you, you probably don't. We got lots of hotels about. I'd say you're not material for the Pontchartrain over in the Garden District," he said grinning and half shrugging. "It's a little on the ritzy-side, if you know what I mean. There's a little place down the street from here, just off Royal. They can probably fix you up. Called the Hotel le Quartier. Nothing fancy, mind you, but it's okay. Clean anyway."

Tom stood up and placed a dollar bill and two quarters on the bar.

"Thanks. This cover it?"

"Yeah, it covers it. You got some change coming though."

"Keep it," said Tom.

Kenneth P. Smith

Tom had not realized how tired he was until he lay down on the narrow bed in the small, dimly lit room. The man at the front desk had hardly looked up from the registration book as he stood there, and the porter had looked at him warily when it became apparent that the only luggage he had was the small canvas bag, his ditty bag from the Corps.

"What can I do for you?" the desk clerk had asked coldly.

"I'd like a room. A room for tonight," said Tom.

"Private bath or shared?" The clerk slid a blank registration card across the counter to Tom. "With bath, it's twelve dollars. Ten without."

"With a bath, I reckon," replied Tom.

"I reckon," mocked the clerk, shaking his head. "Twelve dollars. In advance."

Tom pulled the diminishing fold of bills from his pocket and placed the money on the counter. He then signed his name in the first blank of the registration card.

"Name's all I need," said the clerk as he quickly pulled the card away from Tom. The clerk handed him a large bronzed, tagged key and nodded to the staircase across the room.

The place was second-rate to be sure, but at least there was a private bath. Things looked reasonably clean, not that it really mattered to Tom at this point. Once in the room he had splashed water on his face. The he took off his coat and flopped down on the bed and slept.

When he woke up, the room was bathed in darkness though a faint yellow light blinked at him from the room's one small window. He sat up on the side of the bed for a moment before he realized where he was. He brushed his hair back with both hands and walked to the window which overlooked a small enclosed court yard. The light was reflected from a street light which he could not see from the window. He looked at his watch. Almost nine o'clock. He unzipped the ditty bag and pulled out the one clean shirt that it held. He put it on and combed his hair in the bathroom mirror. Putting on his coat, he left the room. The small lobby of the hotel was empty except for the desk clerk who sat smoking, listening to the radio. It was not the same man who was there when he had checked in. Tom walked over to the desk.

"Excuse me," he said to the clerk, an older man in a dingy white shirt. His stained black tie was loosened. He looked up at Tom for a second as if he had been awakened from a dream, and then sprang from his chair.

"Yes, sir?"

"I'd like to ask you something?"

"Anything wrong with your room, sir?" he asked, in sharp contrast to the surly day clerk.

"No, it's fine," Tom hesitated. "Can you tell me where Algiers is?"

"Sure thing. It's across the river."

"Across the river? How do you get there from here?"

"Well, there's the Huey Long Bridge up the river a ways. But the quickest way is the Canal Street ferry. Say," the clerk continued, glancing at the clock on the wall behind him, "you're not thinking about going over there tonight, are you?"

"I'm thinking about it," said Tom.

"If you want my advice, mister, I wouldn't do it. Not at night, anyway. And you being from out of town and all. No sir, I wouldn't advise it at all."

"Where's this ferry?"

"It's down at the end of Canal Street. That's why they call it the Canal Street ferry," said the clerk, suppressing a guffaw at his own joke.

"How late does it run?"

"On the quarter hour. Operates until midnight, but..."

"What's the fare?"

"You mean what's it cost? Nothing. 'Bout the only thing in this town that's free."

"Thanks, I appreciate the information."

"Canal Street's is down..."

"I know where it is," said Tom softly. "One more thing."

"Sure," answered the agreeable clerk.

"Ever heard of a place called the Yellow Parrot? It's in Algiers."

"Mister, now I know you've lost your mind. Roughest joint in New Orleans. You got to be kidding me!"

"Can you tell me how to find it?"

"Look, if you're bound and determined to go there. It's easy, it's on the Point, just off the water. 'Bout a block from the ferry wharf. But I'm telling you again, I wouldn't do it."

"Thanks," Tom said again and walked out of the hotel.

The hotel clerk was right. When he stepped off the ferry wharf he had spotted the large yellow neon parrot only a couple of blocks away. There were people milling about the street, shadows moving in the dim light of the few street lamps scattered on either side. They seemed to be just wandering aimlessly rather than going someplace in particular. Black people as well as whites. Drunks mostly. And women. Dark, painted women leaning on lamp posts, smoking, talking to each other or to the men passing by them. Some stopped. Most just strode on by, ignoring them.

He turned and walked toward the yellow neon sign. Beside the door, on the sidewalk was a huge, goateed man perched on a high stool wearing a beret cocked to one side. His heavily tattooed arms were folded across his massive chest and he had a bright yellow bird—a parrot—tattooed on his neck, on the left side. He and Tom exchanged quick glances as Tom reached for the door.

"Whoa, mother, just where do you think you're going?"

"Inside. Just want a beer," said Tom.

"Just want a beer, that right?"

"Yeah, that's right."

"You looking for trouble? You appear to me to be looking for trouble," said the big man as he slid off the stool, towering above Tom.

"No trouble. Just a beer, that's all."

"You a tough guy?" asked the man.

"No, I'm not a tough guy."

"You ain't no Algerine."

"No, I'm not."

"I ain't ever seen you around here before. You dressed like a cop. You a cop?

"No, I'm not a cop. I'm traveling, from out of town. Just heard about this place and thought I'd stop in for a beer. No trouble."

"No trouble," the man repeated. Then, "Turn and place your hands on the wall, high up. Tom turned to the building and did what the man ordered. He was being frisked. "Okay, you're clean. There's a dollar cover. You got a dollar?" Tom reached into his pocket and handed the man a dollar bill. He looked at it closely and stuffed it in his shirt pocket. "No trouble."

"No trouble," said Tom as the doorman pulled the door open for him.

He knew immediately that he had stepped into another world. It was a large, dimly-lit room into which it did not seem one additional person could fit. A thin, blue cloud of cigarette smoke hug near the low ceiling. On a low, raised stage a bad Cajun band blared at the far end. The entire middle of the room was the dance floor and it was crammed with people, mostly couples. Here and there a single person—women—swayed to the music, lost in themselves, someplace else. In the crowd, two women, one white, one black, embraced and danced totally out of rhythm with the music. Along one side of the dance floor were tables, scattered along the wall. Along the opposite wall were separate booths, dark and shadowy. The people in the room seemed to be all revolving slowly around its center, drunk, embraced by the music and the alcohol.

Tom entered this surreal scene seemingly unnoticed by anyone. He strode around the edge of the crowded dance floor to the bar to his left. He took the only available seat, a stool beside the cash register. On the other side of the register, a stream of barmaids came with their trays, picked up their drink orders, and disappeared back into the crowd.

"What can I get you, chief?" asked one of the bartenders, wiping off the bar where Tom sat with damp, greasy rag.

"A beer."

"Well, I got two kinds. Dixie on draft and Dixie in bottle. What'll it be?"

"A bottle," said Tom. Almost immediately the bottle of beer appeared on the bar before him.

"That'll be a quarter." Tom placed the coin on the bar.

He turned slightly on the bar stool and looked out over the packed room. The band was into another song which sounded exactly like the one they had just played. He glanced down the row of booths that ran down the wall to his left. Then suddenly something, someone, caught his eye. At the farthest booth, the one closet to the band, was a young woman. He could see her, but not plainly through the blue haze of cigarette smoke. She was talking to someone else in the booth sitting opposite her who Tom could not see. After a moment the woman slid out of the booth and took the hand of the other person, a man. He stood up too. She led him along the edge of the crowd, still holding his hand, to some stairs at the end of the bar which Tom had not noticed before. He was a young man in boots and a straw western hat pushed back on his head. They were both laughing as they disappeared up the stairs. Suddenly he realized that he knew the woman. It was Shelby Jean.

He turned back to the bar and sipped the beer. A barmaid, pretty, stepped up impatiently and set her tray on the bar.

"Two bottles of beer and glass of brandy. The cheap stuff," she yelled out to the bartender. Chomping on gum, she looked over at Tom and gave him a brief, tight smile as he looked at her. The bartender placed the drinks on her tray and made change at the register.

Kenneth P. Smith

"Ronnie Bouchard. Is he here tonight?" Tom asked, looking at the bartender.

"I don't know any Ronnie Bouchard," came the terse reply.

"I was told he owned this place."

The bartender handed the money to the waitress, slammed the register drawer shut, and leaned over the bar, almost in Tom's face.

"Look, chief, I don't know or care who you are or what you're doing here, but I'd strongly advise you to finish that beer and then get the hell out of here. You listening?"

"Yeah, I'm listening," said Tom, looking down at the beer bottle on the bar in front of him. The bartender walked away.

In a few minutes the pretty barmaid was back and placed her order. She then moved over closed to the register, to where Tom sat. She glanced at the bartender whose back was to her.

"He's here. Ronnie's here," she said in an almost whisper.

"Where is he?"

"At the end of the hall. Past the restrooms." She nodded quickly to the hallway across from the end of the bar, beyond the stairs where he had seen Shelby Jean. Just as quickly she moved back to her station as the bartender turned to her with the drinks. Tom put the bottle to his lips and drained the last of the beer. He glanced down the long hallway, past the restrooms where a single light bulb hung from the ceiling. In the dim, yellow light he could see what looked like a blue door. He slid off the bar stool and walked down the row of booths, toward the band. About half way down he stopped abruptly and turned back. He turned down the hallway and stopped at the entrance to the men's room. From here he could see the bartender hunched over, feverishly mixing drinks. He hesitated and then turned and walked slowly down the hallway, toward the blue door.

CHAPTER 11

~

He tapped on the blue door firmly with his knuckles and waited. No voice came from the other side. He tapped on the door again.

"Yeah," came a voice from inside the room.

Tom opened the door and stood in the doorway of the small office. It was brightly lit by two tubes of fluorescent light that hung close to the ceiling. A man sat at a desk at the far wall, opposite Tom in the doorway. Behind the desk, a little to the right, was a closed door.

The thing that struck Tom was nothing about the small, non-descript room, but rather the man himself. He had thick, very dark hair which was swept back from his forehead. His face was smooth and dark, with a thin line of a moustache across his upper lip. He wore what appeared to be a burgundy-colored jacket over a dark blue shirt. His yellow silk tie was knotted tightly and cinched up close to his throat. The silk handkerchief tucked in the breast pocket of the coat matched his tie perfectly. But his eyes were what Tom noticed most. They were small and dark, almost black. More than sinister, they were piercing and cold. There was no feeling in them. Strangely, he felt a slight shudder pass over him as he stood looking down at the man. There what looked to be an accounting journal on the desk top. It was closed and a pencil lay on top of it. There was nothing else on the desk top, but a silver, pointed letter opener.

"What can I do for you, my friend?" asked the man sitting behind the desk. "I am very busy at the moment." He spoke very politely in clear, but accented English.

"I'm looking for Bouchard. Ronnie Bouchard."

"Yes, and you have found him."

"I'm here to see about my brother. I mean, to find out what happened to him," said Tom.

"And may I ask who is your brother?"

"Bud Pruitt. Was Bud Pruitt."

"I know nothing of a Bud Pruitt. Now if you will excuse me..."

"I think someone here at this, uh, at the Yellow Parrot, might know something."

The man leaned back in his chair and interlocked the fingers of his hands, which lay on the desk.

"Please come in, my friend, and close the door behind you." He motioned to one of the two chairs in the room. Tom ignored the gesture and remained standing.

"My brother was found dead here a few days ago."

"Dead here?"

"In Algiers. In some sort of alley or wharf, near your place. Yes, here."

"Look, my friend, I know nothing of your brother, of his murder, if that's what it was. I cannot help you. Go back to the bar and have a couple of drinks. On me. Then go home. It is good advice. I assure you, there is nothing here to find."

Suddenly, the door behind Tom flung open. He did not turn around, but continued to stare at the sitting Bouchard.

Kenneth P. Smith

"Ronnie! Ronnie, I need..."

Tom recognized the breathless voice of the woman and turned toward her. She looked at him, her eyes wild for a second, her hand to her mouth.

"Tom! My god, what are doing here?"

"Hello, Shelby Jean. Just trying to find out what happened to Bud. That's all."

Shelby Jean, gaining her composure, "Well, he sure as hell ain't here. He was, a few days ago. Wanted to take me back to that god-forsaken mill town. But I ain't ever going back there, and I told him so. Just that. He'll probably be back, but he can forget about it. You can tell him that when you find him.

"He's dead, Shelby Jean."

She looked down at the floor for a moment and steadied herself against the door. It was obvious she hadn't known. Finally, "God, I wondered why he hadn't been back around. He said he would be back. Threatened to drag me back to Whittier. I was never going back and I couldn't stand the sight of him, but I never wanted him dead. No, not dead." She turned, her head down, and walked out the door, back down the hall. Back to the world she had chosen.

"One of my best girls," said Bouchard, smiling coldly, "but I did not know her name was Shelby Jean. She is Crystal here. I mean, her working name. I could not care less about her real name or where she is from. It is just business. I am sure you understand, Mr. Pruitt. They come and they go. But Crystal—your Shelby Jean—this life seems to fit her. She is, what shall I say? A natural."

"My brother was killed with a knife. Not stabbed, but cut up. Bled to death."

"You are becoming burdensome, my friend. Take my advice, and go home. Do not come back to Algiers."

"I hear you're good with a knife, Mr. Bouchard."

"And who, might I ask, told you such a thing?"

"A policeman. Downtown. He's working on my brother's murder. He knows you."

Bouchard absentmindedly adjusted his tie and straightened his yellow pocket handkerchief. He never took his eyes off of Tom. For a moment a strange silence fell over the two men. Finally, Bouchard stood up and lightly brushed the lapels of his jacket with his hands. Tom noticed that his fingers were long and slender, like a woman's. His fingernails were manicured. His demeanor suddenly changed. He seemed to relax and he spoke softly.

"It is stuffy in here, don't you think? Let's go out on the wharf. You can leave this way," said Bouchard as he turned and opened the door behind the desk.

He stepped outside, leaving the door ajar. Tom took a deep breath and followed him. As he walked past the desk he glanced down. The letter opener. With his left hand, he deftly scooped it up and grasp it, hiding the handle in his palm with the blade pressed flat against his wrist.

"You see, my friend, the air is much nicer out here under the stars. There is the street," said Bouchard, pointing with the extended palm of his hand.

The air was not nicer. It was hot and heavy, and smelled of decaying fish. It seemed to press down on you. There were no stars. Bouchard stood on the wharf to the left of the door. To his right, in the distance, Tom could see the dimly-lit street. He could hear water lapping against the pilings. Was this where Bud had been killed? Someplace like this? Near here for sure.

"Actually, Mr. Pruitt, there is nothing else to talk about. I would urge you to turn and walk to the street and leave this place. Please do as I ask."

"I don't think so, Mr. Bouchard. Not until I get some answers."

"But, you see, I can give you no answers. Except for, *la vie continue*—life goes on. What can I say? I'm afraid other than that, my friend, there are no answers. You will leave now."

"I don't think that I will," said Tom, softly, almost to himself.

"No, I did not think so, but I had to try. It is unfortunate." As Bouchard said this, there was a 'click-click' in the darkness.

Tom caught the glint of the knife which Bouchard held in his right hand, tapping it repeatedly against his thigh. With his fingers, Tom nimbly flipped the letter opener around in his hand, and grasp the handle. Suddenly Tom felt the knife sweep across his face and a long shallow line appeared on his left cheek as he instinctively drew back to dodge the slash. Bouchard crouched low and a thin, tight smile crossed his lips, showing a row of white teeth. Like a cat, quick and noiselessly, he lunged forward, drawing the knife deeply in a diagonal line across Tom's chest. Tom felt this cut and knew that he was wounded as he staggered back against the wall of the building. He did not look down at his bleeding chest, but kept his eyes focused on the other man. Bouchard smiled and then lunged again, higher this time, aiming at Tom's throat. Tom drew back and caught the wrist of the hand holding the knife. Both men, breathing heavily, glared into each other's eyes, their faces almost touching. Gripping the letter opener tightly, Tom instinctively shoved it forward into Bouchard's chest just below his rib cage. In rapid succession he withdrew the weapon and continued stabbing him, holding him up by the wrist.

Finally, the knife dropped from Bouchard's hand and fell almost noiselessly onto the wharf. Tom let go of his wrist and Bouchard crumpled to his knees. Tom stood over him breathless, watching him as he fell, finally becoming an insignificant pile, a mass of something inhuman, prostrate before him.

Tom dropped the letter opener onto the wharf, and then slid it over the edge and into the murky river with his foot. He reached down and pulled the yellow handkerchief from the dead man's jacket pocket and wiped the warm blood from his hand. He dropped the bloodied piece of silk and it floated quickly to down and came to rest beside the switchblade. With his left arm press tightly across his chest, over the wound, he turned and walked unsteadily toward the streetlight, and the street.

Just beyond the entrance to the Yellow Parrot he grasped a lamp post to steady himself. He was hurt, cut deeply by Bouchard's knife. He was bleeding. He buttoned the three buttons of his coat and drew it tighter around him. Parked at the curb on the block just ahead he saw a Yellow Cab. A woman on the street was leaning over talking to the driver who sat behind the wheel, smoking. Tom stepped out into the street and motioned for the taxi. The driver continued talking to the woman. *Doesn't see me, thought Tom.* He leaned back against the lamp post. He felt tired, weak. After a moment's rest, he stepped back into the street and motioned for the taxi. This time the driver saw him and blinked his headlight. He and the woman continued to talk briefly and then the cab moved slowly down the street toward Tom.

He slid into the back seat.

"Where to, my man?" asked the driver jovially, looking at him in the rearview mirror.

"Train station."

"Which one. We got two."

"I don't know. It's on Canal Street." Tom was weak, his voice almost a whisper.

"That would be the Southern Railway terminal," said the driver. "Going to cost you five bucks."

"All right," said Tom.

"I'm assuming you got five bucks, that is."

"Yeah, I have it." Tom managed to pull a twenty-dollar bill from his pocket, as the driver reached for the meter lever. "Please, don't do that. Here, take this. This fare never happened." Tom leaned forward and handed the driver the twenty.

"Okay, if you say so. You my last ride of the night anyway," answered the driver. Still looking back at Tom, he hesitated for a moment. "Say, you all right? You don't sound so good and you look like hell, if you don't mind me saying so."

"I'm all right. I'm fine. Let's go."

The car pulled away from the curb and turned left on River Road, toward the Huey Long Bridge.

The train terminal was almost totally deserted as he entered it from Canal Street. Griping his coat tightly to his chest, he made his way to the men's lavatory. As he pushed open the heavy wooden door, he saw that the large bathroom was empty—he was alone. Taking no chances, he wet several paper towels at a sink and went into one of the stalls, latching the door behind him. The front of his shirt was bloody, but the cut wasn't as deep as he had thought. He cleaned the wound with the paper towels, dabbing the ten-inch cut with them. He pulled off the shirt and held it stretched against the wall as best he could, and wiped the blood with the remaining wet towels until the dark red stains became a faded pink. He then placed a dry section of towel on his skin against the wound and put the shirt back on. Over this he donned his jacket and buttoned it. Holding his left forearm across his chest as inconspicuously as possible, he walked slowly back out into the empty terminal and sat down. He glanced up at the huge clock on the opposite wall fifty feet away. Three-thirty. The Southern Crescent would board and be headed north at six and he would be on it. In a few moments, his chin fell against his chest and he dozed off.

Kenneth P. Smith

PART 2

CHAPTER 12

~

Jarrard's Store sat in the middle of the Sterling Mill village. It was a low, one-room clapboard structure painted white decades ago, but what paint remained was discolored and peeling, with much bare wood exposed. It sat square and squat in the "V" of Seventh and Eighth Streets where they met to become First Street.

Old Mister Jarrard didn't like to move much, so he didn't. He generally sat on a high stool behind the counter next to the antiquated cash register, puffing a cheap cigar. If you needed to buy something but didn't know where it was in the store he'd grunt and point to it. That was the extent of his 'customer service'. He hired a kid to come in a couple of days a week after school to stock shelves and sweep the floor, and deliver the few orders that customers in the neighborhood sometimes called in. He stocked bread and a few other staples, but they were usually stale or moldy from being left on the shelves too long. The big new super market downtown supplied most of Whittier with the groceries and other things they needed.

But Jarrard and his little store had a couple of things going for it that made it a natural gathering place, especially for the men of the mill village. He was located right in the middle of the village and, more importantly, he sold cold beer. The location and the beer made it a perfect place for the local mill workers and their cronies to meet and gossip. Or as they liked to say, chew the fat.

As he did on most days, Enoch Griffin waited by the time clock, punching out as soon as the four o'clock whistle blew. He walked briskly out the main gate, headed for Jarrard's. He entered the store, nodded to the old man on the stool behind the counter on the far wall, and went straight to the dull red Coca Cola cooler to his left. There were a few sodas in the icy water, but mostly it was filled with beer. Because the distributor offered him a kick-back, Pabst Blue Ribbon was the only beer that Jarrard stocked. And Blue Ribbon was just fine with Enoch as he pulled a bottle from the cooler and opened it with the church key hanging by a string on the wall. Cold beer was cold beer. Old Jarrard, of course, watching this and without moving any part of his body other than his right hand, made a tick in the small spiral notebook on the counter, beside Enoch's initials.

"Um, that's good!" said Enoch, taking a huge gulp from the chilled bottle and wiping the back of his hand across his mouth. "Gets all that lint out of my throat," he chuckled.

He finished the first beer quickly and reached into the cooler for another. Another tick was recorded in Jarrard's notebook.

"I'm going to sit outside and wait for the boys," said Enoch to Jarrard, who nodded almost imperceptibly.

Outside the store, in front, was an old straight back chair and several wooden apple crates. In summer and on mild days and nights the men like to sit outside, drink beer, and, well, chew the fat. It seemed that Enoch Griffin was always the first to leave the mill when the day shift ended and the first to arrive at Jarrard's Store. He took the chair and leaned it back on two back legs against the store building, facing First Street and the direction of the mill. This way he could spot his cronies as they approached from the mill several blocks away. He sipped his beer and waited.

Claude Pruitt finally reached the store and found the usual patrons sitting on the crates out front or squatting against the outside wall of the building. He said nothing, but went inside and reached in the cooler for a bottle of beer. Jarrard entered the inevitable tick mark in his little notebook. He then returned to the outside with the other men.

"Worked a little overtime, did you, Claude?" said Gabby Osteen who was squatting against the building, spitting tobacco and sipping from his bottle. A brown wet stain of tobacco juice ran from the corner of his mouth down the left side of his chin.

"Nah, just had to show the new man something on the loom I'd been working on. He's just started the second shift. That's all."

"Sounds to me like a little brown-nosing going on with the second-hand," teased Enoch from his chair.

"You go to hell," shot back Claude, "I was just trying to help the new man. That's all."

"I remember the days when a new man had to start on the graveyard shift and work his way up. Nowadays, they just seem to start working wherever they want to, or wherever the overseer needs them. Sure didn't see any new man on the day shift or the second, that's for sure," offered Bubba Jack Wilson, sitting hunched over on one of the apple crates, his elbows resting on his knees.

"This new man, Claude, he young? Where'd he come from?"

"Why, it's just Homer Peace's boy. Young? Hell, yeah, he's young. Just got out of the service," said Claude.

"And hired on as a loom fixer right out of the gate. Why I never!" said Bubba Jack.

"Well, you see, he got training. In the army, I mean. No, I reckon it was the navy where he worked on machines. He's pretty sharp to be as young as he is," said Claude.

"It's scary, that's what it is. All these men getting back from the war. Young and strong and needing jobs. They'll have all our jobs before it's over with. I can tell you that," said Gabby after he'd drained the last of the beer from the bottle. He wiped his mouth with his shirt sleeve.

"I don't matter none anyway. They going to sell the mill. Then we'll all be out of work for sure," said Griffin.

"Goddamn it, Enoch, don't start that shit again!" said Claude angrily. "You don't know what you're talking about. Mr. Sterling ain't going to sell the mill, so shut up about it. I'm tired of hearing it."

"Get mad at me if you want to, but I'm telling the mill's going. Sooner than later," returned Enoch to the group.

"I'm going in and get me another beer," said Gabby.

"Bring me one too, will you, Gabby?" asked Bubba Jack.

"Get it yourself. Old man Jarrard will charge me for it and I ain't buying your beer." Gabby pushed himself slowly up from his squat and sauntered into the store. Claude looked over at Enoch.

"What makes you so sure that Sterling's going to sell the mill? Do you know something or are you just bull-shitting us?"

"I know something, that's what, but I ain't supposed to tell anybody. My wife would kill me."

"Your wife? What's she got to do it?" demanded Claude

Enoch looked around the group, whom Gabby had rejoined, and then over his shoulder as if someone might be watching or listening. He took a swig of beer.

"Y'all promise you won't say nothing to nobody, I mean, where you heard it?'

"Yeah, yeah, just tell us," said Claude, looking around at the small group. Bubba Jack nodded his head. Gabby Johnson, back squatting, just shrugged. They all knew that Enoch was bursting to reveal his source. They didn't have to promise him anything.

"Well, you see, it's like this," Enoch said leaning toward the other men, lowering his voice almost to a whisper. "My wife's sister Janice is friends, and I mean close friends, with Ford Sterling's secretary. Y'all know Janice, don't you?"

"For god's sake, Enoch, what'd she say?" said Claude impatiently.

"She, Sterling's secretary, told Janice that Mr. Sterling had an offer on his desk. She didn't say how much, but it came from those gents I told y'all about I saw. They were down here from New York all right. That's the god's honest true. He's going to sell the mill!"

"Damn!" said Gabby.

"Damn!" said Bubba Jack.

"Don't mean nothing," said Claude. After a long moment, "I got to go." Without another word, he rose from the apple crate, kicked it over and walked off, leaving an empty beer bottle on the ground.

"What's eating him?" asked Enoch.

"Hell if I know."

"Well, I'm going to have me another Blue Ribbon," Enoch shrugged and stood. "Anybody want one?" he asked, standing.

"You buying?"

"Hell no!"

"Tell old man Jarrard to tick me for it. Yeah, bring me one more."

"Me, too."

With his hands thrust deep in his overall pockets, Claude strode home slowly, deep in thought. What with new owners, if there were any, and all the boys coming home from the war, he felt uncertain about his future at the mill. It was all he'd ever known. The mill, this town. He was already having trouble keeping up with the work load. He'd strained something in his lower back last month and the arthritis he'd inherited from his mother worsened almost by the day. He already took a fist full of aspirin every day, and his stomach was screaming for him to ease off. New owners, he knew, would change things. Profits would have to be increased, and that meant more and harder work. He did not believe that he could handle it. Not now. He just wanted to work five more years and get his gold watch. Gold-plated anyway. He'd saved a little money and social security would kick in. If only he could make it to then they'd be all right.

Kenneth P. Smith

He shook himself as if shaking off a bad dream, and thought what Jewel had said about Enoch Griffin, how he gossiped, told tales, sometimes maybe lied. At least stretched the truth. Especially when he'd been drinking. Enoch Griffin's full of shit. Sterling would never sell the mill. It belonged in Whittier. To the people. With this, Claude's steps lightened and he increased his pace toward home. Ah, that Enoch Griffin's just full of shit. That's all. Things'll be fine. Just fine.

CHAPTER 13

~

Hatcher handed the girl at the register a quarter and picked up the tray with a hotdog, a bag of potato chips, and a bottle of Coke on it. He then turned away from the counter, looking for a place to sit and scarf down a quick lunch. He was scheduled to be in court at one and he couldn't be late. Joe's Place was packed with the lunch crowd and he didn't see an unoccupied booth or table. He then spotted a booth toward the back with a lone occupant. As he headed toward it, many of the booths were filled with people he knew or that knew him. He nodded to them or spoke in passing, but he didn't have time to stop and chat. Not today. He approached the booth where a young man sat, alone.

"Mind if I sit down. This place is packed today."

Without waiting for a response, Hatcher placed his tray on the table and sat down.

"All right," replied the young man as Hatcher unwrapped the greasy, thin paper from the hotdog and took a bite. He then took a sip of his Coke and looked over at the young man, and extended his hand.

"Theo Hatcher. How are you?"

"I'm fine," replied the young man. "Name's Tom Pruitt. Pleased to meet you, Mister Hatcher." Hatcher looked at him hard and quizzically for a brief moment, and then he remembered. "Say, you're Claude Pruitt's boy, aren't you?"

"Yes, sir, I suppose I am. You know my daddy?"

"Sure do. I guess I know pretty much everyone who works at the Sterling mill. Your dad's been there a long time. A pretty good loom fixer, I hear." Hatcher knew many of the mill workers and, being a small town, most of the townspeople. He had a good memory and an easy-going knack for making you feel like he knew who *you* were, or at least that he knew your family.

"He's been there a while. All my life, at least."

Hatcher took another couple of chomps of the hotdog and it was gone. He then opened the pack of chips and popped one in his mouth.

"I know you too, Tom," said Hatcher. "At least of you. Watched you play ball for Whittier High a while back. Pretty good end as I recall."

"Yeah, but that seems like a long time ago now, Mr. Hatcher." said Tom. Like most people in town, Tom knew who Theo Hatcher was although they had never personally met.

"Well, I guess it has been a while at that. You been away in the war. Like a lot of Whittier boys. How long you been back home, Tom?"

"Just a little while."

"Well, I just want to let you know we're all real grateful for what you boys did over there. And you a hero to boot, according to the paper. Silver Star I believe it was."

"Bronze Star, but I'm not a hero, Mr. Hatcher. Far from it."

"I appreciate your modesty, son, but you had to do something to get that medal. They don't come in a Cracker Jack box," Hatcher chuckled good naturedly.

"I was just trying to survive. That's all. I made it home, the heroes didn't." Tom said and then stared down at the half-eaten hamburger on the table in front of him. Hatcher leaned back in the booth, munching on potato chips.

"I believe you won a Purple Heart too."

"It's not something you win."

"Well, let's just say you earned a Purple Heart. That'll do, won't it?"

"Well, no sir, it won't. I don't mean to be disrespectful, but you don't win a Purple Heart and you sure as hell don't earn one. I reckon it's the only medal they give for being unlucky. The lucky ones, the ones who don't get shot or get a piece of hot metal ripping through their gut, they don't get anything. Maybe an 'at a boy' sometimes and then they go on and do it again. But the unlucky ones, like me, who catch a bullet or a fragment of hot swirling metal, we get recognized. We get a medal. Like I said, it's the only one I know of that's given for being unlucky. I was unlucky, so I got one. That's all."

"Well, Tom, all that may be true. Depends on your perspective I guess. That's the way you see it. But any way you cut it, you did your family and Whittier proud."

Hatcher wadded up the potato chip bag and wiped his mouth with the paper napkin. He ran his tongue across his front teeth, making a slight sucking sound. He then looked over at Tom.

"What are you going to do with yourself? I mean, now that you're out of the service. Got any plans?" Hatcher asked.

"No, no plans. None yet anyway. I probably won't stay around here. My daddy wants to get me a job at the mill, but..."

"Take your time, son, is what I say. Poke around a little. Have some fun. You might find that Whittier's not such a bad place after all."

"Oh, it's not that. I don't think Whittier's a bad place. It's just so..."

"Small," Hatcher interrupted.

"I guess that's one thing. But I don't know. It just doesn't seem like I belong here anymore. Don't know that I ever did, come to think about it."

Hatcher stared at Tom, studying him in some way. Tom glanced up at him, but then looked away. He felt that Hatcher was going to say something, so he waited.

Finally, Hatcher said, "Tom, while you're deciding about things, what you would think about coming to work for me over at the law office?"

"The law office? You mean like cleanup for you?"

"No, no, nothing like that," chuckled Hatcher. "Hell, I got a janitor. I need someone, someone I can depend on, to deliver documents for me. Run errands. Stuff like that. It would be only part time, but it would give you something to do while you're deciding. How about it?"

"I don't know, Mr. Hatcher. Why me? You don't know me."

"I know you were born and raised in Whittier. You dad works at the mill. You're a Marine and decorated war hero. That's all I need to know."

"Well, you know *some* things about me." Thoughts of New Orleans flashed by him.

"Ah, I've been needing someone for a while now. Someone who can take responsibility, who I can trust. Just can't find anyone I can count on. Horace Staley worked for me for years, but he passed away last year. I'll pay you twenty-five dollars a week. How's that sound?"

"That sounds like a lot of money for a part time job."

"Oh, don't worry about that. You'll earn it!"

"I don't know, Mr. Hatcher. How would I get around? I mean to deliver your things, uh, your papers, the documents. I don't own a car."

"Why, you'd use mine. I'm almost always in the office during the day, and I can walk over to the courthouse when I need to be there. I walked here to Joe's today for lunch. Don't need an automobile much during the day in Whittier. Besides, like I said, it would be just part time."

"I don't know, Mr. Hester."

"Well, you take a few days to think it over and let me know," said Hatcher, and then he glanced at his watch. "Whoa, I got to be going. Got to be in court at one." He scooted out of the booth, picking up his tray. He looked down at Tom. "Think it over, Tom, but don't wait too long. Let me hear from you by the end of the week. Just stop by the office."

"All right," said Tom, and Hatcher was gone.

The lunch crowd was thinning out at Joe's, but Tom sat in the booth deep in thought. He felt a vague reluctance about reconnecting. Wasn't even sure he knew what it was. Reconnecting with anything familiar. He knew the longer he hung around Whittier the worse things would get. This life, this mill town life, had a way of getting its claws in you. He did not want that. He wasn't sure what he wanted, but he was sure it wasn't in Whittier. But it was more than that. He was restless. He didn't sleep at night. He couldn't face the dreams he knew were waiting on him. He had left the Pacific and the war, but it hadn't left him. He didn't feel that he would, or could, ever be normal again. He had seen too much and he had become numb to those around him now. He thought about what had happened in New Orleans, but there was no guilt. Just an empty feeling about it all. Self-defense, yes, but he was sure he had avenged Bud's murder. He knew that there would be repercussions. There always were.

Tom finally rose from the booth and walked through a now mostly empty Joe's. As he passed the cash register, one of girls spoke to him and giggled, but he did not hear her. He pushed open the front door and stepped out onto the sidewalk.

CHAPTER 14

~

Tom brushed his hair back and stepped into the office. Without looking up from her typing, Dorothy motioned him with her head to the worn leather chair in front of her desk.

"He's still at the courthouse. Be back any minute I expect," she said absentmindedly, concentrating on the document she was creating before her.

"All right."

Tom slumped down in the worn leather chair across from Dorothy's desk. He watched her for a moment, lost in her work. And then really for the first time, he looked around the office which was plain and somewhat drab. On the pale green walls hung two pictures—one of the Sterling mill and one a bad amateurish water color of a mountain scene. Probably painted by one of Hatcher's children or maybe one of Dorothy's, if she had any; he didn't know. The only other things in the room were a coat rack in the far corner and Dorothy's business school diploma on the wall beside her desk. He glanced at his watch. Almost noon. Suddenly the outside door opened. It was Hatcher.

"Hey, there, Tom. Been to dinner yet?" Hatcher said as he came through the door and immediately began to peel off the coat to his seersucker suit after placing his briefcase on Dorothy's desk, scattering papers that were neatly stacked. She stopped typing and glared up at him, irritated, but said nothing. "Hotter than a two-dollar pistol today," he continued without waiting on Tom's reply. "Come on back to the office. Hold any calls, Dorothy."

"Unless it's Mr. Sterling, I assume?"

"Especially if it's Sterling. I've had a rough morning in court and I've got some work I need to catch up on. Just make up something and take a call-back. Come on, Tom," said Hatcher as he picked up the brief case further sending papers flying, and turned to enter his office, followed by Tom. He hung his coat on the rack in the corner and went behind his desk and plopped in his chair.

"Dorothy, please bring us a couple of cups of water from the cooler," he drawled to the switched-on intercom. "Sit down, Tom. I need you to run an errand this afternoon." Tom took a chair as Dorothy came through the door with two paper cups. She placed them on the edge of his desk and left the room, closing the door behind her.

"By the way, did you see that jeep parked out front, Tom?" Hatcher asked with some excitement rising in his voice.

"That red thing. Yes, sir, I saw it."

"Well, what do you think? About the jeep I mean."

"It's a jeep." replied Tom dryly and shrugged.

"Ford Sterling sent his man down to Fort Jackson last week for the auction. Government surplus stuff from the war, you know. Wanted him to see if he could buy a truck for the mill. Cheap, you know Ford."

"No, sir, I really don't."

"Doesn't matter, just a figure of speech. Anyway, old Moonie—that's Ford's man—buys a truck at the auction, an old army six-by. But he sees this red jeep and bid a hundred dollars just for the hell of it. And by Jove, no one else bid on, so Moonie had to buy it. On the spot! When Ford found out about it he was mad as hell. Almost fired Moonie, and probably would have if he hadn't got such a good deal on the six-by. To make a long story short, I offered Ford what he paid for it and now it's mine. No cash changed hands; I just bartered services. Pretty good deal myself, I'd say."

"Yes, sir. A good deal on a government surplus red jeep," Tom said with just a hint of sarcasm, which Hatcher missed.

"Yeah, it *is* red. Pretty faded though. Don't know why, red I mean. Probably used in a hospital unit or maybe a firehouse. Doesn't matter. It runs good and I got a whale of a deal on it."

"You going to drive it?"

"Well, no. I've got a car. Thought I'd let you drive around for the things you do for me. You can keep it. Drive it home. Have full use of it. Besides, it'll free up my car if I need it.

"All right, Mister Hatcher," Tom said and took a sip of water from the paper cup.

"I need for you to deliver some papers this afternoon, if you will."

"Sure."

"Do you know where the Horse Pasture is?"

"Yes, sir, I think so. Up near the state line I believe." Tom knew where the Horse Pasture was all right. Years ago in high school, on a dare, he and a couple of his buddies had driven up there one night with Emmy Lou Bryant. Emmy Lou was a pretty girl, but she also had a reputation of being a very generous one as well. It was not his proudest moment, he remembered, as he waited impatiently in the car while his two friends, excited and giggling, disappeared into the dark woods with Emmy Lou leading the way. It seemed like a long time ago and he did not remember much about it now. Though tempted, he'd stayed in the car.

"That's right, on up past the reservoir. A real wilderness all right. I need you to take this document to Miss Minnie Ferguson up there." Hatcher slid the envelop across the desk. Tom stood up and retrieved it.

"All right."

"Let me give you a little back ground first," said Hatcher. "This here is an offer to buy her land. Oh, she'll turn it down. Always does, but we still got to deliver it and let her do it. You see, back when the power company was buying up all the land up there, they were able to get almost all of it. Parcel after parcel. If they hit on someone who didn't want to sell, they just took their imminent domain argument to the court and got a ruling. Simple as that. But then one day they knocked on Miss Minnie Ferguson's door. Hers was the last track they wanted. They needed it to run power cables across it. But she wasn't about to sell. She lives on ten or twelve acres up there, more or less, most of it slanted mountain land. No real value. No value, that is, to anyone but the power company and Miss Minnie. You see, her family's been on that land for at least three generations—probably longer. Family cemetery plot and all that too. No way that she was, or is, going to sell it."

"So why are you giving her the offer?"

"Well, the thing is, I'm her attorney. At least of record. She won't let anybody from the power company near her place, not since she won the court ruling. So the power company ups the offer every year, brings it to me, and I take it to her. That's about all there is to it."

"All right. I'll need the car keys," said Tom, having forgotten the conversation about the jeep.

"No problem, Tom, but there's where the jeep comes in. Like I said, while I got it you can drive it. I'll put the gas in it. And it don't take a key. Got a starter button on the floorboard."

"Yes, sir, I know about the starter," Tom said.

"I suppose you saw a lot of jeeps during the war, huh?"

"Yes, sir."

Hatcher smiled up at Tom, shrugged, then tore a clean sheet from the legal pad on his desk and began to draw. Finally, he handed the paper to Tom. "Here. It's a map to Minnie Ferguson house. You'll need it."

Tom took the crudely drawn map and the envelope containing the offer, and turned to the door. "I'll see you later, Mr. Hatcher. Looks like it might be a ways to Miss Ferguson's."

"Oh, it'll like be near dark by the time you get back to town. I'll see you tomorrow. And Tom, be careful. It's rough country up there, especially when you get off the county road. More like a pig trail. Probably be glad you're in a jeep. And tell Minnie hello for me," Hatcher chuckled and turned to the papers on his desk. 'I guess he forgot about dinner,' thought Tom.

Tom lay the envelop in the seat beside him and then placed his hat on it to keep it from blowing away in the open jeep. He then depressed the clutch and pressed hard on the starter button with his right foot. The jeep's engine started immediately and he placed it in gear and pulled slowly away from the curb. He shifted through the gears expertly and drove slowly through town. He glanced to his left at the bookshop as he passed, but saw no one. At the end of town he turned right on the county road and sped up. A couple of cars that he passed honked at the red jeep. The road would run alongside the Wausauki River for about the next ten miles or so. The sun was bright and it was a pleasant drive. Tom pressed down on the accelerator and the jeep responded. The town had disappeared in the rearview mirror and suddenly Tom was aware of a feeling. A feeling he hadn't had for a long time. The sun, the air flowing over him, in his hair, on his skin. It felt good. With the town behind him and gone, he felt free. Free for the first time in a long time. No war, no town, no mill, no New Orleans. This was what it felt like. He breathed it in.

He drove north, almost to the state line before turning east on a narrow, paved road that would take him into McBee County. But just before the county line was the dirt road leading into the Horse Pasture. He slowed the jeep and turned off the pavement onto the dry, deeply rutted road—more a wide trail than a road. He glanced down at the map that Hatcher had drawn for him as his vehicle bounced over the rough ground. He slowed down even more. It would be at least five more miles of this before he arrived at the turn-off to Minnie Ferguson's. He geared down to second as the road started to climb; he could probably leave it there, as it looked like it would be slow going all the way. He finally shifted into first gear and decided to leave it there as he slowed even more. Nothing looked familiar. He recognized nothing from his one trip up here in high school, but then again it had been at night and seemed very dark at the time, and it *was* a long time ago. He dismissed the memory.

Finally, still ascending, he came to a very narrow trail on his right. Looking at the map again, he figured this was the way to Miss Ferguson's place. As he made the turn, the narrow road curved sharply to the left. Once he had made the curve, the road, still slanting upward, opened into a kind of field. Beyond, at the far end, stood an unpainted wooden house with a high porch facing him. He slowed the jeep even more as the trail disappeared and melted into what looked to be the front yard of the house. Further, past the tall grass, a small, frail-looking woman in a faded, but starched cotton bonnet was picking pole beans from a small patch of garden. She did not look up at him as he stopped the jeep, pulled on his hat, and approached her. He held the envelop in his hand.

"Good afternoon, ma'am," said Tom, touching the brim of his hat.

The woman said nothing, and still not looking at Tom, continued plucking the plump, ripe beans from the vine and dropping them into a small wicker basket on the ground at her feet. Tom sighed deeply and glanced up toward the house.

"Are you Miss Minnie Ferguson?" Tom finally asked.

"And if I am?" came the woman's soft reply as she continued picking beans. She still had not looked up at him.

"I'm from Mister Theo Hatcher's office. I've got some papers for you."

"You a lawyer?" she asked disinterestedly.

Kenneth P. Smith

"No, ma'am. I'm not a lawyer, but I do work for Mister Hatcher."

"So just what are you then if you ain't a lawyer?"

Tom was caught off guard by the direct question. He had not really thought about what he was, in working for Hatcher. He thought for a moment and then responded.

"Well, I don't know exactly. I run errands for him. Mostly deliver or pick up papers, you know, documents. Subpoenas, summons. Things like that."

"Then you're a gofer I reckon, ain't you?" she said with a slight, but wry grin.

"I'm not sure what you mean, ma'am."

The woman stopped her bean picking and finally looked up at him.

"You know, a gofer. You go for this, and you go for that. A gofer."

"Why, yes, ma'am. You could say that's exactly what I am. A gofer!" Tom chuckled as the thought occurred to him. He was a gofer for Theo Hatcher.

"I did say it," she replied quickly. And then, "You got a name, son?"

"Name's Pruitt. Tom Pruitt."

"Well, Mr. Pruitt, I reckon I know why you're here. With them papers, I mean. I guess old Mister Hatcher finally got tired of coming way up here hisself, year after year. Can't say that I blame him none. I wager you got my yearly offer from the power company. That right?"

"Yes, ma'am, I do," said Tom as he offered her the envelop. Miss Ferguson turned back to her bean picking, ignoring it. After a moment, Tom dropped the hand holding the document to his side.

"Don't you want to just look at it, Miss Ferguson?"

"No point. I ain't selling my land. Not at any price," she said calmly.

"That's what Mister Hatcher said. You wouldn't sell your land. Can I just leave the offer with you?"

"Nope," she said. "Theo knows it, like you said. He needs to stop fooling around with that power company. They're no good. Trying to take folk's land whether they want to sell it or not. It just ain't right. I'm lucky, I guess. Got a judge with some sense. He put a stop to it!"

Tom looked up toward the house, hesitated, and then turned back to the old woman. "Well, I guess if you're not going to take the papers I best be going. Try to get back by dark."

As he turned toward the parked jeep, she reached down and picked up the full wicker basket by the handle with one hand. With the other, she drew a white handkerchief from her apron pocket and wiped beads of sweat from her face.

"Wait a minute, Mister Pruitt. I can see you're right young. You go off to the war?"

Tom stopped and turned back toward her, pushing his hat back slightly on his forehead.

"Yes, ma'am, I was in the war."

"Japs or Germans?" she asked directly facing him.

"I was in the Pacific."

"Well, I reckon that'd be Japs then, wouldn't it?"

"Yes, ma'am, I reckon it would."

"Come on up to the porch. Let's get out of this here sun. I'll fix us a glass of sweet tea."

"I really appreciate it, Miss Ferguson, but I need to be getting back. It's a long drive."

"Hurrying to get back to Whittier, huh? Got a wife there?"

"No ma'am."

"A girl, then?"

"No, ma'am."

"Then why in the world you so hoppin' to get back to Whittier. Don't make much sense, now does it?"

Tom just looked at her and shrugged. He considered to himself what she had just said. What was so important in Whittier? Nothing.

"I want to tell you about my boy, Mister Pruitt. I think you might understand, being in the war and all. Just a few minutes. That's all." Tom saw a kind of a pleading in her pale, watery blue eyes. He did not know what it was exactly, but he was drawn to it.

"All right, Miss Ferguson, I'll have a glass of tea with you."

He followed her across the narrow yard and up the steps to the porch. She pulled open the screen door and looked back at him.

"Now you just sit down in one of them rockers and I'll be right back," she said and disappeared into the house.

There were two wooden rocking chairs on the porch, both weathered and, like the house, unpainted. Between the rockers was a small wooden crate turned on its end. Tom walked over and sat in the far chair, placing his hat on the porch floor beside him. Miss Ferguson soon reappeared on the porch carrying two pint jars of iced tea. She placed them on the apple crate and sat down in the empty rocker.

"I don't take lemon with my tea. I always say if I'd wanted lemonade, I'd have made lemonade. Do you take lemon, Mister Pruitt?"

"No, no thanks," Tom quickly answered. He sipped the cold, sweet liquid. It tasted good to him, and familiar.

"I got me an electric ice-box right after the war. It's nice to have ice when you want it. I reckon I've spoiled myself," she said, half serious. Tom thought about the irony of her having an electric refrigerator and her feud with the power company. He let it pass.

For a short while neither said anything, just sat sipping the tea and gazing out across the yard and the low, green mountains beyond. Finally, Miss Ferguson spoke, still looking out, not at Tom.

"Boy's name was John David. Barely seventeen when he joined up in in forty-two. He wouldn't hear of being drafted. Too proud, I reckon. He begged me and begged me to sign the paper, but I wouldn't do it. I just told him to wait 'til he was eighteen and let's see what was going to happen. But he wouldn't hear of it, so finally I agreed to sign the paper and he was gone. Just like that. It was a mistake, Mister Pruitt. Don't you see, in a way I killed my own son. I surely and purely did."

Tom looked over at her as she turned to him with the question. Her chin was set hard and there were no tears in her eyes. Just a regretful longing. He did not respond. She continued.

"Pretty soon he was writing me letters from It-lee. Sent some postcards too. Looked like a nice place. Not a place to have a war. The last letter I got from him said he was in the mountains. He said the mountain there were different than what we knew here, but they still reminded him of home. That was the last thing he wrote. They told me later that he was killed the next morning by a shell explosion near a little church that was full of Germans. Don't seem right. Not to me. He was just a boy. It didn't make no difference. He dying like that, I mean."

"I'm real sorry about your boy, Miss Ferguson. They were the heroes, the ones who didn't come back. Anyway, that's the way I see it."

"Hero, my foot! He weren't no hero. He left here just a stupid young'un going on some wild and crazy adventure. I ain't proud, Mister Pruitt. I'm just sad, that's all."

"Yes, sad," replied Tom vaguely, staring out beyond the porch, into nothing but space. They both sat there not speaking for a long time, while the ice melted, diluting the tea in the jars sitting on the apple crate. Then Miss Ferguson spoke, very softly this time, almost reluctantly. Tom could barely hear her.

"I don't see many people to talk to up here. More by choice than predicament. But you being about John David's age and in the war too, I thought you might understand more than most."

Tom sighed deeply, reached down for his hat and stood up, looking down at here. "I do understand, Miss Ferguson. Believe me, I do." He placed the felt hat squarely on his head. "Thanks for the tea. I got to be going now. You sure you don't want to see the letter from the power company?"

"You be careful going doing the mountain, you hear?" she said, ignoring his benign question to which he already knew the answer.

"Yes, ma'am. I'll certainly do that. Good-bye, now."

"Maybe ole Theo will send you up here again next year with a new offer from them robbers at the power company. If he does, it'll be good to see you again, Mister Pruitt."

"We'll see," said Tom. After a brief hesitation, "And Miss Minnie, I'm real sorry about your boy."

He stepped off the porch and crossed the yard to the jeep. He glanced briefly up at Minnie Ferguson still sitting there, rocking, in the shade of the porch. He then stomped down on the starter button and the engine came to life with a soft purr. He backed the jeep up and turned slowly onto the rough, dirt road and headed down for Whittier. It would be dark when he reached home. He negotiated the trail expertly and finally reached the paved county road. As dusk moved over the countryside, he switched on the headlights of the jeep and pressed the accelerator nearly to the floorboard. Then he had a thought that made him smile. I'm a gofer. A goddamn gofer. That's what she said. He chuckled aloud.

CHAPTER 15

~

Tom parked the faded red jeep at the curb in front of the office, and brushed his hair back from his forehead with his hand; he had forgotten his hat this morning. Dorothy was pouring coffee into a mug as he entered the outer office.

"Good morning, Miss Spearman."

"Oh, good morning, Tom. Want some coffee? Just made it."

"No, no thanks." She turned and poured cream into the cup of hot liquid. "Here is the offer I took to Miss Ferguson yesterday," he said, placing the envelope in the in-tray on her desk.

"Hmm, let me see," said Dorothy, teasingly rubbing her chin, looking up at the ceiling. "She turned it down."

"She wouldn't even look at it. She'll never sell that land."

"Nope, she won't. But the power company keeps trying. Pays Mister Hatcher good money every year to draw it up and take it to her. Results always the same. What's that they say about the definition of insanity?" she chuckled as she stirred sugar into her coffee.

"Yeah, I guess you're right about that," said Tom. "Anything for me today?"

"No, not yet anyway. Things are kind of slow around here this time of year. Why don't you check back after lunch? Theo will be in around nine I'd say. He may have something later on."

"All right," said Tom as he turned toward the door which opened suddenly as he reached for the knob. It was Hatcher.

"Tom, my boy. Good morning. You're up bright and early." Dorothy immediately handed him a cup of black coffee. "Thanks, Dorothy. Come on back to my office, Tom."

The younger man followed Hatcher, who removed his jacket and hung it on a hook on the door rather than on the coat rack in the corner. He took a sip of the hot coffee as he sat down at his desk.

"Miss Spearman said there was nothing for me this morning. Do you want me to come back later in the day?"

"How'd it go with Miss Minnie yesterday?" asked Hatcher, ignoring Tom's question.

"Well, she certainly isn't interested in anything the power company has to offer."

"No, of course she isn't, but still I—,"

"But I enjoyed talking with her though. She told me about her boy."

"Well, well, y'all must have really hit it off, I'd say. She would never discuss anything about him with me. I actually took her the news when it happened. Army couldn't locate her, stuck up there in those mountains. She's pretty bitter about it."

"I wouldn't say bitter, Mr. Hatcher. She's just sad. Real sad."

"Maybe you're right. I guess she just needed someone to talk to. Someone she thought might understand, I mean you being in the war and all. I'm glad you were able to go up there and see her."

"That's what she said, I mean that she thought I might understand," said Tom softly and turned to leave the office.

"Tom, you got any plans for Friday afternoon, say around four?"

"No, sir. You got something you want me to do?"

"I sure do, but not business. Fun. Well, business too I guess, but fun. We, well, my wife, is giving a garden party at our home on Friday. Just friends mostly. I'd like you to come. I want to introduce you around. Meet some folks. Like I said, have some fun."

"I don't know, Mr. Hatcher. I don't think I'm ready for a party." It certainly didn't sound like fun to him.

"You ever been to a garden party?"

"No, sir."

"Tom, I'd like you to come to the party. Get out, meet some folks. Rub shoulders with some of Whittier's movers and shakers, if you can call them that," chuckled Hatcher. "Anyway, some important people as far as our little town goes."

"You ordering me to go, Mister Hatcher?"

"Ordering you? Hell, no, Tom, I can't order you to come, but I'd sure like it if you did. Bring someone. A young lady. Got a girl, Tom?"

"No, sir, I don't.

"Nice looking fella like you ought to have a girl. War hero and all. Surely you do."

Tom stiffened slightly when Hatcher mentioned the war. "I'm no war hero. Mister Hatcher."

"Well, then get you a date. There lots of single girls around Whittier. Have some fun. What do you say?"

"I don't know. I'll think about, I guess."

"Good. You do that. Just let me know before Friday so I can let the missus know, okay?"

"All right," said Tom.

Tom didn't know anything about garden parties. The closest he'd come to anything like it was probably the ice cream socials that they had at the church they attended for a while when he was younger. It would be people he didn't know, couldn't know, around Whittier. Upper class people. Unlikely any mill people, certainly not any hourly workers. He'd be out of place. At least he'd feel out of place. But it wasn't just the fact that he'd be expected to mix with people not in his world; it was something else. He didn't know what it was exactly, but the thought of being in a crowd almost nauseated him. Just thinking about it. He wanted to be alone. To be left alone. He felt alone. He always felt alone now. But strange, he thought, I feel out of place now. Here. Alone.

Driving leisurely down Broad Street toward home Tom passed the book shop. He slowed the jeep. Maggie was there, just opening the shop for the day. She did not see him as he pulled to the curb and watched her. She unlocked the door and quickly disappeared inside. Maybe, he thought, if Maggie would agree to go to the garden party with him he could do it. He had told Mister Hatcher he would think about it. He hopped out of the jeep and went inside. Maggie had begun to arrange some books on a shelf. She looked up and saw him as the bell on the door gave a soft tingle.

"Tom," she said quietly and smiled.

"Hello, Maggie. I was just driving by and saw you opening up. Thought I'd come in and say hello." He felt strangely awkward. She looked out the window where he had parked. There were no other cars parked on the street, just the jeep.

"Is that your—uh—I don't know exactly what it is, but you're driving it, right?"

"It's a jeep. Military surplus. Mister Hatcher's. He said he bought it for a song. I guess he did. It's not much, just transportation. Uh, yes, I'm driving it. At least for now."

"Oh, I like it. I've never seen a, uh, jeep. You did say jeep, didn't you?" she asked.

"Yeah, a jeep. I expect you'll be seeing plenty of then around now the war's over. That one's pretty rough, but like I said, it's transportation."

"Well, you'll just have to take me for a ride in it sometime," she laughed and returned to straightening the books.

He picked a book from the shelf and began to thumb self-consciously through it. He placed it back on the shelf and drew another. Maggie glanced up at him briefly as she worked, though he didn't see her look at him. Finally, he cleared his throat.

"Ever been to a garden party, Maggie?" he asked.

"Heavens no, Tom," she laughed. "I read a short story once about one, a garden party I mean. Actually, the story was called 'The Garden Party'. Read it in school, I believe. It's a wonderful story and it's all I know about garden parties. Fancy, fancy, fancy. Nothing like that around Whittier. But why do you ask?"

"Oh, I don't know. Mister Hatcher—you know, my boss—is having one. A garden party. It's actually his wife doing it. At least that's what he said. It's on Friday afternoon. He wants me to come."

"Well, now aren't you moving up in the world? A garden party at the home of the town's leading lawyer." She smiled broadly, as she teased him.

"Yeah, I really don't want to go. I wouldn't know how to act around all those rich people and big shots, but he wants me there," said Tom very seriously, missing Maggie's good-natured ribbing. He placed the book he was holding back on the shelf.

"Well, I think you should go, Tom. You might even enjoy it. I bet you've never been to a garden party."

"That's for sure. I didn't even know what it was until this morning. Actually, I still don't know what it is," he replied.

"Oh, it's nothing. Probably some funny little sandwiches stacked on a glass tray and a big silver punch bowl under a tent. People standing around the yard talking. That's it. At least that's what I remember from the story. You'll do fine," she said.

"It's not that I'm afraid or anything like that. I know it would be awkward for me, but it's not that really." Tom took a deep breathe, looking down at his shoes. "I just don't want to be in a crowd of people. Strangers. I just don't, and I can't explain it."

"You don't have to explain it. Not to me," she said softly, as she continued working with the books. He looked at her for a moment.

Kenneth P. Smith

"Would you go with me, Maggie? I mean, if I decided to go."

Maggie stopped what she was doing and blew a wisp of hair from her face. She looked at him. "You want me to go with you to the Hatcher's garden party? On Friday afternoon?"

"Yes," he said.

"Oh, Tom, I don't know. I haven't gone out or even thought about going out since Eddie was killed. Just that one stupid night you saw me at the Casablanca." She was clearly taken aback. After a moment she wrinkled her eyebrows, then smiled broadly. "Going to the garden party with you. It would be a—uh—like a date!"

"Yes, I suppose it would if you decided to go. We wouldn't have to stay very long. Just in and out. I would take you home right away. That's all." he said.

Maggie looked away and Tom could see the far-away look in her eyes. Then small tears began to roll down her cheeks. She wiped then away quickly with the back of her hand and after a long moment she took a breath and looked at him and smiled.

"Sure, Tom, I'd love to go to the garden party with you."

"All right," he said, returning her smile.

Just west of town was the Whittier Country Club. Like clubs that sprang up in small towns all over the country after the war it was not pretentious in any way, but the lawn in front of the small, white-painted brick clubhouse was well-kept and the golf course itself had a certain manicured look, not quite professionally done, but nice just the same. And beyond the Country Club, not far down the highway, was Windsor Oaks, built just before the war. It was considered around Whittier and the rest of the county to be *the* place to live. That is, if you could afford it. There were, of course, no mill people living in Windsor Oaks other than Charles Woodson, the head accountant at the Sterling mill. Around the mill village in Whittier Windsor Oaks was considered to be 'ritzy' and upper-class, and therefore not desirable, much less attainable. Most people considered it to be *where the rich people lived,* although other than the Sterling's, there were no *really* rich people in Perkins County. Tom had never been to Windsor Oaks and had never given it much thought.

Theo Hatcher lived in Windsor Oaks, though he claimed to hate it. From their comfortable bungalow just off of Broad Street in Whittier where they had lived more than twenty years, his wife had insisted on building a house in the stylish new suburb and had dragged him out there nearly five years ago.

When he turned the jeep off the main highway into the entrance of Windsor Oaks, two thoughts immediately came to Tom. First, he could not connect the Hatcher he knew with this place. With the fine new houses, all set on spacious rolling lawns, everything looked so well-kept and maintained, nothing akin to Hatcher's rumpled, creaseless appearance. He just couldn't make the connection to his boss. And then as he gazed through the windshield, the faded red hood of the jeep was all he saw. If he thought that Hatcher was out of place here, he *knew* that he was.

He glanced over at Maggie, who smiled and shrugged. This was not her world either. But she looked beautiful this afternoon, he thought. Just a few minutes before, he had pulled the jeep up in front of her small frame house—

late—and before he could get out and walk to the porch, she was gliding down the steps out to the vehicle. She was in a pale-yellow sun dress with narrow straps over her shoulders. Her movements were light and graceful. Light as air, he thought. She had, for just a moment, almost taken his breathe away. She smiled broadly and hopped into the jeep. She then ruffled her hair, which she recently had had cut unfashionably short, with both hands and said playfully, "Let's go!"

"I'm afraid your hair is going to get mussed up riding in this old jeep," he said as he pulled onto the street.

"Oh, not be silly. I couldn't care less. I'll run a brush though once we're there. Or maybe I won't!" She squeezed his arm gently. "Oh, Tom, I feel so alive. I mean, just to be out. I feel, oh, I don't know—free! I know that sounds silly and it is, but I don't care. Oh, let's *do* have a good time."

Tom smiled at her, but said nothing. Suddenly, he realized that he was beginning to feel different too. A little, anyway. He didn't know if it was Maggie's happy, carefree attitude or what. He was glad to see her so relaxed and casual. She made him feel better. She seemed so young. Maybe the garden party would not be so bad after all.

As he turned off the main entrance onto Hatcher's street, cars were parked on both sides. He slowed the jeep.

"Oh, lots of people, Tom. Which is Mister Hatcher's house?

Tom took a scrap of paper from his shirt pocket. "Three twenty-two."

"There it is," Maggie pointed at a large, rambling two-story. "Three twenty-two. See it etched in the stone sign beside the driveway."

"Yeah, I see it, but there's no place to park, with all these cars. I guess these are all people come to the party. I'll just go down to the end there and we can walk back. Anyway, I doubt Mrs. Hatcher would want a beat-up, faded red jeep parked in front of her house. Not with all these big fancy cars everywhere. They both laughed.

He parked the jeep and they walked backed toward the house, Maggie took Tom's hand. He flinched a little, but the warm dampness of her soft skin felt strange and fine. He looked over at her while they walked. She returned his glance with a smile, and then looked away.

They mounted the broad front porch and as Tom started to knock on the door, Maggie spied the button for the doorbell and pressed it hard.

"Rich folks!" she said with a girlish laugh, almost a giggle.

A maid—large, black and smiling—led them through the house, to the wide double French doors at the back, and deposited the couple onto a wide stone covered patio overlooking the green expanse of the backyard. There was no one else on the patio, but people were standing around in the grass in small groups, most with a drink in their hand, laughing and talking. Most of the women, all in dresses, wore hats with broad brims. Maggie self-conscientiously fluffed up her short hair. The men mostly were casually dressed in short sleeve shirts, a few wore ties and ascots. Tom ran his fingers quickly down his slightly worn silk tie which belonged to his father. No one seemed to notice them.

Kenneth P. Smith

To the right, out in the yard, was a large yellow open tent. Under it were tables covered with white linen. On the tables were silver dishes of food and in the middle was a large silver punch bowl. A small black man in a white jacket with a ladle in his hand, his smile fixed as if in a poster, served up the liquid from the bowl to the thirsty patrons.

"Lots of people, huh?" said Maggie, surveying the crowd before her. "And there's the punch bowl!" She laughed.

"Yeah," Tom replied, and took a deep breath.

"Let's go get something to drink."

"All right."

They stepped down into the yard and walked across the grass toward the tent. It was then that Mrs. Hatcher, who had pulled away from a small cluster of women to check the level of the punch bowl, spotted Maggie and Tom approaching. She stepped quickly to intercept them.

"Why, you must be Theo's Tom," she said in her best soft Southern drawl, extending a thin pale hand which masked a surprising strong handshake. "He said you were coming."

"Yes, ma'am."

"I'm Sarah, Theo's wife." She then looked at Maggie. "And who is this lovely creature with you?" she smiled broadly, cupping Maggie's hand in both of her own.

"This is..." Tom started to say, but was interrupted by Maggie.

"I'm Maggie. Maggie Porter. Please to meet you."

"Now you two, run over there and get you something to drink and there's plenty of food," said Sarah, releasing Maggie's hand. I'll find that husband of mine and let him

know you're here. Just make yourself at home, dears."
And she was gone.

"She's nice," said Maggie. Tom shrugged and nodded.
They strolled on to the tent.

Tom took the cup of punch handed to him by the
perpetually smiling black servant and passed it to Maggie
and turned back for another, taking it from the servant.

"Oh, Tom, look at all the pretty little sandwiches. I
wonder what they all are. And the flower arrangements,
they're lovely. Let's find the plates and get a sandwich,"
said Maggie who seemed thrilled to be here and *was*
having fun.

"All right."

They spied a stack of small China plates and linen
napkins at the other end of the long table. They both took
one of each and Maggie popped one of the finger
sandwiches directly into her mouth from the stack on the
platter.

"Mmm, that's really good. Delicious, but I don't know
what it is."

"It's watercress," answered a familiar voice from just
behind them, coming up from the yard. "I'm glad
someone likes them because I hate them."

"Mister Hatcher," said Tom, turning toward the voice.

"Hello, Tom, great to see you. I'm glad you could
make it. And I see that you somehow found a date," said
Hatcher teasingly, causing to Tom to blush slightly. "And
damn a good looking one at that."

"This is Maggie. Maggie Porter," said Tom. Hatcher
placed both hands lightly on Maggie's shoulders and gave
her a quick peck on the cheek. He was on his fifth cup of
punch, and perhaps had even sweetened those some, as

there appeared to be the outline of a flask in one of the back pockets of his trousers.

"No kissing all the pretty girls, Theo," said Sarah Hatcher, laughing, as she seemed to appear from nowhere across the tent. She turned toward the small smiling black man. "Mister Hatcher will have no more punch this afternoon, Davis." Davis stopped smiling and glanced at Theo, who opened up his hands and shrugged.

"It's all right, Davis. I've probably had enough anyway," said Hatcher, slyly winking at the servant.

Sarah hooked her arm into Maggie's. "Come with me, Maggie, I want to introduce you to some of my friends. We need to get away from these dirty old men anyway. She dragged Maggie from the tent.

"Don't worry, she'll be fine," said Hatcher. "Sarah will take good care of her. Come on with me. There're some people I want you to meet."

"All right," said Tom, placing his full punch glass on the edge of the table. With Hatcher's arm across his shoulder, Tom followed him out into the yard toward a small group of men talking and laughing in the far corner of the grassy expanse. The taller one was puffing a cigar.

"Here, gents, I want y'all to meet my young protégé," said Hatcher gleefully as the faces of the men in the small huddle turned toward him. "Name's Tom Pruitt." They all nodded.

"Hack Glenn. Glad to meet you", said the smallish man with a firm handshake.

"Good to know old Hack here, being he's the county sheriff," laughed Hatcher. "And this here is Jimmy Buchanan. He'd be my sworn enemy if I tried many criminal cases, wouldn't you Jimmy?"

"I doubt it," said Jimmy lightly and shook Tom's hand. Jimmy was the head prosecutor for the thirteenth district.

"And this here big fellow is Ford Sterling. I guess I don't have to tell you who he is!" Hatcher's speech was not quite slurred, but close.

Sterling pulled the cigar from his mouth with his left hand and extended a large beefy right hand to Tom, eyeing him closely. With Tom's hand still in his grasp he said, "Tom Pruitt. Now you wouldn't be any kin to Claude Pruitt, would you?"

"Yes, sir. He's my father," said Tom, as he self-conscientiously disengaged his hand from Sterling's.

"Mighty fine man, your father. Been with me, well, I don't really know how long. One of our best loom-fixers I understand. Mighty nice to meet you, Tom." He placed the cigar back into his mouth.

"Tom served in the Pacific. Marines. A certified decorated Jap killer. Just been home a few months," said Hatcher. Tom looked down at his feet.

"Yeah, that's right. I remember seeing something about it in the paper. I mean about the medal and all. A gold star or something like that," blurted out Sterling.

"Goddamn, Ford, not a gold star. There's no such thing. I believe it was a bronze star. That right, Tom?" Tom just looked at Hatcher, but didn't answer.

"Well, I don't give a damn what it was made of. You made Whittier proud," said Sterling. "And something else, Tom. When you get tired of working for Theo you just come on over to the mill. I'll have something for you."

"Now, you hold on just a minute, Ford. Tom ain't going to be a lint-head in some old cotton mill. He's going places. We've got plans, huh, Tom," rattled off Hatcher. Tom just shrugged slightly. "I mean we haven't discussed it yet, but Tom's got the GI Bill. That'll pay for college and maybe some of law school. Right, Tom?"

Tom felt foolish and embarrassed as the men discussed him and his future as if he weren't there at all. He could hardly breathe. What was he doing here? He didn't know. He should never have agreed to come. He realized that Hatcher was drunk, or close to it, but they had never talked about college or law school. These things were foreign to him and he wanted no part of it. The future did not exist for him. He didn't know what he wanted other than to be someplace else— anyplace but here—right now.

"Look, it was nice meeting you gentlemen, but I'm going to go get something to drink if you don't mind," Tom said finally and walked away.

"Looks like he's the quiet type, Theo," said Sterling.

"I think he might not be completely used to being out amongst us civilians yet," chuckled Hatcher. "He'll come around. Yeah, he's quiet, but smart as a whip. He'll come around all right."

Ford Sterling shrugged, puffed on his cigar, as the conversation turned toward the upcoming college football season.

Maggie spotted Tom as he strode across the lawn toward the tent. She quickly excused herself from Sarah and a group of women and intercepted him.

"Well, hello, stranger," she said as she approached him.

"Hello."

"You okay?" she asked

"Are you enjoying yourself," he asked, ignoring her question.

"Oh, Tom, these seem like such nice people. There all so friendly. Well, most of them, anyway. Sarah introduced—,"

"Let's get out of here, Maggie. Please."

"Okay, sure. What the matter, Tom?"

"Nothing, I've just got to get out of here. Away from these people."

"Let me just say thanks and bye to Sarah."

"No, let's go now."

They got into the jeep and pulled out onto the highway, with Windsor Oaks fading away in the rearview mirror. Maggie was not angry, but rather puzzled at their hasty departure from the garden party. Neither one spoke as they drove away.

"Maggie, I can't explain it to you. I just couldn't breathe. I just had to get away. I don't expect you to understand," he finally said.

"You don't have to explain it. It's no big deal," said Maggie, flipping her right shoulder forward, then laughing. "Our one big moment mixing with the rich people. I don't suppose they'll ever invite us back. Who cares? But it was kind of fun pretending for just a little while. At least it was for me." She was silent for a moment, then, "It's still early, Tom, let's do something."

"What?"

"Oh, I don't know. Maybe drive up to the lake."

"You mean the old reservoir?"

"Yeah, the old reservoir. My uncle used to take me up there fishing. I mean, he'd fish and I'd play in the water.

Probably scared all the fish away. My uncle didn't mind. He just liked being outdoors. Let's do it, Tom!"

"All right."

At an intersection on their way back toward town Tom turned the jeep left, north, on the old county road that would take then to the reservoir. As they drove, he began to feel lighter; the heaviness of the garden party people lifted from his shoulders, its weight dissipating into the passing air. The things he had felt back there troubled him. He had told Maggie that he would explain it to her, but the fact was he couldn't even explain it to himself. Sometimes he just felt so lost, so inexplicably alone even when there were people around, close by. But he knew that he felt good, at least felt better, with Maggie. He didn't know precisely why, but he did and he would let it go at that.

They finally came to the narrow road that led down to the water, the gravel crunching beneath the tires of the jeep as Tom slowed and turned toward the reservoir. The road ended at a grassy expanse which sloped gently down to the water's edge. The sun was beginning to dip low in the western sky, casting long shadows of the trees across the grass. The lake itself was calm and still, blue-green glistening like a giant mirror reflecting the changing sky of a dying day. The jeep came to a stop, the water's edge about a hundred feet away.

"Oh, it's lovely here, don't you think, Tom?" as she stepped from the jeep. "It's just how I remember it." She slipped out of her shoes. "The grass feels so cool and good!" She smiled back at Tom, still sitting in the jeep. "Come on, Tom, let's go down and wade in the water."

"You go on. I'll just watch."

Kenneth P. Smith

He got out of the jeep and jumped up on the hood. He stretched out his legs, his back leaning against the windshield. He watched her as she strode toward the water. At the edge of the lake she stepped cautiously over into the water, holding the hem of her dress just above her knees, the clear water covering her ankles. She turned backed toward Tom and waved, smiling broadly. As she splashed gingerly in the shallow water, Tom felt a peace, a contentment, come over him that he hadn't felt in a very long time. He breathed the high air deeply and wondered at the quietness and stillness of the place. It was almost serene to him. Other than the girl dancing in the water, nothing seemed to move.

After a while Maggie stepped out of the water onto the grassy bank. She looked up at Tom again, but did not wave this time. She slipped the straps of her sun dress off her shoulders, letting it fall to the ground. She bent down and spread the dress out on the grass. Then she gracefully removed the pieces of her underwear and placed them neatly beside the dress. She turned and stepped back into the water and glided out until just her head and the top of her white shoulders were visible. Tom thought that he had never seen anything as innocent and lovely. At that moment they might have been the only two people on earth.

For a long while he watched her swim in the water. She was a good swimmer and often dove head first, disappearing briefly beneath the surface. Then she would resurface and brush strands of wet hair from her face. As the day turned to dusk, she left the water and stood beside her dress. She motioned for Tom, who slid down off the jeep and walked toward her. Just before he got to her, she lay down on the dress, her face looking up at the sky as tiny specks of stars began to appear in the oncoming darkness. With Tom standing over her, looking down into her face, she took his hand and pulled him gently to her. Water at the lake's edge splashed softly against the low grassy bank as the blackness of the night covered them.

CHAPTER 16

~

They didn't talk much as they drove back from the reservoir. The night air was warm on their faces as the jeep sped toward Whittier and the sky above them was spangled with what seemed like a million stars. Maggie rested her hand gently on Tom's thigh as they made their way along the near-deserted highway. It was all exhilarating to Maggie. The party, the lake, holding Tom close to her in the grass. She knew she had found her freedom, a release, at last, in some crazy way she couldn't explain. She didn't want to be able to explain it. She just wanted, at least for the moment, to feel it. She felt young again, and she knew who she was.

"Well, here we are," said Tom, sighing softly as he pulled the jeep up to the curb in front of Maggie's small frame house. She lived with her parents on a street in town, outside the mill village. Her father worked as a bricklayer, when he worked at all. He drank heavily and worked sporadically. He hated the mill and had often vowed to never work there. Not that he was interested in any steady work. When he was drunk, which was often, he was abusive to Maggie and her mother. Verbally mostly, nothing physical, but bad just the same. He was a bitter man and if Maggie had ever had feelings for him they were so long extinguished by his treatment of her and her mother that she could not recall them. Her mother was a painfully thin woman who had aged way beyond her years living in this dreadful loveless life of near-poverty and loneliness. Seemingly her only reason for living was to love and take care of her daughter. Although Maggie did not understand how her mother could live under these conditions with a man so full of hatred and despair all these years, she loved her and knew that she had always protected her.

As soon as the jeep stopped Tom started to step out, but Maggie had already done so. They stood staring at each other. Although the night was moonless, the stars provided the dim light they needed to see each other's face.

"I'll walk you to the door," said Tom

"No, please just stay in the jeep," said Maggie. She hadn't moved, nor had Tom. She hesitated, then said, "Oh, Tom, I've had a wonderful time. Everything was just perfect. Really it was." Tom started to speak, but she held up her hand to him. "No, you don't have to say anything. I enjoyed being with you. I enjoyed everything. I haven't been out like this, well, I can't remember when. Not since Eddie was killed for sure. I feel so free!"

"I liked it too."

"I'll be seeing you, Tom."

"I'll stop by the bookstore tomorrow."

"I'll be there."

"All right."

With that, Maggie turned and walked across the small dirt yard, and to her front door. Tom watched her as she did, thinking how gracefully she moved, almost as if she was floating, he thought. She pulled open the screen door and looked back at Tom sitting in the jeep. She smiled broadly at him, but in the darkness he could no longer see her. The jeep then drove slowly away and Maggie went into the house.

There was a floor lamp in the living room giving off a dull yellow glow, making the room shadowy and indistinct. A small radio, was on an end-table giving off nothing but a low hum of static. Beside the radio, in a chair, slumped her father snoring loudly. Passed out thankfully, she thought. She quietly slipped off her shoes and strode softly toward the hallway at the far end of the room. But somehow he sensed that he was not alone, that someone else was in the room. He roused slowly and stirred, smacking dry lips together. He raised his head without moving his body in the chair and half shaded his eyes from the lamplight with his hand. Maggie continued to move quickly and quietly down the hall to her bedroom. He would try to spoil what had been a wonderful, dream-like day if she let him, and she vowed to herself this would not happen.

"Who, uh, who's here?" he stammered drunkenly, hoarsely. Then, "That you, girl?"

Maggie heard his growling as she closed the bedroom door behind her. She quickly slipped out of her dress and draped a cotton gown over her body without switching on the overhead light. She slipped effortlessly into her bed and pulled the covers high to her chin. Then she heard him staggering down the hallway. God, let him go on down to his room, she prayed, please.

But he stopped at her door and opened it. He just stood there, his fleshy gnarled face looking into the darkness of her room. She closed her eyes and barely breathed, but he was breathing heavily. He leaned one shoulder unsteadily against the door jamb.

"Eh, I know where you been. Out whoring around just like the rest of 'em. Worthless, just like your ma. I know where you been, all right. I can smell it." He inhaled noisily and vulgarly through his nostrils. "Think you're miss goody-two shoes, don't you? Working in that bookstore. Miss uppity. But you ain't. You're just a slut like the rest of 'em." He stood there for a moment more staring into the darkness. Maggie had not made a sound, but gripped the edge of her blanket tightly with both hands. Finally he growled, "Huh, to hell with you," and made his way down the hall to the bedroom where Maggie knew her mother was asleep. She said a prayer for her. In the morning he would wake sullen and hungover, and would not remember anything about tonight. That wasn't much, but to Maggie it was something.

After her father had left her room Maggie lay in bed, her eyes open in the darkness, staring at a ceiling she couldn't see. A peaceful happiness came over her as she thought about the day with Tom. She liked him. The natural prepossessing air about him of which he was totally unaware. It was like she had never known him before. But there was more to the way she felt, not just about Tom. She felt alive, for the first time in a long time. The war, the hurried marriage to Eddie, then his death now began to seem like a dream to her. Her life was *not* over. There was a world out there and life ready to be lived, and she knew that she wanted to live it! She didn't know how, or if, Tom fitted in, but she knew that she was going to pursue it. Maybe not in Whittier, but someplace else. There was her writing which she would never let go.

Kenneth P. Smith

But she knew she had to get out of this house. She had choices and, unlike her sad mother, she was going to make the right ones. The right ones for her at least.

Maggie then smiled to herself and turned onto her side. Closing her eyes, she fell into a deep dreamless sleep. She did not need to dream, for today had been dream enough for her. But she wanted her life to be real and good, not a dream. She now knew that she could— would make it happen. But it wasn't clear to her, not yet, how it might.

CHAPTER 17

~

Jewel sat on the small sofa in the front room sewing a small patch to the knee of a faded and limp pair of overalls. Claude was much too proud to wear patched pants to the mill, but he *would* wear them to putter around the house and in the yard gathering hens' eggs on weekends. To the mill, he always wore clean overalls over an ironed white shirt with the sleeves rolled up to the elbows. She knew it some way, in his mind, that he equated his dress peculiarities with a certain kind of dignity which she didn't quite understand, but respected just the same. Through the doorway that led into the kitchen she could see him at the table when she glanced up occasionally. His back was to her so she could not see what it was he was fiddling with at the table. Low, nondescript music floated out from the radio in the corner next to the sofa. She absentmindedly hummed along softly, almost to herself.

She loved these quite evenings after supper, when the cooking was done and the dishes had been cleared away. Outside it was starting to get dark earlier and in the falling darkness there was a hint of autumn in the air. Not cool quite yet, but you could feel it coming. She thought that sometimes she could even smell it. With her hands busy sewing or knitting, she could let her mind wander.

Sometimes too much. She thought of Bud every day, wistfully and sorrowfully, and what had happened to him. So young and naïve. His death fathomless and pointless. Something she'd never understand. She worried about Tom. His restlessness and seemingly never to be quite with them even when he was at home. The war had changed him. What was to happen to him? Something, but she had no answers.

But more than anything else, she worried about Claude now. He was no longer the man she had known for so long and, in a way, the one for which had given up her dreams. Over the years they had grown comfortable together, making a life as best they could. She really couldn't call it love, not romantic love anyway, but they cared for each other deeply. Oh, she knew she had given up any dream of real happiness long ago. She had actually given up dreams of any kind for herself. The small flicker of a dream—learning, going to school, becoming a teacher—had been mercilessly and quickly smothered by the harsh realities of life on the mill hill, of a too-early marriage, of a family. She could be philosophical about it now, when she thought about it, but it still hurt a little deep inside her so it was not something she often dwelt on.

The Sterling Mill had indeed been sold. To a large Northern corporation. The people in the mill village had refused to believe it, or rather accept it, almost up to the time that the large gaudy sign over the front gate, 'Sterling Mills', had been unceremoniously torn down and replaced by 'The Arlington Manufacturing Corporation' in large, neat, bold red letters. Oh, Claude had been right about some things. With new ownership change came and it came quickly. But he had *not* been fired. Jewel felt that it would almost have been better had he been. Claude was relieved of his duties in the weave room and offered the job of driving the mill truck, a job typically held by a black man or one who was not capable of holding down a real job at the mill such as a weaver or a loom-fixer. Claude took the demotion, going in each morning, hauling machinery around the mill yard, running errands to the hardware store, or whatever they told him to do. But now he considered himself to be nothing more than a lackey—a flunkey—to use his own word. His pride, that precious commodity that he had for so long clung to, had been violated, and now seemed to be destroyed. And with it, in many ways, the man himself. He stopped going down to Jarrard's store after work to drink beer with his cronies. He stayed around the house mostly, not moping really, but mostly with the quiet sadness of a defeated man.

Around eight o'clock the back door swung open and Tom stepped into the kitchen. Claude looked up at him briefly and then returned to his task on the table.

"Hello, pop," said Tom.

"Hey," said Claude, not looking up.

"Say, that's Uncle Davy's pistol you're working on, isn't it?" Tom sat down in the chair across from his father.

"Just cleaning it," said Claude dryly.

"Why, I haven't seen that thing since I was a kid. I remember you used to pull it out a couple of times a year and let me and Bud look at it. Sometimes you'd even let us hold it. It's a Smith & Wesson, right?"

"Colt forty-five."

"Yes, now I remember."

The pistol was large and black, and gleamed from the reflection of the overhead light as Claude turned it in his hand, wiping an oily rag down the barrel. He then handed it over to Tom, handle first.

Tom took the firearm and looked at it closely. "World War One, right, Pop?"

"Davy brought it home with him. Stole it, I reckon. He was nothing but a private so I don't reckon they gave a pistol like this to a private."

"Did he ever talk about it? Say how he came by it?"

"Only once, maybe. He was about as drunk as I'd ever seen him one night. Came stumbling into the house, mumbling about the war. Wanted to know where his pistol was. Kept talking. I tried to hush him up. Didn't want to wake up the folks. Then he slumped into a chair, still mumbling and wanting his pistol. I told him in a whisper that I didn't know where it was, and that we'd find it in the morning. I figured it was in the chifforobe someplace, but I didn't really know. Then he quietened down for a minute and said in so low a voice I could barely hear him, 'Goddamn captain. At least I got the pistol.' Then, he just passed out in the chair and we never talked about it again." Claude looked down at his hands, sighed and said, "That pistol. It's about all I got left of him."

"I wish I had known him," said Tom.

"You'd have liked him. And he'd have liked you too. Everybody liked him. He was the best of us, Davy was. Except the war changed him some. Like you, I guess. He drank a lot and kept to hisself more after he came back. But you'd have liked him," Claude repeated wistfully and lit another Lucky.

Tom passed the pistol back to his father, got up from the table and went into the front room. He sat down in the stuffed chair beside the radio. Jewel looked over at him and smiled.

"Hello, Tom. I'm glad you're home."

"Yeah, me too, ma. Patching pants, I see."

"Yes, like they say, a woman's work is never done," she said with a soft chuckle and returned to her sewing. After a moment, she lay the overalls in her lap and looked up at Tom. "Tom, you're a grown man and I can't tell you what to do. But I *do* wish you'd not go out to that Casablanca so much. It's not a good place. Seems there's always trouble out there. I read about it in the paper."

"Well, ma, I haven't been to the Casablanca tonight or anytime lately for that matter. I've been in town."

"There's really nothing open this late in town, except the picture show and maybe the book—," she stopped herself and grinned broadly, "The bookstore. It *is* Friday night."

Tom returned her smile wirily, shrugging his shoulder. Jewel returned to her sewing and her humming as they both sat there listening to the music from the radio.

Although it was Saturday, Jewel was up early as usual preparing breakfast. On Saturdays it was always pancakes, one of the few special treats they had allowed themselves in their long marriage. Claude came into the small kitchen from the bedroom. He was fully dressed and was wearing his light coat. Jewel did not notice, but beneath his coat he was wearing newly washed and ironed overalls and a clean white shirt with the sleeve rolled up to his elbows.

"Good morning," she said, not turning from the stove.

Kenneth P. Smith

"Morning. I'm going to step outside. I won't be gone long," he said to her.

"See that you're not. These pancakes will be ready in a jiffy. You can gather the eggs after breakfast."

But he was already out the back door as she spoke. He strode briskly across the yard to the back-alley way and made his way toward the mill. It was Saturday and early, so he encountered no one along the way. He finally reached the mill yard and walked over to the mill pond that stood a few hundred yards from the main building. He glanced over at the mill, huge and foreboding in the early morning light, and then back across the still waters of the pond. As he stepped closer to the water, his right hand slid into the pocket of his coat. He felt the steel, hard and cold, with his fingers. He flicked the butt of the Lucky Strike he'd been smoking into the pond where it died with a quick hiss as it hit the water's surface. He grasped the handle of the pistol and lifted it to his right temple. The sudden blast of the forty-five split the quiet morning air and Claude lunged forward and fell heavily to the ground, his face, fatally shattered, half submerged in the mill pond.

The Pruitt's considered themselves believers, in some vague imprecise way, but they were not religious. Certainly not church-goers. Claude's death had shocked the inhabitants of the town in general, and the mill village in particular. With a formal funeral in the church, long-time friends and co-workers would show up to pay their respects. But many more would come just to ogle and see what the minister would say in view of such an unseemly end to a man's life. The gossip was already bad enough. Jewel would not have it, and she knew Claude would not have wanted it either. He had been a simple but proud man, and that's the way he would be remembered now. At least, that's the way she chose to remember him.

So there was a simple, private graveside burial. Not a service really, but Jewel had asked the minister of the small Methodist church that was on the corner across the street from the mill to

come. He read the twenty-third psalm from the Bible and repeated the Lord's Prayer. Jewel and Tom, with Maggie standing at his side—a little behind him—gazed at the simple casket as the preacher said the words. They were no tears. Only sadness, memories, and regrets.

Kenneth P. Smith

CHAPTER 18

~

Hack Glenn had been sheriff of Perkins County for nearly twenty years. Although there was an election every four years, Hack knew he would have the job for as long as he wanted it. There was not a lot of serious crime in the county and Sheriff Glenn was considered to be straight and honest. He was thinking that he might serve another term and then call it quits. Fishing was his passion and he was already looking at boats. When he retired he would fish every day, or as near every day as he could. He could hardly wait when he thought about it.

Sheriff Glenn put his uniform cap on his head and adjusted it slightly. His stomach had growled twice this morning. He had gotten up early, as always, and he was hungry. As usual, he'd go to Joe's for a quick, if not particularly healthy, lunch. Afterwards he would spend the afternoon attacking the pile of paperwork that continuously accumulated on his desk. He left his office and strolled across the day room.

"Hey, sheriff, phone call for you," called out the desk officer as the Glenn started to push through the outside door.

"Take a message. I'm gone to lunch."

"Says it's important. A detective from New Orleans."

Damn, thought Hack, I don't know anyone from New Orleans. Never even been in Louisiana. He sighed deeply and stepped over to the desk where the officer handed him the phone.

"Sheriff Glenn here. What can I do for you?"

"Sheriff Glenn, I'm Lieutenant Lachance, New Orleans City Police. Got a minute?"

"Sure. What do you need, Lieutenant?"

"Know a Tom Pruitt? Lives in your county, I believe, up in Carolina."

Glenn thought for a minute, then responded, "Yeah, I know him. His family. He in trouble?"

"He got a record?"

"Hell no! He's a damn war hero. Grew up here in Whittier. What's this all about, Lachance?"

"He ought to be in trouble, but he's not. I'd give him a medal myself, if I could, but as you know that's not the way the law works. I just want you to see that he gets a message from me and the New Orleans Police Department."

"What kind of message?" demanded Glenn.

"Just tell him we pretty much know what he did when he was down here, or think we do. But we're closing the case. No hard evidence or eye witnesses. All circumstantial. But if he ever shows his face in Louisiana again, I'll arrest him on suspicion of murder. Or at least bring him in for questioning. That's it."

"Murder! Is this some kind of joke?"

"No, sheriff, it's no joke. Just make sure he gets the message, all right?"

"You're not filing for extradition?"

"Hell, no. Like I said, I'd give him a medal if I could!"

Sheriff Glenn hesitated for a long moment before answering. "Okay, I'll get the message to him, but I don't believe Tom Pruitt is mixed up in anything like you say." There was click on the other end of the line as it went dead.

It was lunch time and as usual Joe's Place was packed. Sheriff Glenn got in line at the counter to place his order. A plain hamburger and ice tea, no lemon. People passing by spoke to him as he waited for his food and he nodded absent mindedly. He was thinking about the phone call he had received from New Orleans and what to make of it. As a lawman, was there anything he should do, or just make sure Tom Pruitt got the message? Obviously, a crime had been committed and Tom may have been the perpetrator. Or at least the suspected perpetrator. But the cop in New Orleans seemed to be willing to let it go. Why? He knew that Tom's brother, Bud, had been killed—murdered—somewhere in Louisiana looking for his wife who had run off. So there was probably a connection.

The line at Joe's moved quickly and Glenn took his tray of food from the girl behind the counter.

"I'd a brought it to you, Sheriff Glenn. You don't have to wait in line here. You know that," she said, smiling.

"Yeah, I know, but we wouldn't want people to think the sheriff was getting special treatment, now would we, Nancy?" kidded Glenn as he winked at her.

"I reckon not," the girl laughed.

He turned and looked for a place to sit in the crowded dining room and then strode to a booth where a couple of city policemen sat.

Kenneth P. Smith

"Have a seat, Sheriff," said one of the policeman as he slid over to make room.

"Thanks, Frank."

"Anything exciting happening down at the sheriff's office?

"Nah, same old, same old. How 'bout with you boys."

"About the same here to," replied the city cop. "Not that I'm complaining, mind you."

Just then sheriff spotted Theo Hatcher at the cash register paying for his lunch. He was about to leave Joe's and return to his office.

Glenn took a gulp of ice tea. "Excuse me, boys. There's Theo Hatcher and I need to speak to him." He slid out of the booth. Hatcher had paid for his food and pushed the door open, and stepped out onto the sidewalk. Glenn was right behind him.

"Hello, Theo. Got a minute?"

"Always got a minute for the county Sheriff. What's up, Hack?"

"Well, I don't know if anything is. Isn't Tom Pruitt still working for you these days?"

"Part time. Why?"

"I got a phone call from a detective down in New Orleans this morning."

"Yeah?"

"Yes, and he wanted to make sure Tom got a message." Glenn hesitated. "In so many words, he said that if Tom ever showed his face in New Orleans again, or Louisiana for that matter, he would arrest him for murder or at least bring him in for questioning. Otherwise, he won't pursue the case. Strange, don't you think?"

"Well, yes, I do. Did he say anything else?"

"Only that he'd give Tom a medal if he could. Tom ever been to New Orleans? As far as you know, I mean."

"Yes, he has, as a matter of fact. He went down there to claim his brother's body and bring it back to Whittier."

"What do you make of it, Theo?"

"I don't know, but I'll talk to him right away. You can bet on that."

"All right. Will you give him the message from the detective?"

"Of course I will, sheriff."

"I've known Tom's people for a long time. Known Tom all his life. This just doesn't sound like him, if you know what I mean. I don't believe it."

"I know what you mean, Hack, but Tom's spent three years in the Pacific killing Japs. He's not the boy who left Whittier to go to war."

"I reckon not, but *murder* in New Orleans?"

"I'll speak with him. I sure it's something he can explain."

"Probably can, but I don't know how. Anyway, I just want to forget about. I don't reckon it's a police matter for me. What do you think?"

"Well, he's not charged with anything and it doesn't appear that he ever will be," offered Hatcher.

"Not as long as he stays out of Louisiana. Never been, but I've always heard they do things different down there. I reckon it's true."

"See you later, Sheriff. I've got to get back to the office. I'll let you know if there's anything you need to do."

"I don't want to know anything more that I already do. I told the detective I'd make sure Tom got his message and I've done that. See you around, Theo."

Kenneth P. Smith

The two men parted and sheriff Glenn stepped backed into Joe's. The cops had left and Glenn stood for a moment looking down at this half-eaten lunch. To hell with it, he thought, and picked up the tray, emptied it in the trash receptacle, and placed it on the counter.

"Didn't eat much today, Sheriff," commented Joe as he rang up the charge. "Food not good?"

"Naw, food's good as usual. Just not as hungry as I thought it was," Glenn said as he took the change and placed it in his pocket. "See you tomorrow, Joe."

Sheriff Glenn strode back to the station slowly, deep in thought. It just didn't feel right. Tom Pruitt involved someway in a murder. But no charges or arrest. Must be a story there someplace. It went against the grain of his decades in law enforcement. But he was glad not to have to go after Tom. Not after all he'd been through. Hatcher would give him the detective's message so he was through with it. Glenn then thought of going fishing, and as the sheriff of Perkins County, he *knew* that this would be his last term for sure.

CHAPTER 19

~

Tom stepped out of the heat of the street into the cool of the office and flopped down in a chair just beyond the corner of Dorothy's desk. The older woman looked up from her typewriter and peered at him over the top of her glasses which were pushed down on her nose. Her raised eyebrow posed a question, but she did not speak. Tom stared back at her for a moment.

"Oh, the court papers," he said, finally realizing her meaning. He got up hurriedly from the chair and placed a manila folder on her desk. "Took me a while to find the charts."

"Plats," she corrected him.

"Yes, the plats. Still learning the lingo."

"You're doing just fine. It takes time, that's all."

"And I got the three subpoenas delivered. Here's the signed receipts." He placed more papers on her desk."

"He's in his office and he said he wanted to see you when you got back."

"All right."

He walked past Dorothy and tapped lightly on the door that was a few feet behind her desk. He then took a handkerchief from his back pocket and mopped his forehead. He tapped on the door again.

"Come in," came Hatcher's voice. Tom entered the office.

"Get those things done?"

"Yes, sir."

"Good. Hot outside, I see."

"Yes, sir. I think you could fry an egg on the sidewalk today." He had heard some of the old men sitting around the courthouse say this. It seemed like the thing to say, but actually he had not even thought about the heat.

"I saw in Sunday's paper where they did just that. Not on the sidewalk, but on the hood of an automobile. A firetruck, actually. Had a picture of them cooking it too. Damnest thing you ever saw. Boy, now that's hot."

"Feels good in here though," said Tom.

"Yeah, how do you like these new window units? They cost me a bundle, but they're the bomb for sure." Hatcher leaned on the desk, toward Tom and lowered his voice. "Get twice the work out of Dorothy now, so they'll soon pay for themselves. Don't know how we got on without them," laughed Hatcher

"I could get used to it. The cool, I mean."

"Pretty hot in the Pacific I would suppose."

"Yes, sir, it was," Tom said softly, looking down briefly at his shoes. "Mrs. Spearman said you wanted to see me."

"That's right, I do. Looks like we got us a little situation here. I just got off the phone with Judge Stover. Have a seat, Tom," said Hatcher, motioning to one of the leather chairs that sat in front of his desk. "Anyway, seems a cab driver was murdered in McBee County last night, or at least sometime before daybreak. Might have been early this morning. I don't know many of the details yet.

However, the accused man can't afford a lawyer and the Judge asked me if I would consider defending him."

"Murder? Are you going to do it?"

Hatcher leaned back in his chair and rested his chin on fingers of his hands, almost as if he was praying. "Well, Tom, it's like this. When the circuit judge asks you to do something like this he isn't really asking, if you know what I mean. He's telling me that I'm going to be Loomis Cartee's defense attorney. Simple as that."

Tom sat up, leaning forward in his chair. "Loomis Cartee?"

"Yep, that's right. Local boy. You know him?"

"Sure, I do. I mean we're not friends or anything, but everybody around Whittier knows Loomis Cartee."

"Well, maybe so, but right now he's charged with robbery and first-degree murder. Supposedly cut that cab driver's throat. That's about all I know right now."

"I can't believe it," said Tom. "Loomis Cartee. I saw him play ball one time when I was about eleven or twelve. Best running back I ever saw. The fastest for sure. I don't how they ever came to play that game. I mean, them being a colored school and all. Seemed like the whole town was there."

"Yeah. I'd forgotten about that. It wasn't really an official game or anything like that, as I recall. At least that's what all the white folks said afterwards. They called it a practice scrimmage. Damnedest thing I ever saw. The coach then, ole Slick Thompson, told me about it later, how they came to play.

"It seems Coach Thompson was sitting in his office at the back of the gym one afternoon and in walks Delbert

Jackson, the football coach of Carver High School. I can just here them now."

"Good afternoon, coach Jackson. What brings you to this neck of the woods?" asked Thompson good-naturedly.

"Oh, thought I'd just drop by to see how the other half lives and talk a little football. How's practice going these days?"

"Hotter than hell. Two-a-days in this August heat is murder, but the team looks pretty good, I think." Thompson twirled a pencil in his fingers as he leaned back confidently in his swivel chair.

"Y'all going to the state again this year? I reckon you will," said Jackson.

"We sure as hell going to try! That's our goal. Conference, Upper State, State."

"I hope y'all make it. It's good for Whittier."

"Well, how's your team coming along? Went seven and three last year as I recall."

"Yeah, that's right. Seven and three. We look pretty good, so far."

"Your boys play pretty good football sometimes. At least that's what I hear."

"I guess so. That's what I came to see you about. I know y'all the defending state champs and all, and I don't know how good we're going to be, but I'd sure like to see. What would you say to us scrimmaging y'all here sometime before the season starts? Might be fun, coach."

Thompson thought for a moment, considering Jackson's proposal. "Oh, I don't know, Coach Jackson. I'd have to get it okayed by my principal and maybe the school board too. You know how it is," said Thompson, shrugging.

"Yeah, I know how it is. Just think about it, will you?"

"Sure thing, coach. I'll think about it."

"Well," Hatch continued, "Slick did think about it, and the more he thought about it the more he warmed to the idea. Not that he was enlightened, racially speaking, or anything like that. He'd heard for years how good some of the black teams were, and he wondered just *how* good. He thought he might have another state championship team on his hands this year and maybe if they just beat the crap out of Carver High this one time, he could stop the rumblings and build his boys' confidence. Anyway, he took it to the principal who didn't think much of the idea, but agreed to present it to the school board, which he did. It just so happened that I was on the school board then and I thought it was a great idea. We argued back and forth half the night. Things got pretty heated, as I recall. We finally voted on the damn thing, and the vote was four to three in favor of playing. I remember the mayor, also a board member and one of the four who favored the scrimmage, saying, 'Let's play this thing and whip us some nigger butt.' So other than mine, the other three 'yes' votes were for reasons other than doing the right thing. At any rate, Coach Thompson was given the go-ahead and the scrimmage was scheduled for the afternoon of the following Thursday. Slick took things a little further than we had approved, or at least the way he understood things were going to be. He, I guess you could say, got carried away. He hired referees and actually set the thing up as a game rather than just a practice scrimmage. Big mistake. News spread through the county like wildfire. White boys going to play the Negroes. Come see the slaughter. You were there, Tom, so you know the rest of the story."

Kenneth P. Smith

"Well, they got the slaughter part right. Fifty-two to nothing, all Carver. Loomis ran up and down the field. Four touchdowns, I think."

"Yep, that's right." said Hatcher. "Needless to say, there was no more practice scrimmages with George Washington Carver High School! The funny thing about it though was ole Slick Thompson coached Whittier to another state championship that season—undefeated—and Carver lost two games. Beat us fifty-two to zip and we then went on to win the state. They must really play some football, those black schools!"

"Yeah, I guess so, but I can't believe Loomis Cartee killed anyone. I just don't."

"I guess we'll see, but I learned a long time ago many times you just can't tell about people. I mean, what they're capable of. Especially when it involves love or money."

"You think he did it?"

"Don't know yet, but that's beside the point. My job is to see that Mr. Cartee gets the legal representation he is entitled to according to the law and that he gets a fair trial. And I aim to see to both of those things."

"Have you worked a case like this before?"

"Well, now, not a capital-one case. No, sir. A few manslaughter cases, I reckon, but this is going to be different. You see, Loomis Cartee will be on trial for his life. And if that's not bad enough, it's the other thing?"

"What other thing?"

"Well, you know. He's a colored man, a negro." said Hatcher, who sighed deeply and turned his gaze to the window at his right.

After a moment Tom said, "I didn't think of that."

Hatch turned and looked at Tom, hard. "You'd better think about it. I'm sorry to say it, but it makes a difference around here. It always has."

Tom stood up. "Is there anything you want me to be doing? I mean, now."

"Naw, not this minute, but we'll pretty much need to put everything else on hold until this trial's over. You go on home, but be here first thing in the morning. I'm driving over to the Corinth jail to interview my new client and I think it would be a good idea if you went with me. Got a problem with that?"

"No, sir, I don't have a problem with it. Not at all," Tom said, as he rose from the chair and turned toward the door. "I'll see you in the morning, Mr. Hatcher."

"Nine sharp."

"Yes, sir, I'll be here."

"And Tom, there's something else we need to talk about. Sheriff Glenn got a call from a police detective down in New Orleans. Said to tell you if you ever set foot again in Louisiana he'd arrest you, or at least bring you in for questioning regarding a murder down there. Something happened in New Orleans when you went down there to retrieve your brother's body, didn't it?"

Tom hesitated for a moment. "Yes, Mister Hatcher, something happened."

"You guilty of murder, Tom?" Hatcher asked carefully, in his best lawyerly manner.

"No, Mister Hatcher, I'm not."

Each man looked straight into the face of the other for a long moment. Then Hatcher said, "Okay, that's the end of it as far as I'm concerned. See you in the morning."

Tom walked out of the office. He and Dorothy exchanged glances as he passed her desk, but neither of them spoke. Tom opened the outer door and strode out into the stifling heat of the street.

Theo Hatcher leaned back in the shrivel chair and clasped his hands behind his head. After Judge Stover's call, he realized that he had become—what was the word—comfortable. He had been cruising along almost mindlessly now for how many years? More than he cared to count. Comfortable in his work. Comfortable in the routine of a small-town practice. Actually, comfortable of the routine of small-town life itself. Comfortable with his home, his wife, his friends. Comfortable. Was that the right word? Complacent? Sure, some. Or was the word that more accurately described his life, was it—had he become *lazy*? He smiled to himself and in a moment of honesty, admitted something about himself that he didn't particularly like. He had become successfully lazy. But then he knew something else. Perhaps lazy he had been for a long time, but that was about to change.

Mac Connelly rose from his chair, holding his hat to his side. He started to place it on his head out of habit, but thought better of it when he remembered where he was—in Judge Stover's chambers. The judge leaned forward; his hands clasped together on his large desk.

"Thank you for the information and the concern, Sheriff. I'll certainly take it under consideration. Have you spoken with the solicitor about this?"

"Yes, sir, I have. But he doesn't seem worried about it at all. I'm not sure he's even thought about it. But my people are on the streets. We hear and see things."

Kenneth P. Smith

"I'm sure."

"Well, it *really* does concern me and I thought you ought to know. I don't like this whole situation. It feels, well, explosive. At least, potentially."

"Thank you, Sheriff Connelly. Like I said, I will take it under advisement."

"Thank you, judge. That's all I came for." Connelly said as he turned and left the office.

When the sheriff left his chambers Stover leaned back in his large leather chair, thinking, chewing on the tip of his eyeglass's temple. He had had murder cases before, plenty of them. But none like this one. They had not had the racial overtones of the Cartee case. And a cold-blooded killing at that. People were angry and their simmering hatred seem to be rising to the top. Especially with the cab drivers. One of their own was killed. But, by god, there would be a fair trial. He'd see to that. He'd tolerate no semblance of vigilantism. Not in his district. He thought for a few moments more and then reached over and flicked the switch on the intercom on his desk.

"Jenny, call over to the jail and see if you can find out when Mr. Hatcher is interviewing a prisoner, Loomis Cartee. Let me know as soon as you find out. It'll probably be within the next day or so. And get me Sheriff Connelly," he said and turned off the speaker. He picked up some papers off his desk and began to read them. In about five minutes he heard the intercom crackle, then his secretary's voice.

"Sheriff Connelly on the phone, Judge Stover."

"All right." Then click. "Hello, sheriff. I've thought about what we talked about a while ago and I'm ordering

Mr. Cartee transferred during the trial. I think the Perkins County lockup will do. Do you agree?"

"Yes, sir. I'll call Hack Glenn, uh, Sheriff Glenn right away and have the prisoner moved."

"All right, that's good. Be sure to notify the defendant's attorney of the move. That would be Theodore Hatcher over in Whittier.

"Yes, sir. I'll take care of it, judge."

"And one more thing. This isn't for public knowledge. Keep a lid on it! Good day, sheriff," said Jasper, hanging up the telephone.

Tom was at Theo Hatcher's office at a quarter to nine. But because Hatcher already had a couple of things on his plate, they were late leaving for Corinth. The officer at the McBee County jail chuckled when Hatcher asked to see his client.

"Sorry, counselor, but he ain't here. Not no more."

"What do you mean he's not here?" asked Hatcher, rankled.

"You just missed him. Transported him this morning to the Perkins County facility. That's where you'll find him."

"Who the hell ordered that?"

"Judge Stover hisself. Security reasons, they said."

Hatcher looked at Tom. "This is worse than I thought. Let's go."

CHAPTER 20

~

Theo Hatcher leaned back in the large leather chair, his left forearm resting on his cluttered desk, staring out the window on the far wall. Beyond the window, the sun was dying in the west and sent long, narrow fingers of bright yellow light across the room. Silvery specks of dust seemed suspended in the rays as if held there by the light itself. He then looked over the desk at Tom. "Well, what do you think? About Cartee's case, I mean," said Hatcher.

"I can't say much about the case. I'm just, well, you know a gofer," Tom replied lightly, "but if you're asking me if Loomis Cartee is guilty, the answer no, he didn't do it."

"Of course, he didn't do it, but we've got a few problems to sort out. All that money on his dresser, for one."

"He had been shooting pool all night and winning, he said. That explains the money. All ones."

"Yes, but cab drivers always have a wad of ones on them, too. I think we can neutralize that argument though. Then there's the blood on his shirt."

"On his shirt sleeve. Only a drop, he said. If he'd done what they're accusing him of doing he'd have blood all over his clothes. I've seen...," Tom stopped talking.

"Yeah, he had a good explanation for the blood too. Other than his being the cabbie's last fare of the night, they really don't have much else when it comes right down to it. All circumstantial. But where the cab was found. I think that's a real key. I mean a key to proving Cartee not being involved."

"You'll need to talk with his mother, won't you?"

"Yes, of course, but I need to talk to Loomis first. We'll go see him in the morning."

"I've got subpoenas to deliver."

"That can wait. I want you to go with me. You got a good ear, and eyes. The other stuff can wait."

"All right," Tom said as he rose from his chair and headed toward the door. Then he hesitated and looked down at Hatcher. "You'll get Loomis off, Mr. Hatcher."

"Maybe. I mean I think we have a good case, but I just don't feel good about all this. They're wanting blood, somebody to pay. Those cab drivers, they're a tight group. A man—a white man— was killed in cold blood, and up there in the jail is the man they are convinced who did it. Loomis Cartee, a colored man. A pretty easy target around here, I'd say. A pretty damn easy target."

"But he didn't do it. The trial will show that," answered Tom.

"I know that, but I still don't like it."

"Good bye, Mister Hatcher. See you in the morning. Tom left the office, pulling the door closed behind him. Hatcher swiveled around, again facing the window. The sun was gone now, below the trees, casting long shadows in the dying light.

The street lights were blinking and coming on as Tom drove the jeep down Broad Street in the gathering dusk.

Kenneth P. Smith

Most of the shops had just closed up for the evening or were preparing to do so. At the bookstore he noticed the lights were still on so he pulled the jeep up to the curb. The bell tingled as usual as he pushed open the door. He strode back to the desk, but no one was there. He looked around.

"I'll be right there," came the familiar voice from the far end of the store, behind the shelves of books. It was Maggie's. Tom did not answer. In a moment she appeared. She placed the few books she was holding in her arms on the desk and brushed back a wisp hair with a hand. Blushing slightly, she removed her glasses.

"Tom, how are you?" Beautiful smile, he thought.

"I'm good. Uh—I saw your lights on and thought I'd—uh—just maybe stop in. Maybe some new books have come in or something," he almost stammered, feeling tongue-tied and stupid. She laughed.

"Oh, we got some new books all right. Anything specifically in mind?"

"No, not really," he said, recovering somewhat.

"Oh, then, let me see. Oh, yeah, we got a new Hemingway in you might like. Well, not exactly new, but new for us. It's there in the stack on the desk. I was planning on displaying it in the window. It's a war story, I believe."

"I don't think so. I mean, I don't think I'd be interested."

"I see. Maybe a ..."

"To be honest, Maggie, I came in to see if you were here."

"Oh," Maggie replied, not smiling, and began absentmindedly straightening items on her desk.

"I'm sorry," he said quickly, "I didn't mean to embarrass you."

"I'm not embarrassed, Tom. I'm glad you stopped by."

After a moment Tom spoke, "I don't know exactly how to say this, but it's just I don't feel connected. I mean to anything here. In this town. Or maybe to anything. Except—except to you. I know this must sound crazy to you, off the wall, but when I first saw you again that night at the Casablanca after all these years, I don't know. The only way I can explain it is I felt something, a connection. Maybe it was just seeing someone from school after so long. When things seemed simpler, or, uh, something. Or Eddie, I don't know. There's just something."

"Oh, Tom," said Maggie as she looked at him. He thought he saw sadness in her eyes.

"I'm sorry, Maggie. I know I sound like such a fool. I *am* a fool. I'm sorry, I've got to go."

As he turned to leave, she placed her hand gently on his arm. "Tom, you've been through a lot. We've both have. It's a different world now. This town, it's the same, but we're different somehow. It will get better for you. It has for me. You'll see, I promise."

"I don't think so. I'm not a part of any of this anymore. Nothing."

"Give it some time, Tom."

"I've got go, Maggie, but I meant what I said."

"I know you did."

With that, Tom turned and walked to the door. Then he stopped and looked down at the floor as if he just remembered something. He looked up at her across the room.

"I know it's been a while now, but I really appreciate you coming to pop's funeral. It meant a lot to ma, and to me too."

"It was nothing, Tom, I just wanted to be..." She stopped, not finishing the sentence. "Oh, Tom."

"Bye, Maggie."

"Tom."

"Yes?"

"Will you come back to see me?"

"Yes."

"Soon?"

"All right."

He stepped out into the early darkness feeling more alone and confused than he had ever felt before. He cursed himself for what he had said to Maggie in the store. He did not know why he had done such a thing. It just came out. I must have sounded pretty pathetic, he thought. But she had not laughed or acted awkward. Maybe she did understand. Understand what? He didn't know himself or what was going on inside him. Inside his head. His chest felt heavy to him, like breathing was hard. As he sat in the jeep, he took a deep breath and exhaled long and slow. The same thing he had done during the war, before a landing. It seemed to help then, but not much now. He was glad he had the work from Mister Hatcher. It kept him distracted. Something to do during the day. But then there were the nights. The long nights.

He started the Jeep and backed it out onto Broad Street. As he drove away, he thought about maybe going over to the Casablanca for a beer. He hadn't been there in a while. But he slowed the jeep and turned into the mill village, toward home.

Kenneth P. Smith

CHAPTER 21

~

The Perkins County jail—a dilapidated, decaying building—was about seventy-five years old, constructed not long after the Civil War. It was a squat, one-story limestone structure that sat hunched cold and gray on a grassless patch of red earth on the county road west of Whittier. It faced south, close to the road. Behind it ran a deep ravine over-grown with kudzu and beyond that, a forlorn jack pine forest entangled with briars and honeysuckle vines. Three concrete steps led up to the porchless entrance—a non-descript steel door—painted with uncountable coats of black paint. Three barred windows stared out from either side. Behind the two far windows on the right there were two rooms and a galley kitchen housing the jailer and his wife, both of which were of indeterminate age and on the backside of their better years. The jailer's wife cooked one decent meal a day— supper—for the inmates, of which there were never very many. For their other meals, the prisoners subsisted on a steady diet of fried Spam, bread, and water. The jail was not large; the crime rate in Perkins County was low, so a larger facility had never been really needed. Occasionally, someone on county council brought up the need for a new, more modern jail, but nothing ever came of it.

Kenneth P. Smith

Just inside the heavy, black steel front door of the jail was a small anteroom. Against the left wall were two wooden, straight-back chairs covered in dust. On the opposite wall was a wooden door which led to the jailer's quarters, and beside it a small curtained window of thick glass. On the back wall was another large steel door. It too was painted a heavy glossy black. Beyond this door were the cells where prisoners were housed. The door opened into a narrow aisle with barred cells on either side. The cells on the right side were for white inmates, the left for blacks. The floor was concrete, worn smooth over the years, its gray paint cracked and flaked away in spots. It was by any measure a small-time jail for a small town, and seemed at the time to be all that was needed.

Hatcher turned the Ford sharply into the dirt yard of the jail, close to the steel door. He sighed and looked over at Tom sitting on the passenger side.

"Ever been here before?"

"No sir, can't say that I have."

"Let's go."

Both men exited the automobile and Tom followed Hatcher, stopping behind him at the foot of the step. Grabbing the handle, Hatcher pushed on the door and it creaked some, but readily opened. He looked back at Tom.

"Not exactly maximum security now, is it?"

Tom just shrugged and followed him into the anteroom. It was empty and the air was heavy with disinfectant and the odor of stale cooking grease. Hatcher walked to the black door at the rear of the room leading to the cells and attempted to open it. It was locked.

"Well, I guess that's something, at least. He then stepped over to the door to his right and knocked on it with three sharp raps. The curtain at the bottom edge of the window lifted slightly and Tom saw two seemingly headless eyes peer out and then disappear. The wooden door opened and the jailer appeared, pulling up the straps of his overalls.

"How'd do, Mr. Hatcher. Just resting a little bit after dinner. Figured you was coming, but I expected you later in the day. Come to talk to Cartee, I reckon." Over his many years of practice, Hatcher had been to the jail many times. The jailer, Jess Tarpley, had been there on his first visit and although he knew that it couldn't be true, it seemed that Tarpley still looked the same then as he did now. "Y'ens want some coffee?" asked Tarpley, glancing at Tom who was standing near the front steel door.

"No, Jess, we don't want coffee. I'm, we're, here on business," Hatcher said sharply. "We're here, like you said, to interview Mr. Cartee."

"All right. I'll need to strap on my pistol and get the keys. I'll be right back." Tarpley disappeared, closing the door behind him.

"Damn, Tom, we've made a lot of progress over the years. In Whittier and the county, I mean, but when I come out here to this jail I feel like I'm stepping back in time fifty years. I declare!"

Tom had his hands thrust into his pockets and raised his eyebrow to Hatcher, but didn't respond. In a short while the jailer came back out into the anteroom. He had buttoned the top button of his flannel shirt and had adjusted his overalls. Around his waist, strapped with a wide leather belt, was a black pistol resting deep in a holster. He shuffled across the room to the door to the cells block.

"I got to tell you, Mr. Hatcher, I don't like this one bit. Not a bit. Bringing a prisoner from another county in here like they done. Not giving me no heads-up or anything. And him a murderin' nigger at that."

"He hasn't been to trial yet, Jess. He's an innocent man until he's convicted. You know better than to talk like that anyway."

"I didn't mean nothing by it. Just repeating what that McBee County deputy told me when they brought him in. That's all," said Tarpley as he bent over the door-lock with the keys. The key finally turned, the lock clicked and he pushed the door open and motioned for Hatcher and Tom to enter.

"This here is Tom Pruitt, my associate. You might wish to record it in your log," said Hatcher. Tarpley looked at him blankly. Hatcher gave Tom a quick wink.

"Follow me. He's in the last cell down this away," said Tarpley as he led them down the aisle of cells.

"On the left side, I assume," said Hatcher sarcastically, looking at Tom.

"Naturally," replied Tarpley, totally missing Hatcher's sarcastic humor.

Loomis Cartee sat on the edge of a narrow cot, his elbows on his knees, his head buried in his large hands.

"Got company, Cartee," announced Tarpley as he unlocked the cell door. He then turned to Hatcher. "I'll be up at the front in the hallway if you need me. How long you reckon y'all will be?"

"As long as it takes," said Hatcher, turning away from the jailer and toward Cartee whose head was still down, in his hands. Tarpley slammed the cell door shut, locked it, and ambled away. Hatcher sat down on the cot opposite Cartee's. Tom leaned against the bards of the cell door, looking down at the hard concrete floor.

"Mr. Cartee," said Hatcher. Cartee looked up at him, his eyes were bloodshot and puffy. He did not speak. Hatcher continued. "Mr. Cartee, I'm Theo Hatcher. I'm an attorney. From Whittier. I've been appointed by the court to be your lawyer. I'm here to defend you." Cartee just stared at him and said nothing. "This here is my associate, Tom Pruitt." Cartee looked up at Tom, and then hung his head, staring at the floor. "Can we talk?"

After a long silence, Cartee said, "About what?"

"Well, about the charges against you for one thing. I've got to hear your story, you know, your side of events."

"They weren't no events," said Cartee.

"Do you know what the charges are against you?"

"Yes, sir, I know all right. They say I killed a taxi driver."

"Well?"

"I ain't killed nobody. I don't know how they pinning this on me. I ain't killed nobody," said Cartee softly and returned his head to his hands. "Nobody," he sobbed silently.

Hatcher glanced up at Tom and then pulled a legal pad from the leather case beside him on the cot and a pen from inside his coat pocket. "Can we just talk some, Mr. Cartee?"

"I reckon," he replied, after a pause.

"Let's just start with a few questions, okay?" Carter nodded, his head still down.

"When and where did they arrest you?"

"They came to my house and got me late Sunday morning. I stay at my momma's."

"Did you resist in any way?"

"No, sir. I was scared. Mama was crying and carrying on. I just went with them. What choice did I have? They put handcuffs on me. I ain't never had no handcuffs put on me before."

"What did they tell you?"

"Not much 'til we got to Corinth. To the po-lice station. They asked me where I was Saturday night. I told them I was shooting pool at the Brown Derby. Then they asked me how I got home that night and I told them."

"How *did* you get home that night, Mr. Cartee?"

"In a taxi cab," finally came the reply.

CHAPTER 22

~

The tiny bell jiggled as the door opened, causing Maggie to glance up from where she sat at the desk in middle of the small bookstore. Blocked by a shelf of books, she couldn't see who had entered the shop. She went back to her work. Just then, and quietly, a woman appeared before her. She was small and frail looking in a long, worn black coat. She wore a long-outdated green wool cloche hat pulled low, almost over her ears. She grasped her purse with both hands in front of her.

"Why, Mrs. Pruitt. How nice to see you," said Maggie rising from her chair.

"Hello, Maggie," she answered, and this was followed by a long, almost awkward silence.

"Uh, how have you been?" Maggie finally asked.

"I'm okay, I think."

"You've been on my mind a lot since, well, you know, since I saw you last.

"Thank you, Maggie. It's all right. I miss him, sometimes more than others. At least I miss some things. We had been together so long, and through a lot too. You know, whether it's love or not, I can't say, but you really get to where you care for someone after a while. What with Bud dying so young and Tom off at war. And the hard times in the thirties," she said sadly. "I hope you young people never have to go through a depression. Not like we did. But I guess mostly I missed the routine. Cooking, sewing, listening to the radio together. Little things like that. He wasn't a bad man. A good man in a lot of ways."

"Yes, the little things. Is there something I can help you with today?"

And then Jewel sort of shook her head, as if waking from a daydream. Her dark eyes brightened and then she smiled. "Why, yes there is. I've come to buy a book."

"Well, that's wonderful, Missus Pruitt! Is there anything in particular that I can help you with?"

"I've never bought a book here before, you know. Or anywhere else for that matter," she chuckled pensively, a little embarrassed.

"Now, I didn't know that. Never?"

"Never," said Jewel almost with a girlish giggle.

Well," laughed Maggie too, "it's high time you started! You know pretty much what we have here in the store. Here, sit down. Let's talk about it." Maggie stood and pulled a straight-back chair closer to her desk. Jewel sat down.

"Oh, just for a minute or two. It's nice to get out of the house for a little while," she said, looking at Maggie. Then she looked down at the purse in her lap for moment. "You know, Claude didn't think much of books. Thought them pretty much a waste of time. I don't think he could read that well himself if the truth be known. He didn't want me to spend any money on them, so I didn't. But I've always loved books. This may surprise you, Maggie, but I was a good student. Once upon a time. In high school. I dreamed of going off to college. Be a teacher.

But you know how life gets away from you sometimes. Well, you're young so I guess you wouldn't know." Maggie looked away, biting her lower lips.

"Not yet anyway. Twists and turns. Interruptions. Delays. We moved down here from the mountains right after I finished the tenth grade. Pa didn't think much of girls getting an education beyond learning how to read and write. He was a lot like Claude that way. I went to work in the mill right away, and soon the dreams started to fade. They just didn't seem real anymore after a while, I reckon. I eventually married Claude; he was a good bit older than me. Worked in the mill too. It seemed like the thing to do if I didn't want to be an old-maid. That's what pa said. Soon had young'uns on the way. Tom, then Bud. We made a life as best we could, but I've got regrets, Maggie. I purely and surely do." Thin tears trickled slowly down her worn face. Maggie handed her a Kleenex.

"Oh, look at me. I'm just a silly old woman," said Jewel, dabbing her wet cheeks with the tissue. "Dragging up all this stuff from the past. None of it really matters anyhow. Not now." She cleared her throat slightly and straightened her shoulders, smiling wistfully. Does Tom ever talk about Claude, I mean the way he died and all?"

"Yes, ma'am, once. Very briefly though."

"Let me ask you something, Maggie. How do you think Tom is doing? I mean do you think he is okay?"

"I think so, but I guess I really don't know him that well. Not as much as I'd like to." Maggie blushed slightly.

"He's different since he got back from the war. He's moody, and he never used to be that way. It's like he's somewhere else. Far away."

Kenneth P. Smith

"I think he saw a lot out there while he was gone. Things he'd like to forget," offered Maggie.

"Does he ever talk to you about it? He doesn't to me."

"Oh, he'll tell me funny stories about boot camp sometimes—Parris Island, his buddies—that sort of stuff. But never about the war itself or his experiences in the Pacific. He never talks about it. At least, not to me he doesn't."

"He just seems so restless. I worry about him. He's all I have left. Things haven't been easy since he got back. His brother murdered and now his papa gone like this."

"I worry about him some too," said Maggie. "But it's been hard on you too, Mrs. Pruitt. I think Tom is going to be all right. Just a little lost right now."

"I don't know. He was such a good boy."

"He's a good man."

"Yes, of course he is," said Jewel, composing herself and rising from the chair. "I didn't mean to get off on such things. Like I said, I'm just a silly old woman." She smiled. "Anyway, I'm going to buy a book today."

"You just take your time. Look around. Find something you'll like," said Maggie.

"Oh, I don't need to look around. I know exactly which book I'm going to buy!" Jewel turned away from the desk and strode to the back of the store to a narrow shelf of books under a neatly lettered cardboard sign that read, 'LITERATURE'. She ran her small index finger across authors' name, as the books were arranged alphabetically that way. She stopped at the 'C's'. She saw the title she was looking for and pulled it from the shelf. She walked back to where Maggie was at the desk and placed the book down before her.

Maggie picked up the book and looked at it thoughtfully, and then up at Jewel.

"The Awakening. Kate Chopin. I love this book, Mrs. Pruitt, but you surprise me. Do you know it? The book, I mean."

"Yes, I know it. My tenth-grade English teacher let me borrow her copy once. Secretly though. Pa wouldn't have approved. It was a long time ago. They say people didn't like it when it first came out. The book, I mean. A woman out on her own, independent and all. They thought it was trashy then. Maybe they still do, but I thought it was wonderful. I *still* do!"

Both women laughed, as Maggie placed the book in a paper bag and passed it back to Jewel.

"Will you let me pay for the book, I mean, as a gift?" asked Maggie.

"Oh, no, but I appreciate your offer. You see, Maggie, it's important to me that I buy this book for myself. My first book. The only one I've ever really owned. I don't know that I can explain it to you, but *I've* got to buy it."

"Yes, Mrs. Pruitt. I think I do understand."

Jewel paid for the book and turned and left the store. Maggie stood beside the shelves and watched her walk to the door, then close it behind her. For a moment, just for a moment, she thought that she was looking at herself. She felt a cold shudder pass through her body as she returned to her desk.

Kenneth P. Smith

CHAPTER 23

~

When Hatcher pulled his Ford up to the edge of Miss Cartee's yard she was on the porch sitting in a rocker sipping lemonade from a jelly glass. He gathered up his brief case from the seat between him and got out of the car. Tom followed. Miss Cartee, rocking gently, watched the two men as they approached the low porch. They stopped at the bottom step.

"Good afternoon, Miss Cartee, I'm Theo Hatcher and this—"

"I know who you are, Mr. Hatcher," she said matter of factly, without emotion.

"Yes, well, my secretary tried to call you and let you know that I was coming, but we couldn't find a number."

"I ain't got no phone."

"Yeah, I assumed that. Can we talk?"

"Yes, I suppose we can."

"This here is my associate, Tom Pruitt."

"He a lawyer too?"

"Oh, no. No. Not yet anyway. Tom's just back from the war. Helps me around the office. May we come up?"

"I'll get y'all some lemonade," said Miss Cartee, rising from her chair.

"No, please, we're fine. Please don't bother," said Hatcher.

Ignoring him, the screen door slammed behind her as she went into the house. Hatcher shrugged and looked over at Tom. "I guess we'll be having some lemonade."

"I guess so."

Shortly Miss Cartee returned, pushing the screen door open with her left hip, with two small jelly glasses of lemonade. She placed them on the small table beside her chair and sat back down. Motioning to the other end of the porch, she said, "Y'all can pull them other two rockers over here if you're going to sit down." Hatcher and Tom each grabbed chairs and placed them into a sort of semicircle facing Miss Cartee. They each took a glass of the lemonade and sipped it. Tom held his, but Hatcher placed his glass on the porch next to his chair, beside the brief case. As he began to speak, Miss Cartee was looking out across the yard, not at Hatcher.

"Now, Miss Cartee, I want you to understand that I'm Loomis' attorney, his lawyer. Appointed by the court. I'm to defend him at his trial. Do you understand?"

With this, she cut her eyes toward Hatcher and seemed to be looking straight through him.

"I'm not an educated woman, Mr. Hatcher, but I ain't stupid neither. The police done been here. They told me about you. I knowed you was coming."

"Of course, Miss Cartee, I apologize. I just have to make sure you know who I am and why I'm here."

"Like I said, I know."

"Good. That's good," said Hatcher as he reached down for the brief case. "I—we—believe Loomis is innocent, but we got to prove it."

"That don't sound right, now does it, Mr. Hatcher?"

"Well, of course we don't have to prove his innocence, they have to prove his guilt. But still I've got to defend him. You know, a fair trial," replied Hatcher somewhat defensively.

"How much all this going to cost?"

"Cost? Well, nothing. Not for you or Loomis. I'm acting as his public defender. I'm paid by the state."

"Ain't that who's trying him?"

"Well, yes, but..." Hatcher sighed deeply and glanced over at Tom with some exasperation. Then he continued. "Look, Miss Cartee I'm on your side. Loomis' side. I want to see that he gets a fair trial. That he's acquitted. I hope you'll believe that."

"All right," she said.

"Then good. I'm going to ask you to tell me about that night Loomis came home."

"You mean the night the taxi driver was killed?" she interrupted.

"Yes, that night. And as you go, I'll be asking you some questions, okay?"

Miss Cartee took a long sip of her lemonade and then took a deep breath. She looked first at Hatcher, glanced at Tom, and then gazed back into the distance. She sat straight in the chair, no rocking. Then she began.

"It was early Saturday afternoon and I was doing some ironing. I always do my ironing on Saturday. Don't know why, but I do. Anyway, Loomis brings me a shirt, his good white shirt, and asks me to iron it for him. I take it from his hand and don't say nothing. He knows I don't like it. I mean, most every Saturday evening he goes over to Corinth. To that damn pool hall! Excuse my language, Mister Hatcher, but it upsets me. Him going way over there. Coming home in the middle of the night. I swear, I just don't understand it. He sleeps so late on Sunday that he can't never go to church services with me. Been out all night. These young folks!"

"But you went ahead and ironed his shirt?" asked Hatcher.

"Yes, I did. Like I always do, but we don't talk much on Saturday afternoons, as you might expect."

"Then?"

"Well, about six o'clock he usually goes down to the Corinth highway to hitch a ride or flag down the Greyhound down if it happens to pass by. Sometimes it does, sometimes it don't, you know."

"So this is what he did on *that* Saturday night?"

"Yes, after we had a little row."

"A row?"

Yeah, he cut hisself shaving. He usually shaves on Saturday. He got a drop of blood on his shirt sleeve. On that bright crisp shirt I just ironed!" Hatcher glanced over at Tom. Miss Cartee continued. "He wanted me to iron him another shirt, but I had done put away all my ironing stuff. I fussed at him some, then tried to lift the stain out with a dab of cold water. 'Course it don't come out, not totally. He says it's running late so he takes off for the highway."

"Gone to Corinth?"

"Yes, sir. I reckon so. Like he does most every Saturday night."

"So when did you next see Loomis? Please think carefully, Miss Cartee, this is very important," Hatcher said, leaning forward in the rocker.

"Ain't nothing to think about," she said. "He came in like he always does. In the middle of the night."

"Do you know about what time he came home that night?"

"Sure do. You see, he's my only young'un living so I worry about him. I mean when he's out so late after dark. And been over in Corinth. I don't sleep until he gets home. After all's said and done, I'm still his mama, ain't I?" Hatcher didn't reply as Miss Cartee took a sip of lemonade. "It was two-thirty."

"You're sure about that? About the time?"

"Yes, sir, I am. My room is on the front of the house and I stand waiting for him to come home, peeping through the curtains. They's a clock on the table by the bed. I keep watching it. And watching it. So that night, when the car pulled up in front of the house, I looked at my clock. Two-thirty."

"A   car   pulled   in   front   of   the   house? "Yes, under the street light, and Loomis gets out, whistling with his hands in his pockets

like it's the middle of the day. I turned around and got into my bed."

"Miss Cartee, what can you tell me about the car? The car that brought Loomis home that

night."

"Nothing special. Just an old Red Bird cab."

"You're sure? A Red Bird taxi cab?"

"Like I just said. It was a Red Bird taxi. No doubt about it."

Hatcher stood, begged off a refill of lemonade, and thanked the old black woman. Tom placed his glass on the porch and stood as well.

"That'll be all the questions I have for you today, but I'll be back probably tomorrow. We'll need to go over all this again, and I'll likely have some more questions. Is that all right, Miss Loomis?"

"I ain't going nowhere," she said and began rocking gently in her chair, not looking at Hatcher.

He and Tom walked to the car and pulled away. Neither man spoke. Hatcher seemed to be in deep thought as he drove back toward town, and his office. Finally, Tom cleared his throat and spoke, without looking over at the driver.

"Are you going to put her on the stand?"

At first, Hatcher drove on as if he hadn't heard the question. Then he glanced over at Tom and looked as if he were waking from a dream.

"The stand? Goddam right I'm going to put her on the stand. She's our key witness. She can clear Loomis!"

"How so?"

"Look, we know, and can confirm with witnesses, that Loomis left the pool hall in Corinth in a Red Bird taxi at around two in the morning. And now we know that he reached home in Whittier at two-thirty. In a Red Bird taxi, mind you, and went straight to bed. How could he be back in that taxi cab which was later found five miles away headed back toward Corinth? Besides being physically impossible, where's the motive? There is none. Money? He had a wad of money from his pool shooting that night. It's as plain as the nose on your face that that cab driver picked up another fare, or at least a rider, on his way back from Whittier after dropping Loomis off at his house. And whoever that was, robbed him and cut his throat.

Kenneth P. Smith

Who, we don't know, but one thing we do know. It sure as hell wasn't Loomis Cartee!"

"It seems like a lot hangs on Miss Cartee's testimony."

"Yeah, you're right, it does. But she'll be a good witness. Believable, and that's what's important. Just remember, Tom, we don't have to prove him innocent. At worst, she will muddy the water and create a reasonable doubt, and that's all we need. A reasonable doubt."

"I hope you're right," offered Tom.

"Oh, I'm right all right. It's the law." Hatcher pulled the Ford to the curb in front of his office and switched off the ignition. "I'll have Dorothy draw up a subpoena right away so you can hustle on back there and serve Miss Cartee. We'll meet with her at least one more time to smooth out any rough edges. I'll need to let her know what questions I'll be asking her on the stand."

"What about cross-examination? They'll do that, won't they?"

"Yes, of course they will, but they'll have to be careful. Very careful. She's an old woman. A Christian, church-going woman. A mother. And her son is on trial for his life. They come down too hard on her and they'll risk alienating the jury. They won't want to risk her gaining any sympathy from a juror. And I'll let her know what they'll likely be asking her. Besides, I'll be there if they get out of line. We'll be fine."

CHAPTER 24

~

Theo Hatcher was at his desk, in the swivel chair moved slightly perpendicular to it, staring out the window. He felt ready. He had done all the legwork that he knew to do. He was prepared. But somewhere, somewhere deep down, there was an uncertainty that he couldn't quite place. Maybe it was the weight of a capital trial. Of the defending of a man, a black man, with his life at stake. Maybe it was just the trial itself. He had been comfortable in his practice for a long time—routine stuff, the same day in, day out, no real personal risks. But this case was different. He wouldn't have taken it on if there had been any real choice, but he knew there hadn't been. Anyway, there was not turning back now; the trial would begin in the morning. Could he do it? He'd damn well better. It was as simple as that. He needed a drink.

There came a tap on the door and Hatcher swung the chair around and placed his hands on the desk. He looked at his watch. It was late and way past time to go home. He had intended to tell Dorothy that she could leave early today, but had been too preoccupied and forgot.

"Come in," said Hatcher.

In the doorway stood Tom Pruitt, not Dorothy. He motioned him in and Tom shut the door behind him.

Kenneth P. Smith

"Oh, hey, Tom. Uh, do me a favor and tell Dorothy she can go. Damn clear forgot how late it's gotten."

"I believe she's already gone. She not out there; her desk is cleaned off."

"Good for her," Hatcher chuckled.

"Here's the contract. Things took a little longer today than usual. Had to drive all the way up to Mount Horath to get Mr. Dooley to sign it."

"Well, how's that old jeep of mine running?"

"It's running just fine."

"Why couldn't Ole Dooley come down to Whittier. Hell, he's the one selling his timber."

"Sent word his truck was broke down," said Tom.

"Sounds just like that old cuss. Laziest white man I ever saw."

"Anyway, I got his signature. I'll put the contract in Mrs. Spearman's in-box."

"Good. Wait," Hatcher hesitated. "Tom, have a seat for a minute. I want to talk to you."

"All right."

"Tomorrow's the trial. I mean it starts tomorrow. I assume you knew that."

"Yes, sir."

"It's going to be big trial, Tom. Damn big! Certainly the biggest ever for me, that's for sure. Maybe in the entire thirteenth district."

"Yes, sir."

"Man's on trial for his life. Murder one. And he's black."

"But he's got you defending him. Couldn't have any better the way I see it."

"Thanks, Tom. I appreciate that, but let me asked you something. You've been in on several of the interviews I've had with Loomis. You've heard his story. Could I have missed something? Anything that you can think of?"

"No, sir, I don't think you have. At least not as far as I understand things."

"You said early on that you thought he didn't do it. Didn't kill that cab driver. Do you still feel that way, Tom? I mean, deep down. Do you?"

"Yes, sir, I still do. I believe he's an innocent man."

For a long moment Hatcher looked hard at the man sitting across the desk from him. At Tom. Or rather it was like he was looking through Tom, at something far beyond, like he was thinking about something.

"I do too," Hatcher finally responded and leaned back in his chair. "I want you to be in court with me and Loomis in the morning. I don't know that Judge Haynesworth will allow it, but we'll see."

"All right."

"Got a coat and tie?"

"I think so—somewhere."

"Well, find it and wear it. Court convenes at nine-thirty. Meet me here in the morning. We'll take my car over to Corinth."

"All right."

Tom found his suit, the one he had worn to his high school graduation, hanging in the back of the closet in the bedroom. Jewel pressed it for him with a hot iron. He woke early that morning and donned it. The coat hung loosely on his shoulders and he had to cinched up the belt to hold the trousers snuggly to his waist. There was a mirror on the closet door and he looked at himself in it. He had not realized how much weight he had lost.

His mother was sitting at the table gazing into her coffee cup when he walked into the kitchen. She turned and looked up at him.

"You look handsome, Tom, real handsome."

"I sure don't feel handsome, Ma," he laughed.

"I could have taken those pants up some if I'd known you'd be needing your suit. Just didn't have enough time."

"It's all right, Ma. I'm fine."

"Well, I reckon you do need to put back on some weight. You just don't eat much now, Tom. It's my cooking, I guess."

"Your cooking's good, Ma. More than good. I just haven't got my appetite back yet. I'll work on it though."

"See that you do," she said. "Sit down here and I'll fix you some breakfast." Jewel rose from the table and moved toward the refrigerator.

"Nah, Ma. I don't have time this morning. We've got to get to the courthouse in Corinth so I best be on my way. Can't be late."

"See! That's what I mean. You just don't eat enough. Can't gain weight that way."

"I'll go to Joe's and eat me a big dinner tomorrow if I can, and I promise to eat supper with y'all this evening."

"Okay, I reckon," she said, and he kissed her on the forehead and was gone.

Tom and Hatcher drove to Corinth without talking much. Hatcher was preoccupied, thinking about the case, mentally rehearsing his opening argument. Tom was wondering what *he* was doing here. When they arrived at the courthouse Hatcher parked the car, retrieved his briefcase from the backseat and looked over at Tom.

"I'm going in to see Loomis right quick before court convenes. You go on into the courtroom. I'll be there directly."

"All right."

As Tom approached the courthouse he could see people, men mostly, milling around on the lawn, under the two large maple trees out front. Some sat in the shade on benches and other stood talking, arms folded or hands thrust deeply into pockets. He noticed that along the street that ran beside the courthouse were parked ten or twelve Red Bird taxi cabs, all Fords. He entered a side door, the one he knew from filing papers for Hatcher. At the end of the long hallway were the steps leading up to the main floor and to the court room.

He pushed open one of the heavy oak doors and entered the courtroom. There were a few grim-faced men he didn't recognize sitting there on the benches that ran along the back on either side of the large, stark room. They were just sitting there, not talking, with their hats on. Tom glanced quickly at them and then walked down the center aisle toward the front of the courtroom. He stopped at the low, polished-wood gate that separated the gallery from the court itself. There was a black man whistling lowly, almost under his breath, wiping tables and chairs with a clean rag. Tom swung open the gate and stepped in. He stood there for a moment, the judge's bench high and forbidding beyond him. To either side of him was a long table with three straight-back chairs facing the judge's bench. The black man did not seem to notice him as he kept polishing the already gleaming furniture.

"Excuse me," Tom finally said softly. The man's back was turned toward him.

"Yes, sir?" he said, stooped over the rail he was briskly rubbing with the cloth, but turned his head to Tom.

"I'm with Mr. Hatcher. Theo Hatcher. Can you tell me where he will be sitting?"

"Oh, sure 'nough. You with the de-fense. Y'all be sitting there to your right. That's where the de-fence always sits." He stood up erect, facing Tom, and pointed to the table to the right of Tom. "Yes, sir, y'all be sitting right over there at that there table." He snickered slightly as he turned and resumed his needless polishing.

Just then a woman appeared from seemingly nowhere and placed a sheaf of paper on the judge's bench. She left briefly through a door behind the bench, but soon returned with a drinking glass and a crystal pitcher of water which she also placed there for the judge. Then she was gone. Tom looked back at the doors beyond the gallery. People were coming in, quietly taking seats. He looked at his watch. It was almost nine. He then walked around the table and sat in the farthest chair. He looked down at his hands folded in front of him on the table, and wondered what he was doing there.

CHAPTER 25

~

From his perch behind the bench the judge, the honorable E. Augustine Haynesworth, looked out over a packed gallery. Cab drivers, thirty or more of them, sat together grimly along the back rows. The judge leaned forward, his forearms resting on the bench. The court room was silent as a tomb.

The judge cleared his throat and rapped the gavel loudly. "Before we begin opening arguments, a couple of housekeeping items to attend to. First of all, where I come from, we were taught from an early age that men— gentlemen—don't wear hats or caps inside a building. I see that many of you, especially you men at the back, have chosen to keep your hats on. I believe we're inside a building now, and I won't allow hats in my courtroom. Remove your hats or leave this court immediately!" Even before he had finished speaking many of the men were reaching for and removing their hats. "Thank you," the judge said with authoritative sarcasm. He then looked over to his left, at the defense table.

"Mr. Hatcher you and the defendant are known to the court. However, there seems to be a third man sitting at your table. To the left of Mr. Cartee there. Who is he?"

Hatcher stood up. "He is an associate of mine, your honor."

Kenneth P. Smith

"So, he works for you?"

"That is correct, your honor."

"Does he have a name by any chance, Mr. Hatcher?"

Hatcher nodded to Tom, motioning for him to stand up. "Yes, sir. His name is Tom Pruitt."

"Is Mr. Pruitt a lawyer?"

"No, your honor, he is not."

"Well then, Mr. Pruitt, if you want to view these proceedings you'll have to do so from the gallery."

Tom glanced quickly at Hatcher. Hatcher leaned over toward him and said in a whisper, "I thought this might not wash. Just go sit in the gallery behind me. As close as you can."

Tom nodded, glanced back up at the judge and squeezed into a seat in the gallery two rows behind the defense's table.

"Now let's get on with it," said the judge. "Mr. Buchanan, is the prosecution prepared to give an opening statement?" The prosecuting attorney, Jimmy Buchanan rose quickly from behind the table.

"Yes, your honor, we are."

"Then you may proceed."

James, "Jimmy" Buchanan had been a prosecutor for the thirteenth judicial circuit for twenty-four years. It was something he was good at. He was by nature a suspicious man, thinking everyone had done something sometime in their lives that they wished to hide. His work was based on this premise though he never shared it with anyone. So to Jimmy Buchanan, everyone was a potential suspect and he liked putting bad people in jail. Tom remembered him from the Hatchers' garden party. He didn't seem so gregarious now.

Buchanan moved slowly but deliberately from behind the table, he pulled and buttoned his suit coat over his amble stomach, and glanced down at his notes in his hands. He then placed the notepad back on the table. He cleared his throat. He loved the theatrics of the court room, and he loved being center stage. He cleared his throat once again for effect.

"Thank you, your honor," said Buchanan as he strode confidently across the room to face the jurors. He then began a long, articulate, and well-prepared speech looking at each juror in the eye, one at a time as he paced back and forth before them, his hands confidently in his pockets. Several times, Hatcher noticed, he pushed his opening statement to near argument, but not quite. He was too smart for that. He knew the limits and he knew Judge Haynesworth would call him on it. He took it slow, purposely but only slightly exaggerating his soft Southern drawl, as he laid out the state's case against Loomis Cartee and stating how apparent it would become to them how the evidence could not be ignored. He was good, Hatcher admitted to himself as he watched the performance. Real good. But there was a long way to go.

Finally, Buchanan finished speaking. He hesitated in front of the jury to let his words sink it. Then he turned, looked up at the judge, and walked back to the table and sat down.

"Mr. Hatcher," said Judge Haynesworth, leaning back in the large leather chair.

"Thank you, sir," said Hatcher as he quickly rose from the table to address the jury. "Well, gentleman, that was quite a speech. There by my counterpart. Quite impressive indeed, but I assure you I will get to the point much quicker so that we may get to the matter at hand." Some of the jurors smiled and nodded their heads.

"I realize that Judge Haynesworth," Hatcher continued, "has already talked to you about evidence. That there are two kinds—direct and circumstantial." Again, several of the jurors nodded. "And that they are equal under the laws of this state. Today you will hear this evidence that the prosecution has cobbled together and presents to this court in the attempt to convict Loomis Cartee of murdering Pick Johnson. And all of this so-called evidence will be circumstantial. There are no eye-witnesses. There is no murder weapon. There are no fingerprints. There is no confession. To be sure, all the evidence you will hear or see *is* circumstantial. The prosecution will ask that you draw a conclusion from this circumstantial evidence that proves that Mr. Cartee murdered Pick Johnson. And being circumstantial, we the defense will clearly show that there are other, more valid explanations for this circumstantial, uh, evidence and that there is, to be sure, no *real* evidence whatsoever linking Mr. Cartee to this heinous crime. Because Mr. Cartee did not kill Pick Johnson!"

Hatcher paused for a long moment, leaning toward the jurors, both hands on the low rail of the jury box. He then stood erect and continued.

"Also, please be aware that the prosecutor, Mr. Buchanan, will tell you things that aren't evidence at all. He will tell you again, as he already has, that Mr. Johnson was a good man, a family man, a man who had many friends. And I believe all of these are true statements, but they are not evidence. So please be careful in considering these things. Ask yourself when you hear this—stuff, 'Is that evidence or is it just smoke?' You'll know the right answer."

Hatcher momentarily half turned his body to the table where the defendant sat. He then returned to the jurors.

"Gentleman of the jury, by the laws of this state and this country for that matter, that man sitting over there at the defendant's table is an innocent man. I want you to keep that fact in the front of your minds throughout this trial. He is an innocent man until proven beyond a reasonable doubt otherwise. Beyond a reasonable doubt. You hear me? Not that he could have done it or that he might have done it. Not that Mr. Johnson was a good man and somebody must pay. No, it must be proven beyond a reasonable doubt, supported by all the evidence, that Mr. Cartee murdered Pick Johnson. I maintain, and I believe you will see, that no such evidence exists. And it doesn't exist because Loomis Cartee has killed no one. He is an innocent man!"

Hatcher then walked back to the defense table and sat down. He had looked into the face of each juror during his opening statement. They, most of them at least, looked to him to be honest men. Men who would listen to the evidence, weigh the arguments, and then decide. If this was true, then he felt confident of successfully defending Cartee. But as he had thought before to himself, there is a long way to go and it would not be easy. Not so easy as he had made it sound to the jury.

"Mr. Buchanan, you may call your first witness," said Judge Haynesworth, glancing at his wrist watch.

"Thank you, your honor. The state calls Raymond Murphy to the stand." Murphy came forward, was sworn in, and took his seat in the chair—the witness stand—just to the right of and below the judge's bench.

"Mr. Murphy, please state your full name to the court and your occupation," directed Buchanan.

"Raymond Eugene Murphy. I'm a deputy sheriff in McBee County."

"Thank you, deputy Murphy. Can you tell us how long you have been a sheriff's deputy for McBee County?"

"Just over two years."

"Deputy Murphy, were you on duty during the early morning of January twenty-six this year?"

"Yes, sir, I sure was."

"And what were you doing early that morning?"

"I was on patrol. In my car."

"Did you see anything unusual that morning when you were on patrol?"

"I'll say! Found a man killed! That's all!"

"Will you please relate to the court the details of how you happened upon this—the dead man?"

"Well, I was working the graveyard shift. Got off at seven."

"That would be seven a.m.?" interrupted Buchanan.

"That's right, seven in the morning's when I got off. Or was supposed to get off. After everything happened it was more near to..."

"If you will, deputy Murphy, just tell what happened that morning."

"Oh, sorry. I was making my last loop out Perkins Bridge Road. To the Perkins County line. I drove out there and crossed the river like I always do. You know, the river is the county line. Anyway, I crossed the river and then turned around and headed back towards Corinth."

"Could you tell the court the approximate time that you turned and headed back to Corinth?"

"Sure thing. It was around six o'clock. Still plenty dark though. Sun's up late in the winter."

"On your way back to Corinth what did you see?"

"Well, I was driving along the highway. There wasn't no traffic. Not that time of the morning, it being Sunday and all. Then off to the right, off the road I seen the taillights of a car. It was sitting kind of slanted like, with the back of the car pointed toward the highway. Kind of in a gully, but with lots of bushes around it. I mean the front of the car. I figured it was a drunk lost control or something like that. Anyway, I pull over and drove up as closed as I could. Kept my headlight on high beam, but I couldn't see anything." Murphy hesitated.

"Then what happened?" interjected Buchanan

"I get out of the patrol car and take my flash light and walk up to the car, on the driver's side. I put my flashlight on the door and saw that it was a taxi cab. I thought that was a little strange, but then I looked inside. At first it was just what I thought it was. A drunk cab driver. A man was sitting in the car with his head slumped over the steering wheel. I tapped on the window. I tapped on it real hard, but he didn't move. Then I grabbed the door handle and it was unlocked, so I pulled the door open. I took the man by the shoulder and shook him. When I did this, he slumped over in the seat. That's when I saw it."

"And just what did you see, deputy Murphy?"

"Blood! There was blood everywhere."

"And what did you do then?"

"Well, I was pretty shook up. I mean, who wouldn't be? I made my way back to the patrol call and called my dispatcher. I reported in like I'm supposed to do in these kinds of situations. I guess I asked for back up. I don't really remember what I said exactly. Like I said, I was shook up. I just leaned against the hood of my car and waited."

"And just how long did you wait, deputy Murphy?" asked Buchanan pointedly.

"Ah, not long. Dispatch sent backup right out. I'd say about ten minutes. It took the coroner, I'd say, another thirty minutes and the Sheriff was right behind him. It's all in my report."

"The coroner pronounced the victim dead, I presume."

"Oh, he was dead all right. Didn't take no coroner to decide that," stated the deputy glancing over at the jury to his right.

"Please, deputy Murphy, just answer the question. Did the coroner pronounce the victim dead at the scene?"

"Oh, I'm sorry, but you see I wouldn't know that. Mac, Sheriff Connelly, sent me back to headquarters as soon as he came up. Told me to write up my report and then go home. It was well past seven in the morning and the county don't like to pay no overtime."

"Thank you, deputy Murphy. I have no more questions for this witness, your Honor." Buchanan sauntered back to his table, unbuttoned his coat, and sat down."

"Any questions for this witness, Mr. Hatcher?" asked Judge Haynesworth, who seemed to be a little irritated.

"Yes, sir, I do," replied Hatcher who was already standing. He approached the sitting witness.

"Deputy Murphy, are you familiar with US Route Forty-Seven? I mean really familiar?" asked Hatcher.

"Why, of course I am. I'm from around here. We usually call it Perkins Bridge Road though. Patrol it every day."

"Yes, I believe we are all aware that US Route Forty-Seven and Perkins Bridge Road are one in the same. Deputy, would you describe Perkins Bridge Road?"

Murphy looked down, rubbing his chin, for a moment. Then said, "I don't believe I know what you mean. It's just a road, a highway. That's all."

"What I mean is this. If I described Perkins Bridge Road—US Route Forty-Seven—as a four-lane divided highway that runs east to west, or west to east depending on which way one is traveling, would you say that is a correct description?"

"Yes, sir, that's right."

Buchanan jumped up from his seat. "Your honor, I object to this line of question as irrelevant to this case. We all know Perkins Bridge Road is a four-lane highway!"

"Your honor, the fact that Perkins Bridge Road is an east-west highway is a central point of the defense," said Hatcher, looking up at the judge.

"Objection overruled. I'm trusting you'll be able to show relevancy at some point soon, Mr. Hatcher.

"Yes, your honor, I surely will."

"You may proceed."

"Deputy Murphy, are you familiar with a town called Whittier?" asked Hatcher.

"Sure am. Lived over there a while back."

"From Corinth, in what direction does Whittier lie?"

The deputy thought for a moment. "Well, Whittier is due west of Corinth if that's what you're asking."

"That is precisely what I'm asking. What is the major highway that connects Corinth and Whittier?"

"Perkins Bridge Road."

"So if I want to get to Whittier from Corinth, I would drive west on Perkins Bridge Road. Is that correct?"

"Yes, sir."

"And if I wanted to get to Corinth from Whittier, I would drive east on Perkins Bridge Road. Correct?"

"Yes, sir, that'd be the quickest way."

"Now, Deputy Murphy, you stated to Mr. Buchanan that the car, the taxi cab, where you discovered the dead man was off to the side of the east-bound lane. Is that correct?"

"Yes, sir, it was."

"So the car, the taxi, was headed away from Whittier going toward Corinth. Is that correct? "Objection, your Honor. The defense is leading the witness. Deputy Murphy has no way

of knowing where the car was headed," Buchanan drawled.

"Sustained," agreed the judge.

"If it please the court, I will restate my question. Deputy Murphy, was the car in question just off the east-bound lane of Perkins Bridge Road?"

"Yes, sir."

"And the east-bound lane of Perkins Bridge Road is heading away from Whittier. Is that correct?"

"Yes, sir," repeated the deputy.

"One final question, deputy Murphy. The east-bound lane of Perkins Bridge Road leads back to Corinth. Is *that* correct?

"Yes, sir, that's right."

"I have no more questions for this witness," said Hatcher.

Judge Haynesworth dismissed deputy Murphy and looked at his watch. "Gentleman, it's a quarter to twelve. This court is adjourned and will reconvene at two o'clock this afternoon." He slammed down the gavel once and then disappeared through the door behind the bench.

Loomis was taken back to one of the holding cells in the court house. Hatcher and Tom walked a couple of blocks to Main Street and entered the City Café in the center of town. It was a large, well-lighted room and was beginning to fill up with downtown Corinth's lunch crowd. The two men took a seat at a small table in the back, against the wall.

Hatcher picked up a menu squashed between the napkin holder and the table condiments. He glanced at it and then passed it over to Tom.

"I don't need it. I'll just have a hamburger," said Tom.

"Me to,"

The waitress came over and took their order. She soon returned with two glasses of iced-tea.

"Burgers'll be up in a minute, fellas. Mind if I go ahead and leave y'all's check. This place is fixing to get crazy. Always does at lunchtime." Hatcher nodded and shrugged slightly. Then she was gone.

"Well, how do you think it's going?" asked Tom

Hatcher leaned toward him, across the table, both elbows on the table. "Pretty well so far, I'd say. I pretty much established this morning that the taxi at the murder scene was headed away from Whittier, back toward Corinth. That in itself doesn't make any sense if Cartee was the killer."

"No, I can't see that it does. What's going to happen this afternoon?"

"Nothing real exciting. They're going to call the coroner and sheriff to the stand. That'll probably take the rest of the day. I'll cross examine, of course. I just want to reinforce what the deputy confirmed about the direction the taxicab was apparently headed. Just for the jury, mind you."

"So, no surprises?"

"Nope, not today. But they are planning to call Moss Bledsoe at some point. Probably be tomorrow. At least I hope so."

"Who is Moss Bledsoe?"

"He's the owner of the pool hall. I sure hope they *do* call him to the stand, but I can't believe that they would do it."

"You mean open him up to cross-examination?"

"Damn, Tom, you're learning," chuckled Hatcher as he leaned back from the table." The only reason I can see that they'd call him up is to establish the fact that Loomis was at the pool hall that night. But I'll tell you one thing. I deposed Bledsoe last week and he is one hostile black man. Hates white people. But he knows that Loomis was playing pool that night and won a lot of games. Dollar games. Boy, I hope they call him to the stand before I do!"

Just then, the waitress brought two plates with hamburgers and French fries on each and set them in front of the two men. They ate in silence, paid their bill and returned the short distance to the court house.

That afternoon the trial went pretty much as Hatcher had predicted. He was able, on cross examination, to hammer home that the taxi cab in question was headed toward Corinth, away from Whittier. Court was adjourned for the day at a quarter to five and the two men drove back to Whittier. Hatcher, driving, seemed to be preoccupied, so there was little conversation on the trip back. Finally, they were in Whittier and Hatcher pulled the car to the curb, beside Tom's old jeep.

"Okay, Tom, here we are. You say the old jeep's running good?"

"It's fine, Mister Hatcher. I'm pleased to have it."

"No problems, then?"

"No, not with the jeep." Both men got out of the car. Hatcher headed to the front door of the building. Tom was following him when Hatcher stopped and turned.

"I got a few notes to go over, but you go on home, Tom. I'll see you in the morning."

"All right."

"I guess we better get a little earlier start in the morning, with traffic being so heaving on Perkins Bridge Road. We cut it pretty close this morning. Besides, I want to speak with Loomis again before court starts. They'll bring him over from the Perkins County jail early I expect. See you about eight then, maybe a little before."

"All right, Mister Hatcher, I'll be here."

CHAPTER 26

~

The Gaslight Bar & Grill was located on a seedy side street two blocks off Main in Corinth. There was a vacant lot beside it where an old discount furniture store had been. This is where the regular customers, mostly cab drivers now, parked their cars. Inside, the Gaslight was a low, dark, gloomy place where the stale odor of cigarettes and dried beer hung in the air. There was a bar along one wall and a few tables with chairs were scattered haphazardly around the room. Country music, usually sad or corny or both, droned on the jukebox in the far corner. The bartender, and owner, was a gruff overweight man who didn't shave often. He jerked beer for his patrons from one of the three taps, but he made more money gambling—he sold parley cards—than he did from selling beer. He didn't have a liquor license so if you wanted a hard drink you had to brown bag. He charged fifty-cents for a set up. That is, for a glass of ice and perhaps some water on the side.

As the banks closed at five o'clock and the office workers began heading home, cab drivers oddly started to drift into the Gaslight. They, five or six of them, took seats on the bar stools and waited for their glasses of beer. They all had vague, serious looks on their faces and no one had yet spoken.

Kenneth P. Smith

"What's up, gents?" asked the bartender almost jovially as he filled glasses from the tap. "Y'all look like you just lost your best friend," he chuckled.

"We just came from the trial," said the driver at the end of the bar.

"Yeah, so what?" said the bartender.

"They going to get that goddamn nigger off!"

"Ain't no way. It's open and shut from what I read in the papers," returned the bartender.

"That's the way we see it too, but they got a slick lawyer. Fellow from over in Whittier. Smart too."

More cab drivers continued to wander into the bar until all the bar stools were taken. Some took seats at the tables. Seemingly out of nowhere a scrawny waitress with mousy hair and bad tattoos on her arms appeared and began taking orders at the tables.

"Bring us a pitcher, sweetie," called one of the men.

"Us one too," said someone at another table.

As she came round behind the bar to get the pitchers, the owner glowered at her.

"Where the hell you been?"

"Where you think, Frank? Out back smoking."

"Why'd you go outback anyhow?"

"Needed some fresh air," the waitress replied sarcastically.

"Well, you better get your skinny ass to work. We got customers."

"Yeah, yeah, yeah," she said and placed an unlit cigarette in her lips. Then she picked up the two pitchers of beer that Frank had poured and delivered them to the tables.

"We just can't let this happen," again from the man sitting at the far end of the bar. "Not after he killed Pick the way he did. Hell, it could have been any one of us."

"I always warned Pick about taking them late fares," offered another man.

"That ain't got nothing to do with. It could have been any one of us. You know that. We all know that."

"He was a good driver," someone said.

"Hell, he was good man altogether."

"Yeah, he was. It could have been any one of us."

"Yeah, any one of us. Cut up like a piece of meat. I ain't going to stand for it."

At this, the men shook their heads and fell silent. Some began taking huge gulps of beer. More cab drivers piled into the Gaslight until nearly every seat was occupied. A couple of men leaned against the jukebox.

"Hey, doll-face, bring us another pitcher."

"Us too and hurry up about it."

As the men drank, they talked to each other in low voices. The more they talked and the more they drank the angrier they became. The man at the far end of the bar was the most vocal and seemed to take on the role of leader. He drained his glass and then slammed it down on the bar.

"We going to sit here talking and drinking while that goddam lawyer is working to get that nigger off? I just know he is. And us just sitting here on our butts doing nothing. Hell, he killed Pick! Don't y'all understand that?" the man said loudly, almost screaming to the other driver in the dark, smelly room.

"We know he did, Bob, but he gets a fair trial, don't he?" said a man sitting at one of the tables.

Kenneth P. Smith

"Fair trial, my ass! Did Pick get a fair trial? The nigger killed him in cold blood. We all know it. What good's a trial but to get him off!" said Bob angrily.

"We can't do nothing. What can we do about it?"

"I say we can do something. We can take that nigger out and hang him. That's what we can do."

"I don't want no part of that, I'll tell you that."

"He killed Pick. Could have been any one of us."

"Hell, Bob, he's locked up in the Corinth jail. No way anybody can get to him even if we wanted to."

Bob took a gulp from a fresh glass of beer, wiped his mouth with the back of his hand and turned on the barstool toward the other men in the room.

"Now that's where you're wrong, Gene. He ain't in the Corinth jail."

"How would you know that, Bob?"

"I know because I know. Got it from my nephew's wife. She works in dispatch at the sheriff's. They got him over in Whittier. And that jail ain't nothing but a tin can. He's in the Perkins County jail!"

"Damn," said Gene.

"Damn," echoed several of the other men.

"I say let's have a couple of more beers and then go get that black-ass killer."

"And do what?" asked someone.

"Take him down to the old canning plant and string him up!" said Bob.

"The one just outside of town, off Route-Thirty?"

"Of course, stupid, that's the one. How many deserted canning plants are in Corinth?"

Kenneth P. Smith

"Well, that would be a good place all right. It's in the woods, way back off the road. Everything's all growed up there I'd say."

"That's right!"

"We got the guts enough to do it? For Pick?"

"Hell, yeah!" came the response from most of the men in the room.

A few of the men sitting at the tables quietly slid back their chair and just as quietly left the Gaslight. They got into their cabs and drove off. They would not take part in a lynching. But most of the cab drivers, now revved up and fortified with alcohol, gathered around Bob as he explained what they needed to do and how to do it. They listened intently as they sipped beer from their glasses, nodding in agreement. Bob had a plan. They were all in this together. Something had to be done.

Other than the four-lane highway, there was a back-road form Corinth to Whittier. The road was dark and winding with thick kudzu growing on either side close to the narrow shoulders. Along this road traveled a string of automobiles, a caravan of taxi cabs all of the Red Bird Cab Company. Other than the driver, several of the cabs carried a passenger or two—all cab drivers. They had left the Gaslight around midnight, all pretty drunk and bent on taking Loomis Cartee from his jail cell at the Perkins County jail just outside Whittier and lynching him. Once this was done justice would be served and life would return to normal. At least for them. Bob was right. They had to do this for Pick. You just couldn't let a nigger get away with a crime like this. Why, it could have happened to any one of them. That's what Bob had kept saying and he was right.

Kenneth P. Smith

CHAPTER 27

~

Jess Tarpley twisted the key with his free hand and pushed opened the door to the cell area. He ambled down the aisle between the cells, balancing the steel tray of food with one hand, the ring of cell keys in the other. All of the cells were empty except one. The last one on the left. The one where Loomis Cartee was, stretched out on the cot his hands behind his head, staring at the concrete ceiling of the cell.

"Supper, Cartee. Evening chow. Looks pretty good too."

Loomis' eyes shifted to Tarpley, but otherwise he didn't move as the jailer worked the key in the cell lock, still balancing the tray in his left hand. Loomis wasn't hungry. His stomach felt like it was all knotted up, but he was thinking about the day in court. He thought that Hatcher had done a good job. He got the jury thinking. He saw it in their faces. Maybe Hatcher was good. He believed Loomis was an innocent man. He knew it, and that had to make a difference. But the charge of murder hung over him like a heavy, lead cloud. He couldn't escape the feeling. He felt sick. But still he knew the trial, in its first day, had gone well.

"Get up and stand against the back wall. I'll set your supper on the edge of the cot. This stuff looks real good.

Smells good to. You'll have to eat it with a spoon though. No knives or forks allowed in the cell. It looks real good. Can't wait to get back and eat supper myself. I got the same thing waiting on me. Wife's a good cook. Purely and surely she is. Now you get up and stand back on that wall."

Loomis slowly swung his legs off the cot onto the floor and sat up. Without looking at the jailed he stood up and backed himself against the wall.

"That's a good boy. Now here's your food," said Tarpley as he carefully placed the tray at the end of the cot. "I'll be back in a little while to get the tray and spoon. Mrs. Tarpley likes to have everything washed up before she settles in for the evening."

Tarpley backed out of the cell, slammed the door shut and locked it. Loomis walked over and munched on a piece of the warm corn bread. He looked at the plastic cup of liquid. Two or three ices cubes floated on the surface, nearly melted. He raised it to his lips and took a few sips of the weak unsweetened tea. He then placed the tray on the floor and lay back down on the cot. He wasn't sleepy or hungry. His only thoughts were about the trial and he wished for tomorrow to be here.

The jail sat low and shadowy in the darkness. Tarpley had switched off all the lights at nine o'clock as he always did, and he and his wife retired to bed soon afterward. This had been the routine all the years he had been jailer. Outside, the only light was a on a pole in the yard at the corner of the building. It cast a pale, yellow light on the front of the building, but did little else to illuminate the area.

Bob's cab, in the lead, pulled into the parking area in front of the jail just outside the ring of the pale light. The other cars began arriving. As the men climbed out of the automobiles, no one spoke. Bob reached into the back seat and withdrew something. He strode to the front of the jail and waited as the other men gathered around him. As he stood in the dim, shadowy aura of the pole-light the others could see and hear what he had taken from his cab. He inserted a shell in the chamber of a twelve-gauge shotgun. With the two dozen cab drivers gathered around him, Bob began pounding on the door, holding the shotgun close to his chest. Finally, a faint light shone from one of the windows of the jailer's quarters. Bob kept pounding.

After pulling the chain on his bedside lamp, Tarpley sleepily rolled out of bed and pulled on a worn, soiled robe from off the bed post. He strapped on the holster that hung on a peg beside the door to the anteroom. He walked across the room and cracked open the outer door and saw the men.

"What the hell's going on out here? What y'all want?" Tarpley yelled out.

Bob did not answer, but forcibly pushed the door open, causing Tarpley to stumble back into the room. He quickly recovered and reached for the holster. As the men crowded into the small room, Bob placed the barrel of the shotgun under Tarpley's chin. Tarpley instinctively raised his hands, his eyes wide with terror.

"We got no truck with you, jail keeper. We just want one of your prisoners."

Kenneth P. Smith

With his hands still in the air and eyeing the shotgun still pressed against his throat, Tarpley managed to speak. "I ain't got but one."

"He a nigger name of Cartee?"

"Yes," answered a terrified Tarpley.

"He's the one we taking," said Bob.

CHAPTER 28

~

After the mob had rushed out of the jail dragging Loomis Cartee bound and crying, Tarpley sat shaking uncontrollably on the edge of Loomis' cot, or what had been his cot. The cell door was standing open, flung wide, and he was trying to calm himself and think straight. He could still feel the cold steel of the shotgun barrel pressed against his neck. A shiver ran through him. They would have killed him for sure. What else could he have done? Nothing. They would have killed him for sure.

Finally, after he had calmed himself some, he strode back to his apartment in the front of the jail. When things had first started that night, when the mob of cab drivers showed up, he told his wife to stay in the bedroom, which she had obediently done. He flopped down in the large chair. There was a console radio on one side and a small table on the other. There was a black telephone on the table. His wife came in from the bedroom, distraught.

"Jess, Jess are you all right?" Before he could answer she continued. "Oh, my god, I was scared to death! Are you all right? What did they want? Oh, Jess, I was so scared? I saw all them cars! I was so glad when they left! Are you all right?"

"Yes, woman, I ain't been harmed. Quiet down, will you? Everything's okay now. I got to think." He did not tell her about the shotgun. "They took Cartee away with them. They going to lynch him for sure. That's what they said. They going to kill him." His wife put her hand to her mouth, shocked. "I got to let Sheriff Glenn know."

Tarpley picked up the receiver and dialed the sheriff's office. Most telephones in Whittier and everywhere else for that matter were on a party line, but the county had had a direct line installed last year between the jail and the sheriff's office. No one understood exactly why this was done at the time, and Tarpley hadn't appreciated it. That is, not until now.

As he dialed the number, he figured he'd have to let it ring until the dispatcher was waken. It rang twice.

"Perkins County sheriff's office," came the clear voice at the other end of the line.

"McNeil, that you?"

"Yeah, it's me. What do want at this hour?"

"I got to get in touch with Sheriff Glenn. I mean right now! I don't have his home number. Never needed it before."

"So why you need him now?"

"Goddammit, McNeil, they's been a jail break out here. I mean a mob come and got one of my prisoners! A lynch mob! You need to call Glenn right now and let him know. I mean right now!"

"All right, I'll let him know."

"Now, McNeil. Call him now!" Tarpley was almost shouting into the receiver.

"Okay, okay. I try and call him now."

Tarpley slammed the phone down and fell back in the chair. Nothing like this had ever happened to him before. Not at the jail. He was still shaking.

"Better put on some coffee. I expect Sheriff Glenn will be up here in a few minutes. I guess I better put some clothes on myself," Tarpley said to his wife.

Tarpley was standing in the anteroom when Sheriff Glenn's car pulled up to the jail fifteen minutes later. He was almost instantly in the anteroom with Tarpley.

"What the hell's going on, Jess?"

"They come and got Cartee. They was a whole bunch of them," Tarpley rattled off, excitedly.

"Who were they?" asked the sheriff, though he already knew the answer to his question.

"Taxi-cab drivers! Red Bird taxi drivers! At least most of them were, as I seen it!"

"Why didn't you stop them?"

"Hell, sheriff, they put a shotgun to my head right off! What could I do?"

"Nothing, I guess. How long have they been gone?"

"I don't know twenty or thirty minutes. I don't know. You want some coffee?"

"Did you hear any of them say where they were taking him?" asked the sheriff, ignoring the coffee offer.

"No, I didn't hear them say."

"Get any names?"

"They called the one with the shotgun 'Bob'. He looked to be the leader. I didn't catch any other names. Hell, Sheriff Glenn, I was scared shitless!"

"All right, settle down, Tarpley. They're likely headed back to Corinth, but who knows. I've got to radio Sheriff Connelly over in McBee County," said Glenn and he left the jail and returned to his car. Tarpley stood at the door of the jail and watched the sheriff's car back out and speed onto the road, the rear wheel spewing gravel behind it. He then shut and locked the black steel door and returned to his chair beside the telephone. He realized he was very tired, but wide awake as he sipped the coffee his wife had made. It's time, he thought, I quit this job.

As he sped toward his office in Whittier, Sheriff Glenn managed to contact the deputy dispatcher in Corinth and inform him of the situation. He would wait on a call back. Once he got back to his office, he would call Theo Hatcher and let him know what had happened and probably what was happening to Loomis Cartee. Then what would he do? Wait to hear back from Connelly. That's about all he could do now. He knew what was happening, but was powerless to do anything to stop it. It was a helpless feeling and he didn't like it.

On the drive back to Whittier, Glenn's car radio crackled, but sometimes he could not get good reception this far out.

"Sheriff Glenn. Come in, Sheriff Glenn," came the voice through the haze of static.

"Glenn here."

"Sheriff Glenn, this is Mac Connelly. Can you read me?"

"Yeah, I can hear you, Sheriff Connelly—barely."

"I got the word and have patrol cars out looking. Do you know anything?"

"Just what I told your dispatcher. A mob came up here and took Cartee from the jail. Seems it was cab drivers from Corinth. Leader named Bob. All of them were driving Red Bird taxis."

"How many?"

"Jailer said it looked to be about two dozen. A real mob."

"The folks at your jail couldn't stop them?"

Folks, thought Glenn. He took a sigh deeply out of embarrassment. He knew that they should had more security at the jail, at least he realized it now. But it had just been the jailer and his wife there. It looked bad. He would look bad. But it just wasn't in his budget. How hard had he fought for it in the past? He would speak with county council again.

"They were armed. Threatened the jailer. He didn't have much choice it seems." There was no use it trying cover anything up. Get things out in the open and move on. That's the way he'd always operated.

After a brief moment, "All right. I'll keep you posted. If I were you, I'd put some extra cars out. You know just in case. I'm out."

"Ten-four," said Glenn, but the radio had already gone dead on the other end.

Sheriff walked past the dozing dispatcher and went into his office. It was nearly two o'clock, as he glanced up at the wall clock. He took a black and worn address from the desk drawer and dialed Theo Hatcher's number. He'd had to make bad phone calls over the years—sons killed in car wrecks, husbands arrested and in jail, even a couple of kidnappings—but he had never liked it or had gotten used to it. He knew he'd have to tell Cartee's mother, but he'd wait and go out to the house later in the morning.

On the fifth ring a groggy Hatcher picked up the receiver. Glenn needlessly identified himself and told him what had happened as clearly and succinctly as he could. When he finished, there was no sound on the other end of the line.

"Theo, you there?"

"Yes, I'm here. I wish I wasn't, but I am. Have you not heard anything back from the McBee County sheriff?"

"No, not yet, but I will. He'll let me know as soon as he finds out something. I'll let you know."

"All right," said Hatcher as he placed the receiver back on its cradle. It was bad news. He knew that. As bad as it gets.

"Theo, what is it? Who was that on the phone?"

"Sheriff Glenn. There's been some trouble at the jail, that's all. It's nothing. Go back to sleep." With that, she pulled the covers to her shoulders and turned away from him. Hatcher lay there, wide awake now, staring into the darkness of the bedroom. He waited. He knew the phone would ring again soon. He knew it would not be good.

After a while, and with no call coming in, Hatcher pulled on his clothes and drove to the office. Once he was there, he called Sheriff Glenn back, but there was no news. Both counties had an APB out and were combing the county side. Hatcher made some coffee and sat at his desk, and waited.

CHAPTER 29

~

Loomis Cartee sat wedged between two men in the backseat of Bob's cab as the caravan of cabs sped back toward Corinth on the same back road on which they had driven to the jail. The rope that tied his hands together behind his back cut into his wrists, and he was scared. Plenty scared. His breathing was quick and shallow, and he felt he couldn't get enough air. His heart pounded in his chest.

"I don't know what y'all going to do to me, but I ain't done nothing wrong. Please let me go!" said Loomis weakly.

"Shut up!" said one on the men beside him.

"Please let me go. I ain't killed nobody. Please!"

"I ain't telling you again, nigger, to shut up," the man repeated.

"Please!" said Loomis, and with that the other man slammed his fist hard into the bound man's unprotected chest, leaving Loomis in great pain, gasping for breath.

"I told you to shut up now."

Just after the automobiles passed into McBee County, the lead cab slowed and turned down a narrow dark road where deep woods crowded the shoulders. It had been paved long ago, but was now dotted with potholes and cracks in the surface. In several places the ubiquitous vines of the kudzu snaked their way across. Except for occasional young lovers, the road was now seldom used. It then curved sharply right and descended just as sharply before coming to a dead-end at which several deserted and dilapidated buildings were huddled around what was once a circular parking lot. Bob's cab pulled up and stopped, and the other cars soon followed.

Bob got out of the car with the shotgun and yanked opened the back door of the car. The man sitting beside Loomis crawled out dragging him by the shirt collar.

"Bring him over here," commanded Bob, leading the way between two of the buildings, toward a large live oak tree in the rear near heavy undergrowth. The man holding Loomis followed, as did the rest of the mob.

"Please y'all got to let me go. I didn't do nothing," pled Loomis, tears streaming down his face. With this, Bob turned and swung the butt of the gun to Loomis' face. Loomis' eyes rolled back in his head and his chin feel to his chest. He had been knocked unconscious. Bob slapped him hard in the face.

"Don't you pass out on me, nigger. I want you wide awake for this. Just like Pick was when you cut his throat!" Loomis did not move. "They's a bottle of whiskey in the trunk of my car," said Bob, tossing a set of keys to one of the men. "And bring that rope that's in there, too. I forgot to get it out." The man, who was holding a flashlight, turned and ran back toward the car. He quickly returned with a full bottle of liquor and a coil of rough, thick hemp rope. Bob splashed some of the whiskey into the face of Loomis who was still out and supported by a man on either side of him. Loomis didn't move. Bob splashed more whiskey on Loomis.

"Waste of good bourbon whiskey, Bob," said one of the men and they all laughed. Bob slapped Loomis again, but not as hard as before. Loomis groaned groggily and half opened his eyes. The beams of a dozen flashlights blinded him. Bob punched Loomis in the stomach as the two men held him up. The other men then walked up to Loomis, one by one, and hit him, or slapped him. Some spat in his face. Finally, the two drivers holding him released their grips and Loomis fell to the ground. He lay there, weak and exposed, barely conscious. Several of the men kicked him in the groin, some in the face, all cursing.

"I think he's out again, Bob."

"Don't matter none. He's fixin' to be out for good," said Bob. "Shine your light on that tree there."

Bob took the coil of rope and tried to toss one end over a large limb about ten feet above the ground. He missed. He tried again. Missed. On the third toss, the roped went over the limb enough for one of the men to pull the end down to the ground.

"Tie it around his ankles."

"He's still out, Bob."

"I don't give a damn. Tie the rope like I said."

One of the men lifted Loomis' ankle together off the ground and another wrapped the rope around them and pulled a tight knot. They then dragged him over beneath the limb.

"Y'all help me hoist him up. We going to give this here nigger what he deserves!" Along with Bob, several of the men grabbed the rope and began pulling it over the limb. When the slack was gone, Loomis was dragged further along the ground. They continued pulling until Loomis's legs and most of his torso was up; only his shoulders and head were still on the ground. They gave a final long pull on the rope and Loomis was up, upside down, dangling from the limb, his head just off the ground. He groaned and tried to speak, but nothing came out. Blood poured into his nose and eyes. All was a blur.

"Damn nigger's heavier that I thought he'd be. Let's pull him up some more." The men yanked on the rope again until Loomis was well above the ground. He struggled, trying to move, but just swung slightly in the night air like a human pendulum. He was breathing, but barely. He could not see the men around him, blinded by the bright flashlights and blood. He was past pain, his battered body numb and bleeding. Then a strangeness came over him. He could no longer hear the mob of men, their slurs and curses. He was floating. He was a boy again. A little boy. His mother was holding his hand as they walked up the path to the little white church. He felt safe at last, and warm. His hand in his mother's felt good. Everything was going to be all right.

"Let's just leave him here, Bob. It'll be days before anybody finds him. He's near dead already."

"He ain't getting off that easy. Not this nigger," said Bob, who then strode over to where Loomis hung, place the barrel of the shotgun to his head and pulled the trigger.

PART 3

CHAPTER 30

~

At twenty minutes of eight, Tom parked the jeep on the street in front of the office and noticed that Hatcher's car was already there. Hmm, thought Tom, he's always late. Maybe just anxious to get to the court house and get things started. He went in, walked past Dorothy's unoccupied desk and tapped gently on Hatcher's closed door.

"Come in."

Tom pushed the door open and stepped into the room. The room was dark, lit just by the dull yellow light of the early morning sun reflected through the window across the room. But he could see the shadowy figure of Hatcher at his desk.

"Mister Hatcher," said Tom quizzically.

"Good morning, Tom," came the low, hoarse reply. "Come on in. Switch the light on, will you?"

Tom flipped the wall switch and suddenly the office was bathed in the bright artificial light. Hatcher sat slumped in his chair behind his desk. His seersucker suit seemed more rumpled that usual and he had not shaved. The knot in his tie was loosened and pulled away from his throat. Tom thought he was wearing the same white shirt as when he left him the day before.

"Mister Hatcher, have you been home since yesterday?"

"Sit down, Tom," he said, gesturing with his hand toward a chair.

"Hadn't we better be getting ready for court?" Tom asked. He then noticed an empty glass on Hatcher's desk and a half-empty bottle of bourbon on the credenza behind him.

"Oh, I'm not drunk, Tom. Don't think I could be. Sit down—please." Tom sat down in the chair. Hatcher took a deep breath and exhaled with a loud sigh. "I suspect Loomis Cartee is probably dead. They broke him out of jail last night. This morning, whenever. Doesn't matter. Bunch of cabbies from Corinth it seems," Hatcher continued despondently. "Don't know where they took him or what they've done with him, but I know it's not good. Sheriff Glenn's supposed to call me when he knows something."

"Damn," said Tom, looking away. "Damn." He then rose from his seat and strode over to the window, his back to Hatcher.

"There's nothing we can do, Tom, but wait. And even then, there's nothing. It's a police matter now," Hatcher said, and hesitated. "I think they've lynched him, Tom. I purely and surely do. And there's not a damn thing we can do about it."

The word 'lynch' struck Tom as something unbelievable and absurd as it rolled off Hatcher's tongue. After all he'd been through, to a different world that had been hell, and to come back to a place where the word 'lynch' still meant something. Back long ago, when he was nine or ten, he remembered a gathering of men at the edge of town. He had snuck out there that night just to see what it was like. He remembered the huge cross aflame and men with torches, their heads hooded. But then he had run home as fast as he could, and it all came to seem like a dream to him. But it was no dream. The hatred and the violence were still here. Lynched!

With both men lost in their thoughts, with nothing more to say, the phone on Hatcher's desk rang splitting the silence. He grabbed the receiver.

"Hello, sheriff, any news?" There was silence on the other end of the line. "Sheriff?" The voice, low and gruff.

"This Theo Hatcher?"

"Yes, this is Hatcher. Who are you?"

"Just wanted to let you know that nigger won't be needing a lawyer. Not no more."

"Who the hell is this?" Hatcher shouted into the receiver, his face red with rage and whiskey. "You son of a bitch!"

"But I'm a live son of a bitch, your nigger's a dead one. I just called to tell you where you might could find him."

"You son of a bitch!" Hatcher repeated angrily.

"You'll find him at the old cannery off Route-Thirty. At least what's left of him," said the voice on the other end, laughing wickedly. Then the line went dead.

Hatcher looked up at Tom who was standing over his desk now. "He said Loomis was at some old cannery off Route-Thirty. Hell, I don't know of any old cannery. Do you?"

When Tom heard the words 'old cannery off Route-Thirty' he shot out the door before Hatcher could finish his sentence. Hatcher got up quickly from his desk and pursued him. But by the time he got to the door Tom had already hopped into the jeep and sped away.

Tom knew exactly where the old cannery was. During high school they had gone there a couple of times after a football game. Just the players. They had a few bottles of cheap, warm beer. Laughed and cut-up like the teenage boys they were. They had even met some players from Corinth High School there one time. They hadn't stayed out late, and were usually home by midnight. As he sped down Broad Street, through town, and turned left on a back street that would offer him a short cut to Route-Thirty, Tom inexplicably wondered if the empty beer bottles that the boys had left strewn on the ground would still be there after all these years.

The cannery had been shut down for a long time. At least twenty-five or thirty years, maybe longer. It was in a very isolated spot off the old two-lane county road between Whittier and Corinth, Route-Thirty. The turn-off was just inside McBee County, so it was about the same distance from Whittier as it was from Corinth. The winding one-lane road once paved was now rough, with the pavement cracked and missing in some places. Lush kudzu was everywhere on both sides of the narrow trail and had probably covered most of the road by now. It descended sharply into a large flat area where the plant was located. There were two buildings still standing, both made of concrete blocks. The boys had never tried to enter the buildings, but rather partied under a large oak tree beyond, next to a narrow swift creek.

There was very little traffic on the road so Tom was able to push the jeep to its limit. It did not take him long to reach the narrow turn-off. Because the road was so twisting and in such bad repair he had to slow down and maneuver the jeep carefully. Finally the road opened up some, and he saw the deserted buildings of the cannery before him. They looked old and dilapidated as streaks of the early morning sun poured through the trees of the thick forest surrounding them. He stopped the jeep before the larger building which had actually been the cannery itself. He looked down, and on the ground around him were many tire tracks. All fresh. His heart was racing, but the place seemed so peaceful and quiet; the silence only broken by the occasional chirping of birds or a squirrel rustling in the dead leaves. He saw nothing else. He got out of the jeep and began walking past the building, back to the rear, by the creek, where they had drunk beer and laughed and grabbed-assed at what now seemed now like so many years ago. There were several empty whiskey bottles lying about. They, too, looked freshly discarded.

Tom strode a little further, until he could see the old oak. He looked up. Hanging from a large limb, almost like an apparition, was the body, still and lifeless. It was inverted, as his feet were tied to the rope that had been flung over the limb and hoisted up. He walked slowly over to where it hung. There were cigarettes butts scattered on the ground and more whiskey bottles. Then he saw the two spent shotgun shells lying in the bloody grass, close to what was once Loomis' head. It was now a mass of ragged, bleeding flesh, unrecognizable and grotesque. Tom knew he had found Loomis.

Though the sight was sickening and horrible, Tom felt no emotion, not at first at least, to the mutilated body hanging from the tree. The war in the Pacific had long since desensitized him to such atrocities. Later, he would feel differently as he came to recognize what had been done to this innocent and helpless man by a lawless mob of his fellow citizens. It wasn't the same as war.

Just then Tom heard an automobile pull up beyond the cannery. He turned and saw that it was a police car. A county deputy emerged from the vehicle. Another car was close behind this one, and another arrived shortly thereafter. When the deputy spotted Tom, he stopped and withdrew the revolver from its holster.

"Stop where you are! Don't move!" shouted the deputy across the two-hundred feet of overgrown yard where Tom stood, looking at him. "Spread your arms and place your hands on your head! And I mean slow!" the deputy screamed, as he strode cautiously toward him. Tom did as he was told.

By now the other policemen were out of their cars, following the first deputy with guns drawn. Tom was standing a few feet from the oak tree and he did not think the deputies had yet seen the body hanging there, as there was much overgrowth, creating a kind of canopy around and above them. It was shadowy even as the early morning sun shot piercing, narrow shafts of light here and there through the thick vegetation.

"What are you doing out here?" demanded the deputy.

"Same thing you are," answered Tom softly, as he turned his head toward the hanging tree.

"I told you—my god!" said the deputy as he suddenly saw Loomis' body suspended from the oak. The other men had arrived at the spot and saw it too.

"Who are you?" the deputy asked nervously.

"Tom Pruitt."

"Got ID on you?"

"Yes. In my back pocket."

The other deputies had moved over to the hanging body, walking around it, inspecting it, but not touching anything on it or the ground around it.

"Goddamn, Sorrell, this nigger's a mess. He's really messed up?

"Is he dead?" asked the man holding the gun on Tom.

"I'd say so, since half his head is gone and his brains are all over the ground," replied the policeman as he continued to gaze at the gore.

"You're under arrest," said the gun-holding cop to Tom. "Put your hands behind your back. Put the cuffs on him, Garrett."

Tom was placed, handcuffed, into the backseat of one of the police cars. Shortly Sheriff Glenn arrived, followed by what looked to be a police photographer. He began snapping photos of the scene. He took about a dozen of Loomis' body before they cut it down from the tree. With it lying in the bloody grass, he took several more. Another officer was furiously writing in a small leather-bound notebook he had pulled from his uniform coat. Finally, Glenn walked over to the car in which Tom sat, and snatched open the door.

"Well, well, Mister Pruitt. It seems you beat us to it."

"I was with Mister Hatcher when the call came in. The one telling us where we could find Cartee. I knew the place, so I rushed over here. That's all," said Tom coolly.

A deputy stepped up behind Glenn and then bent to look in at Tom sitting in the backseat of the police cruiser. "You know this man, Sheriff Glenn?"

"Hell, yes. He's works for Hatcher, Cartee's lawyer. Take those damn handcuffs off him," said Glenn gruffly.

Sheriff Glenn strode over with Tom toward the jeep. "Sorry about this. They didn't know what to expect out here. A case like this can rattle you sometimes, you know."

"It's all right," said Tom who, rubbing his wrists, got slowly into the jeep and drove away. He drove to Hatcher's office and was told by Dorothy that he'd gone home to clean up and change shirts.

"They found him. They found Loomis," said Tom.

"Yes, I know. Mister Hatcher spoke with Sheriff Glenn on the phone. A terrible thing."

Tom did not respond to Dorothy's comment, but said, "If you will, Miss Spearman, tell him I'll be back here this afternoon."

"I'll let him know."

Tom felt nothing but turmoil. His brain was spinning. In the war, he had seen more than his share of bloodshed and death. Things no man should have to experience. He knew after a point it had hardened him. It had stolen his youth, like it had so many others. But this, the killing of Loomis Cartee, was different. In war, at least in the Pacific, there had been no rules. Not really. You knew who the enemy was. It was kill or be killed. You knew you were existing in a world where gravity didn't work. You lived with it day by day. The only instinct was to survive. But no matter how small or faint there was always hope. You knew there was another world. One that was real and safe. And you might just survive and make it back to that world. To home. To where there were rules to live by and goodness. At least that is what he had clung to for a while.

Kenneth P. Smith

But somehow in Tom's mind these two worlds had just collided. Lawlessness and murder were the same anywhere. How could this happen here? How, he thought? But it did. He could make no sense of it and he just wanted to escape. Escape to where? He didn't know. He just didn't know.

For a long time he had just driven around, trying to clear his head and think. He drove up to the old reservoir and parked the jeep. He knew that he needed to talk to someone, to see someone. He had never felt so alone. Of course, up here he thought of Maggie. He thought of that warm summer night when he had held her, and anything seemed possible. He knew that he could talk to her. At least she would listen and try to understand. But how could he explain to her how he felt when he really didn't understand it himself. He only knew that he was damaged goods. Surely, she could see that. He got back in the jeep and drove back to Whittier, to Hatcher's office.

Hatcher was sitting slumped behind his desk, his chair turned toward the window, staring into space. Tom sat down in a chair across from him. Hatcher turned slowly about and looked at him directly.

"Tom," said Hatcher looking at him as if waking from a dream and not realizing someone else was in the room. "Some bad shit, huh?"

The young man stared at the floor and did not respond. He then looked up at Hatcher. He could see that his boss had put on a fresh suit and shirt. He was clean shaven, but his eyes were bloodshot from drink and lack of sleep.

Kenneth P. Smith

"Sheriff Glenn said you were over there at the cannery when his men arrived this morning. Damn, the way you shot out of here I didn't know what to think. You okay?"

"It's just when I heard you repeat what the caller was telling you, I knew where the old abandoned cannery was. I thought maybe he—Loomis—might still be alive. I thought—"

"Well, you thought wrong, didn't you?" said Hatcher sarcastically, unsmiling.

"Yes, sir. I couldn't have been more wrong."

"Sheriff Glenn's going to want to get a statement from you."

"All right."

Hatcher turned in the swivel chair, his back to Tom, and pulled something from the credenza behind his desk. He then set two glasses before him and poured whisky into each of them. He slid one across to Tom and emptied his with one gulp. Tom reached for the glass, held it for a moment, staring into it, and did the same.

CHAPTER 31

~

Tom stood up abruptly and left Hatcher's office without a word. The whiskey hadn't help. He knew it wouldn't. He just wanted to be away from here. The office. Hatcher. Everything. He drove slowly down Broad Street and pulled the jeep up in front of the bookshop. Maggie was on the sidewalk, her back to him, locking the door to the shop. Then she turned.

"Tom!" she said. She was not expecting to see him there. He had gotten out of the jeep and was walking toward her.

"Hello, Maggie. I didn't realize it was so late."

"We close a little early on Wednesday's," she said. "What's the matter, Tom, you look awful."

"I guess you didn't hear about it yet. Last night they took Loomis Cartee from the county jail and murdered him," Tom blurted out, staring down at the sidewalk. "I found him early this morning. Hanging from a tree."

"Oh, Tom, that's awful! Who did it? Do you know?"

"A lynch mob. Cab drivers mostly they think. They just strung him up and killed him. Blew his head off. They've killed an innocent man." Tom spoke without emotion.

"That's terrible. Just horrible," replied Maggie. They both just stood there for a moment. Maggie looking at him, and he the ground. "Are you all right?"

"Yes, I guess so. He hesitated. "No! I'm not all right. I just wanted someone to talk to, that's all. And you're the only one." He glanced up, looking her into her eyes.

"Oh, Tom, I want to talk to you too, but I can't now. I've got some things I've got to do this afternoon."

"Yeah, well, I understand. Maybe later, huh?"

"Of course," she said, biting her lower lip in dismay. Then, "Why don't do something Sunday? Go on a picnic." Then she continued, excitedly, "I know, let's go up to the reservoir. We will be alone up there and we can talk to our hearts' content. I'll make us a picnic basket. It might be fun, Tom. What do you say?" She touched his arm.

He looked down for a moment at her hand on his arm. "Funny thing, I drove up to the reservoir this morning. It's nice up there." He was in his own thoughts for a moment, then he looked back at her. "Sure," he said. "A picnic would be nice."

"Pick me up at ten, then?"

"Sure. At ten."

"Will you be all right until then?

"Yes, I'm all right now really. Just want to talk to somebody."

"I know you do and so do I," she said, glancing at her wristwatch. "I've got to go. See you Sunday."

"Good bye, Maggie." He turned and strode back to the jeep. She walked up the street toward home.

She placed the picnic basket in the back of the jeep, got in the passenger's side and kissed Tom lightly on the cheek. He smiled, said 'good morning' and turned the jeep into the street. The day was warm, with sunlight exploding off the leaves of the trees, washing everything in its brightness.

Kenneth P. Smith

It is good to be alive, thought Maggie. And to be here this moment. This moment in time. It's all we have when you think about it. Tom's demeanor had brightened too. She could tell he had things on his mind, but it seemed some of the heaviness, what she had seen earlier on the sidewalk in front of the store, had left him. She hoped so.

There was almost no traffic as they drove through town. Only the church-goers were out. Maggie waved to them gaily as they passed. She and Tom talked little as the jeep sped up the highway to the lake. Finally, they were there as he turned the vehicle slowly onto the unpaved road leading down to the water. He stopped the jeep in the same spot where they had been before. He looked over at her, smiled, sighed and slightly shrugged.

"Here we are," he said softly.

"Tom, it's just perfect, isn't it? The day, the water, just everything. Let's go up in the shade of that big elm tree."

"All right."

They got out of the jeep, he grabbing the picnic basket, and strode up the gentle grassy slope to the elm. She took his hand into hers as they walked.

"Here, there's a blanket in the basket," said Maggie as he set the basket in the grass. "Help me spread it out, okay?" They took opposite ends of the old quilt and spread it out smoothly on the soft grass.

As they both sat down on the blanket, Maggie reclined, propped up on her left elbow. Beside her, Tom sat with his arms wrapped around his pulled-up knees. They stared out at the water before them. In the distance, near the water's horizon, was a small boat bobbing gently in the breeze that swept across the lake. In the boat, they could just make out a lone figure as he fished, but the fisherman could not see them where they sat in the shade of the elm back from the bank.

"Are you feeling better, Tom? I mean, after what all happened?

"I guess so. I just can't make any sense out of it. I need to let it go."

"Can you? Let it go, I mean?" she asked.

"Yeah, I can. Maggie, I've had to let a lot of things go, but this is the hardest, I think."

"You've been through a lot for someone your age."

"Seems like a lot."

For a long while they just sat there on the blanket gazing out across the silver, shimmering lake. They both had things on their minds, with no one but each other to share them with. Finally, Tom stretched out on the blanket, his hands interlocked beneath his head staring up at the pure azure sky with Maggie beside him breathing softly, her eyes closed. It seemed so peaceful here, a world away from the Pacific, New Orleans, the suicide, the old cannery. Those things almost seemed like a dream now, like they never really happened. But Tom knew that this—here by the lake with Maggie— was the *real* illusion, not the ugly things of life. They were real. He turned toward Maggie.

"I talked with Mister Hatcher on Friday. Or rather he talked to me. I just listened mostly," he said suddenly.

She didn't open her eyes. "What about?"

"His plans for me. He wants me to become a lawyer. Go to college, then law school. Just crazy stuff like that."

Maggie then opened her eyes, turned and looked at him. "Tom that would be a wonderful thing if you could do that! What did you say to him?"

"Not much. I told him I could never afford something like that and he reminded me that I had the GI Bill at my disposal. And he's right, I guess I do, but—"

"You could do it, Tom! I just know you could!"

Tom was silent for a long moment, then said, "I told him I'd think about it. And I have. You see, Maggie, that's not me. I could never be a lawyer or go to college. I've done things. Things I'll never live down."

"What kind of things?" she asked

He sat up and looked out across the reservoir, but didn't answer her immediately. The lone boat with the fisherman was gone. Without looking at Maggie, he told the story of his trip to New Orleans to bring his brother's body home. He told of going to the Yellow Parrot, ostensibly to find Shelby Jean. He told her of meeting Boucharde and then of the fight, and the killing. He told her everything. When he finished neither of them spoke for a long while.

"You see, Maggie," he finally spoke, "I could never be anything more than what I am, and that's not much. At least, I finally realize that. I'm just a mill town boy. Nothing more."

"But, Tom, you've got a chance to get out. Get out now while you can. Make a better life for yourself."

"Run away from myself, you mean?"

"No, that's not what I mean at all." She hesitated and then continued. "I need to tell *you* something. I've been meaning to, but just—I don't know, I just didn't. Tom, I want to be a writer. I mean, I *am* a writer. But I want to be a good writer. I need more education. I need to be around other writers." He did not look at her, but out across the expanse of water. "Ever since, even before, I took the job at the bookshop I've been saving my money. Living with mama and daddy, as hard as that's been, I saved most everything I made. I don't buy clothes; I don't go out. I've saved my money. Do you want to hear this?"

"All right," he said.

"I applied to a school for writers. In Vermont. It's a kind of writer's workshop and they accepted me, but I didn't have the money. Now I do and I'm going. I'm getting out of Whittier!"

"That's good, Maggie. You should."

"You can too. You can come with me. Go back to school. We can do it, Tom!"

He looked at her for a long moment, then, "I don't think so, Maggie."

"But, Tom, why? Just tell me why?" she pleaded, near tears.

"I already did."

"Tom, I care about you. I mean, I really care. I want us to be together. This would be our chance." She took his hand. "Do you care about me? About us? Or is all this just, I don't know, a—fling? Just something to do? Please tell me!"

"No, it's not a fling. I care for you very much. Fact is I love you. I want to be with you. We can make a life here in Whittier. A good life together."

"Yeah, some life. You working in that damn cotton mill until you're an old man. That is, if you don't die of brown lung first. Me taking a second shift job there too. Until the first baby comes along. And then the second. Then the third. Being forty and looking like sixty, and feeling older than that. I've seen it happen. To my mother. Your mother. Some life together. Not me. I told you, Tom, I'm a writer and I'm determined to be a good one. That's my dream. My dream, Tom, don't you understand?" Huge wets tears tracked down her cheeks.

"I'm sorry, Maggie, I just don't see it. I don't think I can do it. That's all. I can't."

She rose from the blanket and strode down to the edge of the water, wiping the tears away with the back of her hand. She wanted to be with him. Every inch of her body, soul, and mind yearned for him. But she understood choices. He had made his. She would make hers. If it meant losing him, that was a price she was prepared to pay. She had come too far with this dream. She would not let it go now.

After a while Maggie walked back to the blanket, knelt and fixed them both plates of food from the picnic basket. They looked at the food and picked at it, neither of them eating much. Whatever they had, or thought they had, was fleeting, gone now really and somehow without speaking about it again they both knew it. Tom had come home from the war confused and disillusioned, but with Loomis Cartee's murder—his lynching— his thoughts had seemed to crystallized. He felt that he saw things now as they really were. He saw himself in this harsh new light and he knew he could not escape it. He was who he was.

After a while Tom spoke, gazing out over the lake, not looking at her. "We were on ship board once, near an island to rehearse a landing we were going to make, when the ship was struck by a torpedo. We, Marines mostly, were all in our quarters below deck—trapped. Water began rushing in, filling the compartment. No one could open the hatch. Men were thrashing around, some screaming, and some beating on the bulkhead with their fists. We were going to all drown and I knew it. The moment I realized it, a strange peace came over me. It was like it just wrapped itself around me. The water was almost up to my chin as I just stood there, waiting death. Then a strange thing happened. There was a loud crash, almost like a car crash but much louder. And then a jolt. But the funny thing was the water stopped rising and even receded some. The captain of the ship had realized that men were trapped below deck after the ship was hit, so he purposely turned the ship toward the nearby island as best he could and ran it aground in shallow water. We were all saved, most of us anyway. But I didn't feel saved. You see, Maggie," he said, turning to look into her face. "I was already dead." She took his hand, and he continued. "It was when I found Loomis hanging from the tree that morning, I said to myself or maybe I said it out loud, I don't know. I said 'Welcome home, Loomis. I'm already dead, now you're dead, too. Welcome, home.' Like I said, I don't know if I actually said it or not, but that's the way I felt. 'Welcome home, Loomis. You and I are the same now."

"Tom, that's terrible. I'm so sorry. It's just the war. It makes the absurd seem normal and the normal seem absurd. But you can survive this. I just know you can."

"I don't know, Maggie. I really don't know." And then they were silent again for a long while. Something had passed between them and neither of them knew exactly how to put it into words, so they didn't try. But they both knew it.

Finally, she gathered up the picnic things and placed them in the basket. He helped her fold the quilt in the silence. They walked backed to the jeep without speaking.

Kenneth P. Smith

His foot pressed the starter and the engine came to life. Before he pulled the gear shift lever, she touched his arm and looked at him.

"It doesn't have to be like this, Tom. You know it doesn't."

"Not if you stay here with me, it doesn't," he said, unconvincingly.

"I'm going to Vermont, Tom," she said, removing her hand from his arm.

"Yes, I know."

She turned and stared through the windshield, her eyes glistening with tears. Tom drove slowly up the dirt road and out onto the highway toward Whittier.

Kenneth P. Smith

CHAPTER 32

~

Early Monday morning Tom pulled the faded red jeep to the curb in front of Hatcher's office. Dorothy's old Dodge was in the small gravel parking adjacent to the building, as he knew it would be. Hatcher's Ford was not there, as he knew it wouldn't. He opened the front door and stepped inside, quietly shutting the door behind him.

"Hello, Miss Spearman."

"Good morning, Tom. My, you're here awfully early. I don't have anything ready to go yet, but I'm working on a couple of subpoenas. Should be ready in an hour or two. You want some coffee?"

"No. No, thanks. I—I just came by to drop off the jeep. Mister Hatcher's jeep."

"Why, I think he meant to *give* you that old jeep. You need something to drive for the work here. Now, you didn't go out and buy yourself a new automobile, did you?" She said jokingly, with her head turned slightly and her eyebrows raised.

"No, ma'am, nothing like that." He hesitated, and then continued. "I'm quitting work here. I'm—I'm not working for Mister Hatcher anymore." Tom lowered his eyes to the floor.

"I'm sorry to hear that, Tom. I suppose you've told him, Mister Hatcher."

"No, ma'am. I've not told him. I think it's better this way. For both of us, him and me. I expect he won't be too surprised."

"Oh, I see," said Dorothy. "Well, you know we'll miss you. You did a good job."

"Thanks, Miss Spearman. I appreciate that. I do. I liked the work, too. Tell Mister Hatcher that, if you will."

"I certainly will, Tom."

"Just tell him—" Tom started to say something, but hesitated. "Just tell him the jeep's out at the curb. I cleaned it up." He turned to leave.

"You know, Tom, that lynching was a bad thing. It has affected us all here. Real bad. A funny thing, not ha-ha funny, but crazy, I guess. Some people from over in Corinth called Mister Hatcher last Friday afternoon after you left. You know what they asked him?"

"No, ma'am, I don't."

"Those people—fools really— wanted to know if he'd defend those cab drivers. The one's they've arrested and charged with the lynching! Can you believe that? You'd have thought Mister Hatcher would've cussed them out or something. But he didn't. You know what he did?" she asked, but continued without waiting for Tom's rely. "He didn't say a word to them. Not a word. He merely quietly placed the phone back on the hook and poured himself a drink. That's what he did. He was just sitting there at his desk when I left for the day. Staring out the window."

"He's a good man," said Tom.

Dorothy signed and placed a clean sheet of paper in her typewriter. "So, what are you going to do, Tom? I mean for work, or are you leaving town?"

"I'm going to work at the cotton mill, I guess."

Kenneth P. Smith

"Oh," said Miss Spearman softly, her voice almost cracking. "Good luck, Tom."

"Thanks, Miss Spearman. See you around." He opened the door and stepped out into the morning.

On the walk from town back to the mill village Tom wondered why he had lied. He knew that he would never go to work at the Whittier mill or any other mill, for that matter. It just seemed the simplest answer to Dorothy Spearman's question. Clean, no explaining. He could have just replied, 'I don't know', but he didn't. He thought about Maggie, then Loomis, then his father. He knew then that he had to get out of this mill town.

He came into the house and went straight to his bedroom. From the chifforobe, he pulled out the olive-green ditty bag, the one he had from the service. He stuffed a shirt, a pair of pants, and some other odds and ends into it, and zipped it up. He then walked into the kitchen where his mother was busy peeling potatoes near the sink.

"Hello, ma."

"Hey, Tom," she said without looking up from her work.

"Ma, I need to talk to you."

"All right," she said, wiping her hands on her apron and turning to face him.

"Ma, I'm leaving. I put some money on your dresser. It's a good bit and I'll send you more when I can."

Jewel blew a wisp of hair from her face and went into the living room. She sat down heavily in her chair as tears welled up in her pale blue eyes. They were tired eyes. Tom followed her, but did not sit down. He was leaning against the door frame.

"Well, son, when are going?"

"Now."

"Oh, Tom!"

"I can't stay here, ma. It's just too much. I don't expect you to understand, but I've got to go."

"Have you told Maggie?"

Oh, ma, Maggie's leaving, too. Probably already gone. She has dreams and they don't include me."

"Did she say that?"

"It doesn't matter, ma, not now."

"Where will you go, son? Where will you go to get away from yourself?"

Tom sighed deeply. "I don't know. Out west, maybe. Canada—I don't know. I need space or something. Please try to understand. This isn't an easy thing for me either."

"No, I don't suppose it is. How long you planning to be gone?"

"I don't know. I'll write."

"Sure you will," she said despondently. "Won't you wait until tomorrow? You know, sleep on it."

"No, ma, I can't wait. I've made up my mind."

He went back into the bedroom and retrieved his bag. When he came back into the living room his mother was still in her chair, huge tears streaming down her thin pale cheeks. He bent down and hugged her, and kissed her on the forehead,

"I love you, ma."

"Oh, Tom!" She buried her face in her hands.

Tom left her there and walked quietly out the door and down the street through downtown, toward Route Forty-Seven. When he reached the highway, he stopped at the gas station on the corner. A large trailer truck, a big yellow Diamond Reo eighteen-wheeler, was idling at the pumps.

Kenneth P. Smith

A man in greasy overall, apparently the driver, was standing near the truck.

"Are you the driver?" asked Tom above the low, deep rumble of the diesel engine.

"I reckon I am. Why?"

"Where you headed from here?"

"A goddamn far piece, if it's any of your business."

"West?"

"Hell, yeah, west. That is, if you call Portland, Oregon west. 'Bout as west as she gets," said the driver chuckling as he turned his head and spat a stream of tobacco juice onto the payment. "Got a load of textile equipment to deliver,"

"You take a rider?" asked Tom.

"You?"

"That's right."

"How far you going?" asked the driver, glancing down at Tom's ditty bag.

"All the way!" said Tom.

"Well, I reckon I could use some company. There's some mighty lonesome miles between here and Oregon. You'll likely get tired of it long before we get there."

"No. I won't," he said solemnly.

"Then get in and let's go."

"All right," said Tom, as he climbed up into the passenger side of the truck.

CHAPTER 33

~

Theo Hatcher rose from his desk and wearily pulled on his seersucker suit jacket, and stepped into the outer office. Miss Spearman stopped her typing and looked up at him.

"Dorothy, when you finish whatever it is you're working on, why don't you call it a day and go on home. I won't be back today," he said.

"Going over to the courthouse, Mr. Hatcher?"

"No, but I wish I was. I got to make one of those visits that I'd rather do anything but. I'm going to drive over and see Miss Loomis. I figure I owe her that. I don't know how she'll receive me, though."

"Yes, sir. That's got to be tough."

"Not as tough as she's had it. See you in the morning, Dorothy."

"Sure thing. Good luck," she replied and resumed typing.

When Hatcher pulled his car up at the street in front of Miss Loomis' house he could see her sitting on the front porch, rocking gently in her chair. He took a deep breathe, exhaled, opened the car door and walked up to the porch. She watched him closely as he approached.

"Good evening, Miss Loomis," he said softly.

"Evening," she replied coldly.

Kenneth P. Smith

"May I come up on the porch?"

"You a white man, I reckon you can do most whatever you want to do around here." There was a sad bitterness in her voice. Hatcher mounted the steps and stood to one side of the black woman.

"Miss Loomis, I -,"

"You what, Mr. Hatcher?"

"I'm sorry. I came out here to tell you I'm sorry. That's all," said Hatcher

"Sorry? Now that don't bring my boy back, does it Mr. Hatcher?"

"No, ma'am, it doesn't. Nothing can do that. But *we* can grieve, can't we?"

"Grieve," she chuckled sarcastically. "Grieve you say. I reckon you can if that makes you feel better. I'm beyond grief, Mr. Hatcher and it scares me. I'm real close to hate and hate is way past grief. I've tried to live my life as a Christian woman. When things be good and when they be bad. But a Christian ain't given the luxury of hate. I'm s'posed to love everybody, my brother, but I don't. Not right now. I'm struggling, Mr. Hatcher, because I'm awfully close to hate. As I sit here, I declare I am close to hate."

"Miss Cartee, if anybody has a right to hate, it's you."

"No, that's where you're wrong. Nobody's got a right to hate. Not if they love the Lord. You ain't got no right, and I ain't got no right. But I do." Her voice was soft and bitter.

"But you're only human. It's only natural for you to hate those men for what they did to Loomis. Purely natural."

"Did you come to the funeral, Mr. Hatcher?"

Kenneth P. Smith

"Yes, ma'am, I did. I was there. It was a real nice service."

"A nice service you say. They couldn't even open the casket so I could see my dead boy. Couldn't even open the casket, Mr. Hatcher, with what and all they done to him." Tears rolled down her weathered cheeks. Hatcher had no response.

Hatcher sighed and glanced across the porch. Near the screen door there was an old large suitcase. He then looked back at the old black woman.

"You planning on going on a trip, Miss Cartee? I see that suitcase sitting over there by the door."

"Chicago, Mr. Hatcher," she said, wiping the tears away with a small white handkerchief that she gripped tightly in her hand. "I'm going to Chicago. I got a sister who lives up there. I'm going to Chicago. Waiting on the taxi now to take me to the bus station." She hesitated. "One of them yellow taxis." She adjusted the small black straw hat she was wearing which Hatcher had not noticed before.

"Why that sounds like a real good idea, Miss Cartee. Get away for a while. It'll make you feel better, I'm sure."

"Won't be for no while. I'm going to Chicago and I ain't coming back here. I want to forget this place. I ain't got much, just what's in that suitcase. I been renting this old house for a long time. Raised my boy here. But I done give the key to the landlord. Told him he could have it because I was going to Chicago."

"Well, I'm sorry to hear that," he said as she looked away. "I've got to go now. I'm real sorry about Loomis. He was an innocent man. A good man as far as I knew."

She looked up at Hatcher standing there and then looked away into the distance.

Kenneth P. Smith

"Good bye, Miss Cartee. And good luck." She did not answer him and Hatcher wondered if she had even heard him as he left the porch, got into his car and drove away.

CHAPTER 34

~

Jewel Pruitt felt as if her life had come full circle. The feelings took her back, in some kind of vague, inexplicable way to the same feelings she had experienced that day long ago when her father had told her that there would be no more school for her, and that they were leaving the mountains for good and moving down to this town called Whittier. She hadn't said anything then, but had done what she was told. It seemed that was what she had always done—what she was told to do. The feeling that she finally identified, and which griped her now, was that she was alone. She felt alone. Bud, her youngest, was gone. Mysteriously murdered a long way from home in New Orleans. How or why was never explained to her, at least explained in a way she could understand. He had never been a smart boy, but was gentle and kind. A good boy. She wished he had never gotten involved with that girl. Oh, Shelby Jean. It was difficult to understand why someone should want to kill him.

And Claude. Poor Claude. She didn't really understand *that* either. Maybe if she had listened to him more. His worries and insecurities she had accepted as just being a part of who he was, nothing more. Although she knew that she had never really loved him, she cared for him. He was a good man. Somehow they had built a life together in this mill town. And the dreams. She had let go of them gradually and perhaps a little reluctantly, at least at first. She now wondered if they could have ever become a reality, or were they just that—dreams. Anyway, she had let them die on the vine, the vine of hope, and she had made life work with Claude. But somehow it had become a life that he couldn't live with, so he got out. She was sad about it, but angry too.

And Tom was now gone too. He had left her some money and said he would be in touch, but he didn't really tell her anything. Hugged her warmly and kissed her, and then was gone. He had come back from the war changed. He had often seemed to be somewhere else, seeing things he couldn't, or wouldn't, talk about. He kept it all inside of himself. War does that to people, she thought. He had seemed to be getting better when he took the job with Mister Hatcher. And when he met Maggie. But the brutal and senseless death of Loomis Cartee had hit him hard. That and the old war memories just flooded back upon him, and she lost him. Maybe for good, but perhaps not. She didn't know. But seeing Tom again was a hope she clung to. It was all she had.

She finished her coffee, rinsed the cup at the sink, and sat down in her chair in the front room by the window. She chuckled to herself. After all these years, most of a lifetime really, she had worked. First, there had been shift work at the mill, then taking care of her two boys and Claude. The cooking, the cleaning, the washing, everything. Day in, day out. But now she realized there was nothing to do. She could eat when she wished, go to bed whenever she felt like it, or just do nothing. In other words, she was in a sense, free. This thought caused her to chuckle ever so softly.

Jewel just sat for a while thinking. Then she got up and went back into the bedroom and pulled a worn black sweater from the chifforobe and put it on. She placed a small red hat on her head and ran a hat pin through it, and then looked at herself in the mirror. This hat makes me look frumpy and old, she said to herself. So she quickly removed it and flung it onto the bed. She brushed her dark but graying hair and put just a touch of rouge on both cheeks. She smiled at herself and thought, 'not too bad for an old woman'.

It was a beautiful cool, clear morning and Jewel decided to walk the mile or so to downtown. There was no particular reason she had for doing so other than she just wanted to. Maybe she'd stop by the book shop and buy another book. She could, after all, do whatever she wished to do. The new freedom felt strange to her, and she was not altogether comfortable with it. Not yet, anyway.

She walked briskly through the mill village and didn't really slow her pace until she came to Broad Street, downtown. She turned right at Joe's Place and strode leisurely down the town's main thoroughfare. She stopped at Freeman's Family Store and gazed upon the things in the large display window. On the ever-smiling and shapely mannequins were some lovely and fashionable women's clothes. Hmm, she thought, I'm not quite ready for such lovely things. Maybe later, she shrugged and walked on.

As she came to the bookshop, and as she reached for the brass door knob, she saw the sign in the window beside the door. It read HELP WANTED in bold red,

neatly printed letters. Without a second thought she
opened the door and reached down and picked up the
sign from the window. Carrying the sign, she strode back
to where the desk and cash register was located. She was
surprised to see a woman she didn't know sitting at the
desk. She had expected Maggie. The woman looked up at
her.

"May I help you?" she asked.

"Is Maggie not here?" asked Jewel.

"No, I'm afraid not. Maggie no longer works here."

"Oh, I see," said Jewel. "I'm sorry to hear that. I really
liked Maggie. She was very helpful. At least to me she
was. We had become friends, of a sort. She and my son—
oh, never mind. She was a good girl."

"Yes, I liked her too. A good girl, but she up and quit
last week. I don't really know why. Said something about
leaving Whittier. Going away. She was vague. I hated to
lose her, but what can you do? Young people," laughed
the woman as she shrugged.

Jewel placed the sign on the desk, looking straight at
the woman sitting there, who turned and glanced down at
the sign and then back up at Jewel.

"You wish to apply for the job?"

"I do. I would guess there's an opening because Maggie
left."

"Well, yes, that's right." The woman stood up and
extended her hand to Jewel. "I'm Thelma Hendricks. I
own this shop. That is, me and the bank."

Jewel took and shook her hand. "I'm Jewel Pruitt, Mrs.
Hendricks," she said softly. "Maggie's told me about you.
She really liked you and said you were good to work for."
Although they had never met, Jewel knew who Thelma

Hendrix was, as she had been the high school librarian for many years before she retired. She had heard the name from her boys.

"Fact is Maggie's gone and I'm not up to working fulltime, not every day anyhow. I need someone to help out here."

"I'd like to apply for the job," said Jewel matter of factly.

"Sign's been up for a week, and other than a couple of high school kids no one has been interested. Do you have any experience, Mrs. Pruitt? I mean retail experience."

"Please call me Jewel. No, I've never worked in a store. Worked in the mill when I was young, but I've been a housewife for the last twenty-five years or so."

"Well—,"

"But I love books," Jewel interrupted. "I purely and surely do. And I think I could learn the cash register."

"You know, the job doesn't pay much. You don't get rich running a bookshop."

"I don't need much. I just want to keep busy, and...," Jewel hesitated.

"And what, Jewel?"

"I don't know. Just to be around all these books. I think I'd love it, Mrs. Hendricks. That's all."

Mrs. Hendricks rubbed her chin softly with the back side of her left hand. She sighed, then smiled and said, "Why not, Mrs.—uh—Jewel? I'll give you a chance. Might even work out. Who knows? When can you start?"

"Now!" said Jewel, beaming with a broad smile.

They talked for a while and then Jewel left, but returned to the bookshop later that afternoon. Thelma first showed her how the cash register worked. A skill that

Jewel quickly mastered. Then the two women worked on book arrangements on the various shelves before reviewing ordering and invoicing and the other various tasks involved in the day-to-day running of a small bookshop. After overcoming her initial uncertainty, Jewel easily absorbed everything Thelma taught her. Just to be surrounded by books was exhilarating. Their smell, their feel, their hopefulness. She would be happy here.

The day dawned into one of those late winter days that you often get in the South. The sun shone brightly and although cool early, the sun promised warmth and newness. Spring could not be far behind. With the sun on her face, Jewel strode purposely that morning to her job at the bookshop. She had never felt freer and more hopeful. Life was good. Maybe dreams do come true, she thought. Sometimes.

Acknowledgements

Thanks to Rita Hedden for her wonderful and professional assistance in formatting the manuscript for publication. And a special thanks to my first reader and wife, Mary, whose comments and suggestions were invaluable in completing this novel.